Yellow Tapers for Paris

BOOKS by BRUCE MARSHALL

Father Malachy's Miracle

The World, the Flesh, and Father Smith

Yellow Tapers for Paris

BRUCE MARSHALL

Yellow Tapers
for Paris

1946

HOUGHTON MIFFLIN COMPANY BOSTON
The Riverside Press Cambridge

All the characters in this novel are entirely
imaginary and any similarity between
their names and occupations and those
of people at present alive is accidental.

The Riverside Press
CAMBRIDGE · MASSACHUSETTS
PRINTED IN THE U.S.A.

Yellow Tapers for Paris

ON THE ROOF opposite, the electricians were trying out the new advertisement for Balto cigarettes. Red and blue and white they flashed it in and out across the dark sky. Bigou watched the crisp jewels come and go and come again without knowing it, because he was trying to find an error of thirty centimes in the trial balance of the Entreprises Françaises d'Installation de Chauffage Central, S.A. Like furry caterpillars the platoons of figures stood, towering and spreading with friendly familiarity. Bigou loved his work, and this was the fourteenth time running he had made up the company's accounts. Away back into 1923 other trial balances stretched, with their violet ink getting more and more faded, but somehow the contemplation of them gave Bigou a sense of immortality: because he had made the accounts up so often now and knew that he would make them up so often again. Immersed in his task, Bigou forgot that he was poor and earned only two thousand francs a month. Up on the roof opposite the high dusty room in which he worked, the electricians went on trying out the new advertisement for Balto cigarettes and the reflection of their flashes fell in pools of crimson and blue on Bigou's trial balance, like the sun dappling the floor of a chancel. Down on the black shine of boulevard the buses ploughed up and down the chaussée like lighted pleasure boats, with the lamps of invisible taxis as will-o'-the-wisps

1

to guide them. The shop of the Trois Quartiers was all white and icy and lighted up. Sleek prostitutes sailed the pavements on glass legs, promising bowler hats and mackintoshes that they should see God face to face for two hundred francs. It was the evening of the sixth of February, 1934.

'So you don't want to go home? It's struck six long ago.'

Bigou looked up and saw Oppilliard, the head invoice clerk, eyeing him with hostility. Oppilliard wore a short shiny black jacket, coarse trousers striped like sticks of peppermint, and thin yellow shoes. Bigou hated him because the other's poverty was so accurate a reflection of his own.

'I've got an error of thirty centimes in my trial balance to find,' he said.

Oppilliard took two small coins from his pocket, and then, admitting that the joke was a poor one, put them back again.

'You had better not stay too late all the same,' he said. 'They say there's going to be trouble tonight over this Stavisky business.'

'There's been trouble for some days now,' Bigou said.

'But they say that tonight there's going to be real trouble,' Oppilliard said. 'Not just debagging gardes mobiles in the Place Beauveau and making them say their prayers. They're going to sack the Chambre des Députés. And about time, I say. If you ask me, they're all in the racket together: Right, Centre, and Left. In any case I'm off home before I get my mug broken.' He winked at Bigou with empty benevolence and sauntered away.

Bigou worked on until he found his error, which turned out to be a five copied down as an eight. Then he closed the general ledger and balance book and put them both away in the safe for the night and went out and got his coat and hat, which were both shabby. On his way down the stairs he overtook the managing director's new secretary, a girl with golden holy hair and with her blue dress frisking up into a blue saucer about her knees. Bigou smiled at her and tried to keep the hating hunger out of his eyes, and the girl smiled back as though she noticed all the lines on his face, and Bigou wondered if it were really true that she had been away to Deauville with old Dupont. Down on the tessellated ground floor he met Terrasse, the company secretary, getting out of the directors' private lift. Bigou took off his hat and the padded secretary raised a benign finger back.

'Going home?' Monsieur Terrasse asked.

'Yes, going home.' Bigou never knew quite what to say to Monsieur Terrasse, but he thought that it might please his employer to learn that he had been putting in overtime. 'I've been working on the trial balance,' he said. 'I had an error of thirty centimes, but I've found it now.'

'That's good,' Monsieur Terrasse said. 'And it may please you to learn, Bigou, that you aren't the only one who's been working either.' Both men raised their hats as the pretty secretary passed them smelling of the taste of chocolate. 'Monsieur Dupont and I have been working too. At the War Ministry, my dear Bigou. You'll be pleased to learn that we've landed the Maginot Line central heating contract.'

'That's excellent,' Bigou said. 'That's wonderful.' He tried to speak with enthusiasm and soon succeeded so well that the tears of brotherly love came smarting to his eyes. Monsieur Terrasse looked so handsome standing there in his new thick overcoat with the big broad belt and the fur collar that it was impossible not to feel pleased when he was pleased. And perhaps landing a big thing like the Maginot Line contract might mean more money for other people besides the directors. Perhaps. Who knew? 'Yes, that's really magnificent.'

'Of course it wasn't just as easy as it sounds,' Monsieur Terrasse said. 'Monsieur Dupont and myself had no end of trouble trying to make those fools at the War Ministry see reason, but in the end we succeeded. After all, in the next war public opinion will insist that our soldiers enjoy all possible comforts. Of course there isn't going to be a next war, but the Ministry's too stupid to realize that. All this talk about Hitler is stupid.'

Bigou didn't listen much to Monsieur Terrasse's last words. While the other was talking, he was wondering. After all, it wasn't every day he saw the company secretary alone and in a good mood. Perhaps, though, it was a little mean to strike when the iron was hot. But with Marie ill and Odette going to make her first communion next year . . .

'Monsieur Terrasse,' he began, licking hard at his suddenly parched lips, 'I ask you to believe that it isn't only for myself that I am speaking.'

'What is it that you're trying to say, Bigou?' Monsieur Terrasse's expression was now hard and penetrating. 'Am I to understand that you are asking me for a rise in salary?'

'In a manner of speaking, yes, monsieur,' Bigou said. 'You see, I've been with the company some time now and I am earning only two thousand francs a month and it isn't very much . . .'

'And you believe in striking while the iron's hot, eh?' Monsieur Terrasse gave Bigou a heavy playful thump on the shoulder, but his eyes weren't smiling at all and his mouth stretched like a dent in a Homburg hat. 'I shouldn't worry about money if I were you. We all of us think that we could do with a little more of it than we've got, but health is after all the main thing. Of course I don't say that when the results of this new contract materialize — but in the meantime we must all be patient, must we not? Good evening, Bigou.' He waved a thick hand and walked out through the glass door and got into his limousine and was driven off. Bigou watched him unhappily.

'One more and one less,' the night watchman shuffled up and said behind him. 'I said: "One more and one less,"' he repeated when Bigou did not answer.

'The swine,' Bigou said.

'Who are you talking about?' the night watchman asked. 'The Pope?'

'I was talking about Terrasse,' Bigou said. 'He's just refused me a rise.'

'He refused me one last week too,' the night watchman said. 'What do you think of that? A chap who earns at least forty thousand francs a month refusing to give a rise to a chap who earns eight hundred francs a month. It's a disgrace.'

'There's worse than that,' Bigou said. Then he saw that the night watchman's rheumy eyes were too interested and he realized that he would be dismissed if he divulged any of the firm's secrets. 'No, I haven't said anything,' he said.

'You were going to talk about commissions, weren't you?' the night watchman said, bringing his sore mean red face close to Bigou's. 'All right, I shan't ask you to give away anything, but you needn't think I don't know that the directors get a big commission on profits as well as their salaries and their dividends. But that won't last forever. Not after tonight, it won't. Listen: I hear on very good authority that there's going to be trouble tonight. People are fed up with the big bugs: Stavisky and Chautemps and Daladier and the rest.'

'What have Stavisky and Chautemps and Daladier got to do with Terrasse refusing you and me a rise?' Bigou asked.

'Just this,' the night watchman answered. 'Stavisky and Chautemps and Daladier and Terrasse are all big bugs. They all go to Saint-Jean-de-Luz in the summer for three months at a time. Well, all that's going to stop. The Croix de Feu are going to make it stop.'

'But the Croix de Feu are big bugs too,' Bigou said. 'They're all mummy's darlings from Passy and Auteuil and Neuilly. And then they're fascists, aren't they?'

'Fascists or not they're going to put a stop to all this roguery,' the night watchman said. 'And the communists are going to join in too. It's going to be a proper cleaning-up. If I were you I'd go and see for myself. I'd come with you, but I've got to go round and stick a key in all those rotten locks every half-hour. Well, good evening, Monsieur Bigou.'

Afraid that he had perhaps talked too much, Bigou went out into the street. Perhaps the night watchman was right. After all things couldn't be worse under the fascists than they were at present under the republicans. Perhaps the workers would get a fairer deal. Perhaps he would be able to earn enough money to send Marie away to a sanatorium. Perhaps there wouldn't be any longer such a difference between his overcoat and Monsieur Terrasse's overcoat. The memory of a suspicion he had once briefly entertained as a

boy recurred to him: that the apparently meaningless be-
haviour of his fellow men was a comedy staged for his
especial delusion; that when he wasn't there, people laughed
at him for being so simple as to believe that Christians found
it difficult to love one another; that somewhere was a cellar,
where, when the trapdoor was battened down, men wor-
shipped the Father in spirit and in truth. Smiling at the
folly of his bygone sense, he bumped into a pretty woman
in furs and with eyes like Our Lady of Perpetual Succour.
Her shoes made a squeaky noise as she walked, and her cor-
rugated fur cape looked like a tippet made of cucumbers.

'Coming, darling? We'll do beautiful things.' She stopped
the catalogue of her prowess when she caught sight of his
battered overcoat. 'I beg your pardon,' she said. 'I didn't
know you were broke too.'

'Everybody's broke these days,' Bigou said.

'But not forever.' The girl's eyes were friendly now. 'Things
are going to happen tonight. Just go out and take a look at
the rue Royale if you don't believe me. The rich aren't going to get it all their own way much longer. And a good job
too. Do you know why I'm selling my body? Because of a
swine of a burgess doctor. My husband ran away and left
me and I had to have my little girl of four operated on for
appendicitis, and the dirty fellow stood over her with his
knife poised in the air refusing to operate until I'd promised
to pay him three thousand francs. *Ce n'est pas gai, la vie
d'artiste.* All the same, it's no use worrying.' She made a
white sign on the night with her glove and vanished into the
gloom.

The girl's words aroused his own desire for vengeance.
What if she were right? What if one had but to strike to

obtain? It was not right that Dupont and Terrasse should
earn so much and he should earn so little. He hurried along
the boulevard. The frost in the air struck his cheek with
a pleasant tang. He saw that the coloured destination
boards had been removed from the sides of the buses and he
remembered reading that on the previous evening the rioters
had used them as weapons.

The pillars in front of the dark bulk of the Madeleine
grew like cool trees in a forest, but the surge of people in
the rue Royale was so great that the AB and AS buses had
to turn up the Boulevard Malesherbes. The chairs had been
removed from the pavement in front of Larue and Weber.
Before Bigou stretched a vast black sago of hats. He asked
a lighted cigarette on his left what was happening.

'We're going to the Chamber.'

'And then?'

'We're going to throw all the deputies into the Seine.'

'And then?'

'We'll govern ourselves, of course.'

'That's just the trouble with France,' another cigarette on
Bigou's right said. 'The people of France are not fit to govern themselves. At least that's what la Rocque says.'

'To hell with what la Rocque says. It's what Blum says.'

'To hell with what Blum says.'

'Listen: I was in the trenches for four years and I know
what I'm talking about and I still say: "To hell with what
la Rocque says."'

'I was in the trenches for four years too, and I say: "To
hell with what everybody says,"' Bigou said.

Both cigarettes laughed at Bigou's sally. Far away toward
the Place de la Concorde somebody shouted:

'Down with Daladier!'
The crowd took up the cry:
'Down with Daladier!'
'Down with Chautemps!'
'Down with Frot!'
'Down with Cot!'
The last two ejaculations seemed to please the crowd most, perhaps because they rhymed. They kept shouting them over and over again. It was like calling Our Lady mirror of justice and tower of ivory in the litany, but very much more amusing. Then the darkness started the *Marseillaise* and the crowd sang with sad hope beneath the stars. They sang at first self-consciously, then with enthusiasm, then almost not at all. The song died away as suddenly as it had begun. The night hung silent again, with the centuries velvet in its folds. Then the shouting broke out once more:
'Down with Daladier!'
'Down with Frot!'
'Down with Cot!'
'*A la Chambre!*'
The last cry was repeated with especial force. The crowd began to ooze forward toward the Place de la Concorde as though sucked by a sluice-gate. Bigou oozed with them. 'Come on, Frenchmen,' somebody cried, and a man with matter running from his right eye trod on Bigou's foot. Bigou almost screamed aloud with pain, but he swore instead. When the surge forward stopped, he found himself squeezed up against the man with the running eye. He scowled at Bigou as though it were Bigou who had trod on his toe and not he on Bigou's.
'Don't look at me like that,' he said. His half-finished

cigarette bobbed about on his underlip as he spoke and he smelt of sour wine.

'A cat can look at a king,' Bigou replied as aggressively as he dared.

'Who do you take me for?' the man said, thrusting out his chin. 'I didn't fight in the last war for nothing, I can tell you. Four years in the trenches. And then I met Painlevé in 1927. There were a lot of us ex-service chaps there, but I had more medals than the rest, and when Painlevé met me he stopped and shook me by the hand.' But before he could say any more he was sucked into a pocket of permutation. Bigou was left with other faces muttering, 'Down with Frot, down with Cot' in a bored rosary of imprecation.

'They're all in it,' somebody said. 'Daladier, Chautemps, Tardieu, Laval, Blum, they're all in it.'

'The only thing to do is to sack the Chamber and throw all the deputies into the Seine,' somebody else said.

'France for Frenchmen!' somebody else said. 'Down with the dirty foreigners!'

In the middle distance a figure stood against the sky. Bigou wondered how the man had got there and supposed that he must be standing on horseback or on somebody's shoulders. The man took off his hat and held it in front of his face. There was a clamour and a sudden silence and the man said something which Bigou couldn't quite catch. There was another silence, and then a shout of defiance and derision which rolled over the heads of the crowd with a grand rumble. Bigou found himself shouting without knowing why. When he grew tired of shouting, he turned to his neighbour. 'What's up?' he asked. 'That was Bonnefoy-Sibour,' the man answered. 'He says that he's given orders to the

garde mobile to fire on us if we try to cross the bridge.'
'You're a liar,' a man a little farther away said. 'It was Frot
himself and he said he was going to fire on us anyway.'
'Three cheers for Chiappe!' somebody else cried and the
crowd took up the chant.

'Follow me, all good Frenchmen!' The command was
rapped out with a crack, and once more Bigou was carried
forward in the surge. For the first few minutes he allowed
his movements to be controlled by others, but suddenly his
arms and his legs were his own and he was striding through
those who had strode through him. Exhilaration filled his
soul as he found himself floating into the Place de la Concorde. He felt happier than he had felt since he had
marched off to the war in 1914 with the women throwing
flowers. He didn't know whether it was the stars or the
lamps which were shining on the helmets of the gardes
mobiles drawn up at the neck of the bridge, but he knew
that they looked beautiful. He knew, too, that it couldn't
really hurt getting a bullet in your belly, because justice was
going to prevail forever. From now on, nobody was going
to earn less than five thousand francs a month. Workers'
wives would no longer be ill with tuberculosis in garrets: if
they were ill, they would be sent to sanatoria in Switzerland,
and if they weren't ill, they would be able to sit comfortably
at home and read André Maurois. 'Three cheers for liberty!'
he shouted, and rushed on toward the so beautiful helmets.

He did not stop running forward as soon as he heard the
first rifle-shots: they sounded harmless, like someone being
bad-tempered in Spanish a long way off. He did not stop
running forward until other people running backward made
him turn and fly too. Then, indeed, he took to his heels

with all his new certainties frozen to fear about his heart. The shots rang out again. 'Sweet Jesus, they're firing on us!' a man cried. 'It'll be our turn tomorrow,' somebody else said. Bigou heard a bullet whistle past his ear: it made a noise like silk being torn. He tasted blood and salt in his mouth. 'The swine,' his mind said, but his tongue could make no sound, because it was dry and hanging out of his mouth.

When he reached the entrance to the rue Royale, the Madeleine still stood dark and friendly like an enlarged reflection of the Chambre des Députés on the other side of the river. Bigou heard the sound of horses' hooves and, turning, saw a seethe of golden helmets come bobbing toward him, like a giant's helping of tapioca. More shots rang out. There was a sound of glass being broken and yells of anger and yelps of pain. Everybody seemed to be saying 'merde.' A seethe of macaroni came to meet the seethe of tapioca: Bigou realized that the police were charging with their white bâtons from the Madeleine as well. On his right he saw letters above a shop: BAS LYNÉS, with the space inside the 'B' all solid and blocked out to make it look like a character from a foreign language. He pushed toward it and fell through overcoats and hats onto stone. The hooves crashed past like a hexameter from Homer. Bigou found himself lying in a shop doorway. In the window beside him a wax mannequin showed her legs.

The main fighting seemed to be going on both outside the Madeleine and at the other end of the rue Royale, although all around him he could see policemen's bâtons rising and falling. Cramming his hat over his eyes, Bigou tried to burrow his way down toward the rue du Faubourg Saint-

Honoré so as to be able to take the underground at Saint-Philippe du Roule.

His fever for justice had cooled: he wanted only to get home and tell Marie what he had seen. His brain swam with love for her. He was still loving her when a policeman's bulk stood in front of him, blocking his way. At first Bigou couldn't distinguish his uniform, but only the silver buttons, like holes punched in the night.

'Where are you going?' the policeman asked Bigou.

'I'm going home,' Bigou said.

'That's what they all say,' the policeman said.

'I'm doing nobody any harm,' Bigou said.

'That's what they all say,' the policeman said.

A rush of clothes and boots and hats separated them. Somebody trod on Bigou's foot and somebody else kicked his ankle. He was carried along in pain for several yards until the walls of the world fell away and he found himself in the rue d'Anjou. His feet made a fine clam-clam as he ran along the empty street, but when he reached the point where it intersected with the rue Pont l'Evèque he saw a platoon of policemen drawn up. He turned immediately and ran back toward the rue du Faubourg Saint-Honoré. The policeman from whom he had escaped came running to meet him with his raised bâton slitting the sky.

'Dirty swine!' the policeman exclaimed.

Bigou closed his eyes and prepared to feel being hurt. Often when lying awake in bed at nights, he had wondered how he would stand being guillotined and if he would have the strength of character to be disembowelled if his suffering would save his wife a similar fate. He tried to feel brave against the red screen of his closed eyes, but all he knew was that he didn't wish to be hurt. When he opened his eyes, the policeman had lowered his bâton and was leaning against the wall.

'It's no use; I can't do it,' he said. 'When a chap hits me, I can hit him back, but when he stands there doing nothing I can't hit him. Funny, isn't it?'

'I suppose I ought to be thankful that you're a merciful chap,' Bigou said.

'Not that that excuses you for rioting against the Government,' the policeman said. 'It's very wrong to riot against the Government.'

'But I wasn't rioting against the Government,' Bigou said.

'It's very wrong to riot against the Government,' the policeman said.

'In any case I shan't do it again,' Bigou said.

The policeman pointed to where a small café was hollowed out in amber.

'Let's go and have a quick one,' he said.

There were no customers in the café when they entered it. The counter was a horseshoe covered with tin. Behind it a woman was washing glasses in a sink. She went on washing them for several seconds before she looked up with sullen inquiry. When she opened her mouth, the absence of molars made the upper row of her teeth look like a Spanish comb.

'Well?' she asked.

'Two brandies,' the policeman ordered.

The woman produced two small glasses shaped like silver tulips. When she had filled them with brandy, they became golden tulips. She filled them so full that the liquor ran over the side and down onto the counter. When the policeman raised his glass, the drops fell on his tunic, but he did not trouble to wipe them off.

'Here's to us,' he said.

Bigou tinkled his glass against the policeman's and some more brandy fell on the floor. A splash fell on the policeman's boot and made a shiny stain with rays sticking out of it.

'It was nice of you to bring me in here,' Bigou said.

'As long as you understand that it's very wrong to riot against the Government,' the policeman said.

'Who else is there to riot against?' the woman asked. 'It's the politicians that are at the bottom of all the trouble.'

'It's wrong, all the same, to riot against the Government,' the policeman said.

'What about the revolution?' the woman asked, skewering a dirty cloth round the inside of a tumbler. 'Why should it have been right to riot against the Government then and wrong now?'

'Things have changed since then,' the policeman said.

'As far as I can see they haven't changed at all,' the woman said.

'Of course they've changed,' the policeman said. 'For instance, look at photography.'

'That's stupid,' the woman said.

An advertisement for Byrrh caught Bigou's eye: it represented a pretty girl in a scarlet blouse with grapes like purple balloons all about her head. Staring at her with elation, Bigou knew that he had discovered the secret of the universe; when he had drunk the remainder of his brandy, he knew that he could make the policeman discover it too, but when he sought for the words to communicate the secret, they would not come.

'What about another?' Bigou asked the policeman.

The woman refilled the glasses and stood regarding Bigou with surly expectation. Bigou pulled out his pocketbook and extracted a fifty-franc note which he handed to the woman. 'Easy seen it's the beginning of the month,' the policeman said.

The woman's bust moved along the counter toward the cash register and her shoulders moved along the mirror behind the bottles. When she pressed the key of the register, it was like hearing a lot of rusty bicycle bells rung simultaneously. Bigou raised his glass and clinked it against the policeman's, but the policeman's eyes had a far-away look. The policeman tossed his drink off at a single gulp, so Bigou did the same. When the woman came back along the counter with the change, Bigou found that she had kept back the money for the policeman's round as well as for his own. He was still recounting the change when the door opened and twelve more policemen entered the café. They all wore helmets like blue pork pies and had vertical sprays of silver buttons on their tunics. They kept changing their truncheons from hand to hand and stood along the counter making manly faces at their reflections in the mirror.

'What a business!' one of them said.

'I caught one chap a slosh on the ear he won't forget for a long time,' another of them said.

'Daladier'll have to resign all the same,' another of them said.

'If this sort of thing happened in Berlin, I'll bet Hitler'd know how to deal with it,' another of them said.

'Albert Lebrun's no good,' another of them said.

'It says in *Paris Soir* that the Pope is following the present crisis with great interest,' another of them said.

'So's Madame Stavisky,' another of them said.

There was a general laugh at this and five or six subordinate conversations broke out. Bigou put his change back into his pocket and, turning to bid farewell to his own policeman, found that he had already been absorbed by his colleagues. In one grand blue clot they stood, yammering at one another without listening back. Bigou went out into the street, waving a vague benevolence at the bisected woman behind the counter. The rue d'Anjou was deserted and no policeman stood at its junction with the rue du Pont l'Evèque. Bigou ran along it until he came to the Boulevard Malesherbes, which also was almost empty. The stars looked like holes in a lighted pepper-pot. As he ran, he could hear the sound of shouting in the distance and the occasional crack of a rifle or revolver, but as he drew near the patient bulk of Saint Augustin, these sounds had become an almost friendly blur.

Down on the platform of the underground an employee was killing bacilli. With a perforated pail he walked slowly from one end of the platform to the other leaving a sticky trail of damp spots behind him. An advertisement for Persil represented three pretty girls hanging brassières on a clothesline and three elderly lechers taking off their hats to them. Through the tunnel the lights of the station at Miromesnil could be seen glittering like the city of God. A train rattled in at the far platform filled with people sitting in amber casements. The second-class carriages at either end were painted green, but the first-class carriage in the middle was painted red, with the metropolitan arms stamped on it and a scroll: *Nec Fluctuat Nec Mergitur*. It rattled away out again and turned into a slowly disappearing red light.

The second-class compartment at the tail of the train which Bigou entered was filled with passengers wearing humble shabby clothes unlike the occupants of the first-class coach two carriages ahead which was plastered with notices which said: DON'T FORGET THAT THE NUMBERED SEATS ARE RESERVED FOR THE WAR WOUNDED, but nobody bothered much about that any longer. Bigou sat down on the hard wooden seat opposite a man reading an unfolded newspaper on the back of which Bigou could make out the words: 'The Papal Nuncio says that the preservation of peace is among the most earnest desires of His Holiness Pope Pius XI.'

When the train had gone a little way into the tunnel, the newspaper was lowered. A stern puckered red face looked inquiringly at Bigou.

'You been in it too?' the man asked.

Bigou nodded vigorously. Then he looked to see if anybody was watching him. Two girls sat next the window, but their eyes were as empty as spittoons. 'You can get them at the Printemps for fifty francs,' one of them was saying. 'Real silk, too.'

'How did you know?' Bigou asked.

'That's easy,' the man said. 'Your face is all flushed. You've an eager look in your eye. Not many people in France have eager looks in their eyes these days.'

'That's true,' Bigou said.

'Listen: we've been beaten tonight, but tomorrow night we shan't be beaten. Daladier and Frot are going to pay dearly for this. We are Frenchmen all the same.'

'That's right,' Bigou said.

'We fought in the war. At least I did. Four years of it. The Marne, the Somme, Verdun. They told me I was a hero when I was in the trenches, but when I came back they wouldn't even give me a job.'

'I fought in the war too,' Bigou said.

The train crashed into Miromesnil. Opposite where their window stopped was a notice which said that the Petits Chanteurs des Croix de Bois would sing vespers at Saint-Germain l'Auxerrois next Sunday, with Pontifical Benediction.

'That sort of thing oughtn't to be allowed,' the man said. 'Not a single hymn should be sung while there's an empty belly in France. In case you don't know it, I'm a communist.'

Bigou nodded again. Now that he came to think of it, he was a communist too, but the man got out before he could tell him and the wall of tunnel was again singing in black on yellow, DUBO, DUBON, DUBONNET. The train clanged on down the iron tripes of the city. Rond-Point-des-Champs-Elysées, Alma Marceau, Iéna succeeded each other like days strung past a god.

The station at the Porte de Saint-Cloud smelt of lubricating oil, brilliantine, and wet cement. The platform was strewn with pink and green tickets although there were receptacles for used tickets at all the exits. A ticket-puncher in a blue uniform was shouting to another ticket-puncher in a blue uniform on the opposite platform. 'Speicher's a dead cert for the Tour de France this year,' he said. His voice was drowned in the noise of a train rushing in from the Pont de Sèvres. Bigou ran up the steps two at a time.

The avenue de Versailles stretched in broad dreariness with the railway bridge at the Point du Jour looking like a balcony slung out of heaven. There were not many pedestrians on the pavements, but there were a lot of cars moving along the roadway. The revolution of their tyres made a noise like sticking-plaster being ripped from a wound. The house where Bigou lived was situated near the Point du Jour. He made his way quickly to it beneath the cold candles of the stars.

On the door of the concierge's loge a little oval red notice was hanging. It was an advertisement from an undertaker's establishment and said: 'LA CONCIERGE REVIENT DE SUITE'; but the concierge was there all right, having forgotten to remove the notice. Framed in gold she sat at the table which occupied at least half of the tiny room. She had frizzy black hair like a bath-sponge soaked in ink. Her husband, in shirt-sleeves and cap, sat opposite her, with a camembert cheese jammed on the point of a knife. Between them on the oil-cloth cover of the table a cat was eating off a plate. Their eyes rounded with disinterested hostility as Bigou opened the door to say good-night. Bigou both hated and feared them. He resented the fact that Madame Lacordaire made him pay fifteen francs a quarter for taking his letters upstairs, which she never did, since he always called for them at the loge; but he nevertheless hoped that behind her dirty apron she invisibly loved him.

'Good evening, monsieur et dame,' he said.

'Good evening, Monsieur Bigou.'

'Nothing new?'

'Nothing new.'

The concierge and her husband stared solidly at the cat. Bigou hoped that they would say something nice about his wife being ill because he would much rather love people than hate them. He knew that they were waiting for him to go away so that they might go on thinking about nothing in peace; but he could not go away without trying to squeeze out of them at least a semblance of sympathy.

'There's been rioting tonight,' he said.

'Ah?' Monsieur Lacordaire said.

'France is rotten,' Madame Lacordaire said.

'I'm glad it's not here because of Madame Bigou,' Bigou said. 'The rioting, I mean.'

'Naturally,' Madame Lacordaire said.

'Money's a small blessing compared with good health,' Bigou said.

'Health above everything,' Monsieur Lacordaire said.

Bigou hoped that they were going to say something more personal, but they didn't. Monsieur and Madame Lacordaire sat on with concentrated apathy. The cat's tail stuck up in the air like a mast. The camembert fell from the point of Monsieur Lacordaire's knife and broke with a splodge. Monsieur Lacordaire crammed a portion of the yellow sludge into his mouth and washed it down with a gulp of wine.

'Cheese and wine's the best thing in the world,' he said.

Fumbling in the dark for the button of the minuterie, Bigou pressed that which opened the front door instead. A bell in the Lacordaire's loge rang with a ping and Monsieur Lacordaire swore so loudly that Bigou knew that he was intended to hear. The lamps on the stair burned feebly when he eventually succeeded in pressing the right button and he ran up swiftly so as to reach his own landing before they went out automatically. There was no carpet on the stair. Each landing looked exactly like the landing below it. There were two blistered doors facing each other with a great brass knob in the middle. There was also a communal lavatory in the centre of the landing with its door half-open. Even Bigou could distinguish his own landing only because he knew that he had to climb six flights to reach it. The minuterie went out as he came panting up the last few steps, but deep down in the well of banisters he could still see a haze of light coming from the loge.

The flat consisted of a bedroom, a kitchen, and a recess known as a *cabinet de toilette*, but the family always washed in the kitchen, as Madame Bigou kept the coal in the cabinet de toilette in order to save having to carry it up from the cellar. There was no room for a table in the kitchen, so the Bigous ate their meals in the bedroom. At present the table was laden with the remains of her own and Odette's supper which Madame Bigou apparently had not felt well enough to clear away. There was also a clean plate set for Bigou. An unshaded electric bulb hung like a lighted tear from the ceiling and a crucifix and a portrait of Sainte Thérèse de l'Enfant Jésus had been nailed above the small bed in which Odette, aged eleven, was now sleeping. Bigou bent and kissed the child's warm pudgy cheek and stood for a moment looking down at her in loving pity. Then he bent over his wife who was lying in the other bed. She opened her eyes as Bigou's lips touched her hot brow.

'Where have you been all this time?' she asked. 'I was beginning to worry. You're not going to tell me that you've been working late again.'

'Just a little late,' Bigou told her. 'And then I got caught in the rioting in the rue Royale. There's been terrible rioting tonight, Marie. Shots fired too. I shouldn't wonder if people hadn't been killed.'

'Poor France,' Marie murmured. She lay on her back
without moving, her dark hair spread out on the pillow,
shining like wet seaweed. In the pupils of her eyes two
miniature Bigous were reflected, like heads on very small
coins. 'One wonders how it's all going to end.'

'This time I think they're bound to clean the mess up,'
Bigou said. 'There's been serious rioting, I tell you. The
politicians are bound to realize that dishonesty in high
places can't be kept hushed up forever. And then I met a
fellow in the underground and he said that even if the police
had won tonight they wouldn't win tomorrow.'

'Jean, promise me something.'

'Anything you like, Marie.'

'Promise me you won't go rioting tomorrow.'

'Of course I'll promise, Marie. I came near enough to
getting my head broken tonight.'

'You see I want you still to be here to look after Odette
when I'm gone. She's getting a big girl now. She'll be making her first communion next year.'

'I know, Marie, but, Marie, you're not going to die.'

'Of course not, Jean, but all the same I feel so ill sometimes.'

'We all feel ill at times, Marie, but that doesn't mean that
we're going to die.'

'Sometimes, Jean, I can't help wishing that we had just a
little more money. Two thousand francs is a good salary, I
know, but it's not a fortune all the same.'

'Perhaps I'll have more soon, Marie. Listen: I was talking
to old Terrasse tonight. He was telling me that the firm had
just landed a big new contract. That's pretty certain to
mean a rise for everybody later on.' He tried to speak as
though he believed what he said.

'And by then the cost of living will have gone up so much that we'll need a rise, anyway. Jean, forgive me for talking like this. I'm depressed and I'm not feeling very well to-night. Jean, do you still love me as much as you did?'

'Of course, Marie.'

'Jean, do you remember the day we met in Nancy?'

'Of course, Marie. You were wearing your red dress and the hay got caught in your hair.'

'Jean darling, we've grown old since then.'

He sat stroking her hand until she fell asleep. Then, be-cause he was hungry and couldn't be bothered cooking him-self anything to eat and because he wanted to talk to some-body about the night's events, he went downstairs and across the road to the café for a beer and a sandwich. Baco, the proprietor, Chanu, the butcher, Latérade, and Verneuil and the tart's mother were all there, sticking their mugs into jugs along the counter. The new wireless was on full blast, blaring advertisements from Radio-Paris:

> *Bien l'bonjour Monsieur Lévitan,*
> *Vous avez des meubl-es,*
> *Vous avez des meubl-es,*
> *Bien l'bonjour, Monsieur Lévitan,*
> *Vous avez des meubles qui durent longtemps.*

But the noise didn't seem to bother either Baco or his cus-tomers who were used to talking at the top of their voices.

'Talk of the devil . . .' Baco said as Bigou entered.

Bigou grinned unhappily because he suspected that the others had not been talking about him at all and that Baco had only made the remark in order to make him feel uncom-fortable. He knew that both Baco and Chanu rather de-spised him because he did not make as much money as they did. Latérade, too, was richer than Bigou, because he had two pensions from the Government: one for having served fifteen years as a sergeant in West Africa and another for having worked for twenty years in the post-office; and he earned another seven hundred francs a month by working as a filing clerk in the Boulevard de Latour-Maubourg. Verneuil, who worked as a conductor on the buses, was the only one of the group who was poorer than Bigou.

'And how is Madame Bigou?' asked the tart's mother, who had a kind heart.

'Not too well, I'm afraid,' Bigou said.

'Perhaps when the spring comes,' the tart's mother said.

'That's it,' Latérade said. 'You mustn't worry. Perhaps when the spring comes.'

Bigou nodded and changed the subject, because he knew that they were already tired of looking sympathetic. It was impossible for human beings to feel the tin tack in the other fellow's belly. 'A beer and a sandwich,' he ordered. 'There's been rioting on the Place de la Concorde,' he said. 'Shots fired.'

'Verneuil's just been telling us about it,' Baco said as he ran out Bigou's beer.

'Were you in it too?' Bigou asked the bus conductor.

'Hell! They set my bus on fire,' Verneuil said. 'We were trying to get up the Champs Elysées so as not to have to cross the Place Beauvau and a crowd of students stopped us and made us all get out and then set fire to the petrol. It was a beautiful blaze.'

'All the same, things are going to finish badly,' Baco said.

'We'll muddle through,' Chanu said. 'France has always muddled through. And then there's only one thing to do:

put a clean man at the head of the Government, a fellow like Doumergue. Perhaps he could make things better.'

'Politicians never make things better; they only make things worse,' Latérade said.

'Of course,' Verneuil said. 'Doumergue'll just mess things up like anybody else. They're a dirty lot, politicians, always on the make.'

'That's why I cheat on my taxes,' Chanu said. 'Because I don't want to pay for politicians' mistresses. Every time I take ten francs at the till, I write it down as five.'

'I keep two sets of books,' Baco said. 'One for my wife and myself to look at and one for the tax inspector.'

Everybody grinned all along the counter. It was evident that they didn't care who paid for France as long as they didn't. But Bigou didn't grin; he wanted to say something about the need for paying for public services and armaments, but he knew that the others would only think him a prig if he did and say that he was jealous because he couldn't cheat on his own taxes, as his earnings were returned by his employer.

A stick came tapping into the café: it was Etienne Bacqueroët from the rue Claude Terrasse. Bacqueroët had lost his eyes and half his face at Verdun. He wore a wig with long red hairs like a bedroom mat.

'And to think it was for swine like these that one got one's mug smashed up,' he said when he had ordered a beer.

Nobody said anything, because everybody felt a little ashamed when Bacqueroët was about, because he had suffered so much and all apparently for so little. Then the tart herself came in in her new fox fur fresh from dalliance with her lover. High on her heels she stood, pouring bénédictine into her porcelain face. Behind her back everybody called her 'the yellow tart' because she was so blonde, but to her face they called her Mademoiselle Turbigo.

'She's the dead spit of Marlene Dietrich,' her mother said.

Everybody laughed except Bacqueroët whose tortured face looked as though he were imagining the yellow tart as even more beautiful than she was. Bigou paid for his beer and his sandwich and went away back across the road to bed. He opened the window to let the smell of sickness out and then closed it again in case Marie would catch cold. When at length he fell asleep, he dreamed of columns and columns of figures, like ants walking.

II

THE POLITICIANS began to get down to things. Albert Lebrun wept in the Elysée and Henri Béraud wrote an article. Gaston Doumergue came galloping back from Tournefeuille to be Prime Minister and everybody was glad because he smiled so nicely. Philippe Pétain became Minister of War and nobody was afraid of Hitler any more. It was decided that the auditors of public companies ought to do more than check the trial balance with the general ledger and that Paul Reynaud was talking nonsense when he said that France could not possibly retain her foreign markets with the franc at seventy-seven to the pound. It was decided to suppress tax evasion and to do away with wooden railway carriages. It was decided that Monsieur Frot was bound to be killed one of these fine days. It was decided that it was

only fair not to be unfair too soon to Gaston Doumergue,
and besides the old gentleman had been such a good-hu-
moured President of the Republic and had presented football cups so pleasantly. A *fête de nuit* was held at Long-
champ, and the horses raced beneath arc lamps, and Gaby
Morlay and Sacha Guitry and everybody who was anybody
were all there, and the green grass grew all around, only it
didn't look green, and afterwards there was a special edition
of *Paris-Soir* to say that Hitler had just had to have a purge
in Berlin which proved to the directors of Schneider
and Renault that the German menace was all my eye and
Betty Martin. Of course it was a pity that Planeta had
to go and murder Dolfuss, but one knew what these Austrians were, and a war could never start twice in the same
place, and after all Mussolini had been very decent to his
widow. The curé of the Madeleine was consecrated Bishop
of Nevers and Maurice Chevalier brought out a new song.
King Alexander of Yugoslavia was assassinated at Marseilles,
but Cardinal Verdier prayed for the repose of his soul beneath the Arc de Triomphe and took off his biretta to the
archimandrites who did their stuff afterwards. The wise
man of Tournefeuille went back to Tournefeuille, but
whether he went before or after the murder of King Alexander nobody could quite remember and nobody cared, because behind the smile there had lurked the desire to become a dictator, or at least so Monsieur Pierre Laval said,
or perhaps it was Monsieur André Tardieu, so they shunted
him out on the *douzième provisoire*, which was obviously
an excuse, as it had to do only with taxation. It was decided
to suppress tax evasion and to do away with wooden railway carriages. Monsieur Pierre Laval and Monsieur Pierre

Etienne Flandin went for a sail in a boat with Mussolini at Stresa. They also went to London, but which of them was Prime and which of them was Foreign Minister everybody soon forgot, because the more it changed, the more it was the same thing, and Ray Ventura was a great discovery, and *tout allait très bien, Madame la marquise,* and there was a posh new whorehouse on the Boulevard Edgar Quinet, where the girls cost only fifty francs, although of course you had to pay extra for the room.

III

BIGOU would have preferred to go alone with his wife to Odette's first communion, but Mademoiselle Turbigo and her mother insisted on coming, too, because first communions were so pretty, so they said. Madame Bigou wore her best black satin dress and the fox fur for which she had been inveigled by the advertisements in the underground into paying twelve monthly instalments of seventy-five francs, and Bigou wore his new black suit, or at least it had been new ten years ago. Madame Turbigo was wearing her best clothes too, and Mademoiselle Turbigo herself was dressed up to the nines as usual, but of course she wasn't wearing her best clothes because all her clothes were best clothes nowadays now that Monsieur Frimandière of the Société Anonyme Frimandière was her lover.

Baco and Chanu waved them off, and Baco said that they must be sure and look in at the café and have a snifter when the ceremony was over. It was a fine day, and above their

heads the sky stretched, blue and silken, like Mary's girdle.
The pavements were full of little girls in white going to their
first communion at the chapel of Sainte Géneviève. The
flutter of their veils smeared the world with new daubs of
Christ, and even those who had lost their faith looked at
them with a tender smile. Bigou walked with a self-conscious air and wished that Marie's new shoes wouldn't
squeak so much, but he soon grew accustomed to his new
feeling of importance because there were plenty other self-
conscious-looking men about with wives and squeaking
shoes. Odette walked with her prayer-book firmly in her
hand and with her head demurely lowered.

There was a terrific jam in the church because all the
front seats had been reserved for the communicants and the
parents and friends had to hugger-mugger together at the
back. A mincing cleric in surplice and cassock ushered
Madame Bigou and Bigou and Mademoiselle Turbigo and
her mother all into a row together and smiled at them with
insistence as though to say: 'I'm not really as holy as
you think I am and I know you're not really as worldly as
you pretend you are.' Bigou knelt and tried to pray when
he saw that Marie and Mademoiselle Turbigo and her
mother were also kneeling and trying to pray, but a woman
came side-stepping along the kneeling cushion and jabbed
him in the stomach with the ferrule of her umbrella so he
had to begin all over again. It was a long time since he had
prayed and he started off on the first prayer he could remember: 'Hail, Holy Queen, Mother of Mercy, hail,' but
when he got a little way he found that he had forgotten the
words, so he prayed instead: 'Make Odette a good girl, not
too religious, but make her a good girl; make Marie well

again; and make me soon earn more money.' Then he sat
upright and saw that, although Madame Turbigo was sitting
upright too and was gazing at the rest of the congregation
with beady birdy curiosity, Marie and Mademoiselle Turbigo were still praying with their faces jammed right down
on top of their arms almost as though they were weeping.
Bigou wondered if Marie was praying that she wouldn't die,
but of course she wasn't going to die because she had been
looking so much better of late and had been able to get
through the week's washing in a single day instead of taking
two days like this time last year; but he couldn't understand
what Mademoiselle Turbigo had to pray about, because she
couldn't very well wish for a richer lover than she had.

The lame priest who lived above the bakery limped in
to say the Mass in stiff white shining vestments. The children in front all knelt down for the *Judica me, Deus,* and
the *Confiteor,* but most of the parents stood up because they
didn't wish to look too pious in front of their friends. When
the celebrant had read the gospel, the abbé Pécher entered
the pulpit to preach the sermon. He was a tall, thin, emaci-
ated ill-looking priest who loved God a lot. Bigou knew him
well by sight, because he was always scurrying about the
district in his cassock taking off his hat as politely to those
who didn't go to Mass as to those who did.

This was a great day in the life of those children who were
going to receive the Body of Christ for the first time, the
priest said, turning his sore lighted eyes on the parents as
though trying to make them love God too. It was a great
miracle which God wrought each time that a priest consecrated the Host at Mass, because He poured Himself Body,
Soul, and Divinity into the species of bread and wine and

was as truly present on the altar as He had been on Calvary. If men and women could only realize this beautiful truth, was it too much to hope that social unrest and wars might one day cease? In Germany Hitler had given a wrong creed to youth and youth had lapped it up and become strong and purposeful. If the children of France would only besiege the altar rails, it was certain that French youth would become stronger and more purposeful than German youth, because God was very much more powerful than Hitler. We must also remember that in the Eucharist God slaked his thirst for us as well as we our love for God. The priest preached on with enthusiasm for a little and then began to repeat himself wearily as though despairing of making the people understand. Then he stopped and held his lined sad face over the boys and girls as though praying that Christ would cool them. Then he made the sign of the cross high over the congregation and vanished into the sacristy.

The Mass went on. The priest, who lived above the bakery, prayed with Peter and Paul, with Clement, Xystus, Cornelius, Cyprian, and Lawrence. God smote Himself down into the Host and His Precious Blood welled up in the chalice and the sacring bell rang out and the hen choir in the organ loft bleated: *'Benedictus qui venit in nomine Domini.'* At the *Agnus Dei,* Bigou had to bury his face in his hands so as to hide his tears. He remembered his own first communion and how he had sworn that no matter how much his friends laughed at him he would serve God forever, and he remembered how he had failed. By the time the sacring bell rang out again for the *Domine, non sum dignus,* he was blubbering away in ecstasy and swearing that he would never lie, cheat, or look lewdly at women again. 'Corpus Domini Nostri Jesu Christi custodiat animam tuam in vitam aeternam' he heard the priest say over and over again as he passed and repassed along the altar rails laying the frail flake of God on the tongues of the kneeling children, but he was unable to look up in case people would see that he had been weeping. When at last he raised his head, the communion was over and the priest was back at the altar and the candle flames had blurred to shafts of gold through the haze of his tears.

He still felt humble and good and pious as he stood in the street afterwards and kissed Odette because she had just made her first communion, and he was surprised to see that his wife and Mademoiselle Turbigo and her mother had been weeping too. Perhaps deep down in themselves everybody wanted to love God and be pure and brave and kind, and were deterred only because they were afraid that other people might think them silly if they tried. After all, it was just as likely that the world was 'about' loving God and being pure and brave and kind as 'about' aeroplanes and cinemas and wireless sets and book-keeping and central heating systems.

They were all rather subdued as they walked back down to the Boulevard Exelmans towards Baco's café, but Baco's red face was as unconverted as ever above his waistcoat as he stood behind his counter arguing the toss with Chanu who had just dropped in for a quick one in between diddling customers. 'So everything went off all right?' he shouted at them through the doorway and came out onto the terrace to serve them with drinks. A cluster of concierges gathered round Odette and began to congratulate her on her first communion. Odette stood gravely and showed them her new prayer-book and communion card. The concierges made a great clatter about how beautiful Odette was and about how beautiful the Blessed Virgin was and then went back to their kitchens to peel potatoes.

Bigou and his wife had intended asking only Mademoiselle Turbigo and her mother back to lunch, but Baco was so generous with the drinks that they felt they had to ask him too, and then Chanu kept hanging about, so they had to ask him as well. And then, as they were about to leave the café, Verneuil, who had just finished an early shift on his bus, came along with Bacqueroët, who had been too badly smashed up in the war to work at all, and of course they had to ask them also. Madame Bigou said that she was afraid that she mightn't have enough for them all to eat, but Baco said that that wouldn't matter at all, and Verneuil said that, as long as there was plenty to drink, that was all that mattered to him. Bigou felt rather proud being seen crossing the avenue with Baco and Chanu because they were so much wealthier than he was and had motor cars in which they drove their fat hams of wives out to Fontainebleau on Sundays, but he was also pleased that he had the grace of God back golden and bubbly within him and wasn't ever going to want to commit adultery again, and he knew that it wasn't just drink, but because he had seen his own daughter, flesh of his flesh, make her first communion. Madame Lacordaire and Lacordaire, who was home for his lunch from his morning sail down the city's sewers, were standing about in the entrance and looked as though they wanted to be invited too, but Madame Bigou pretended not to notice because she knew that she wouldn't have enough plates to go round.

Baco and Chanu were already pretty well stewed and they put their arms round one another's necks and sang as they took a good look at the legs of the yellow tart who was going up the stairs in front of them.

'*Quand un pompier Rencontre un autre pompier ça fait deux pompiers,*' Baco sang.

'*Quand deux pompiers rencontrent un autre pompier ça fait trois pompiers,*' Chanu sang.

> '*Quand un vicomt-e*
> *Rencontre un autre vicomt-e*
> *Ils se racont-ent*
> *Des histoires de vicomt-e,*'

Baco sang.

But behind them again Bacqueroët, climbing the stair on Verneuil's arm, was prophetic and serious.

'One of these fine days France is going to pay for the selfishness of Frenchmen and for her unwillingness to think logically,' he said.

Bigou, bringing up the rear with Odette, wondered what the child, who had just received the Body of Christ for the first time, must make of Baco's and Chanu's hilarity. His soul still shining with zeal, he wanted to shout at them to shut up and to tell them that this was a holy day because Odette had just made a vow to love God and to keep His commandments, but he knew that he couldn't do so without being guilty of the solecism of asserting that religion was true outside church as well as inside.

They all crowded into the tiny flat and stood about making it seem tinier. While Marie was hunting out extra plates, Bigou poured vermouth for his guests. Odette moved among them in her white dress, gravely showing her prayer-book and her communion card. Some nodded at her absent-mindedly and some came back from their potations to be little again and to walk for a flicker with Christ. Bigou could not read from her eyes whether the child was loving Jesus because she had a sacrament in her soul or because she was wearing a pretty dress. On the communion card Our Lady looked like Lilian Gish and had round her head a printed hoop which said that she was the Immaculate Conception.

Before they sat down to eat, the gentlemen asked if they might put themselves at their ease, which meant that they took off their jackets and put on their caps. There weren't enough chairs to go round, so Bigou sat on the bed. Baco said that he would sit on the bed if Mademoiselle Turbigo sat on the bed with him, but the yellow tart said that she would be afraid to risk her virtue, at which there was general laughter. The first course was *hors d'oeuvres variés* and all the guests heaped their plates with slodging great helpings of sardines, anchovies, shrimps, olives, potato salad, herrings, Russian salad, beetroot, meat paste, and *oeufs durs mayonnaise*. Napkins were tucked under collars and bodices and knives seized halfway down the handles as though they were entrenching tools. Bigou was sad at the thought of the money the feast was costing him, but he soon worried no longer when he caught sight of Marie's friendly face.

'It's funny, this God business,' Verneuil said. 'Everything evolved from mud so there's no God.'

Odette looked sadly up from her plate. 'I'd like there to be Our Lady all the same,' she said.

Bigou was so shocked that he dared to be angry.

'Of course there's a God,' he said, stretching across to the table and patting the child's hand. 'Don't you worry about that. You've only got to look at the stars at night to understand.'

'Our friend Bigou's becoming a parson,' Baco mocked.

'There are parsons and parsons,' Bigou declared, with a courage which was not due wholly to the wine he had drunk. 'And the abbé Pécher's as good a parson as any in France, and what's more he preached a very good sermon this morning. And after all, what the priests say about loving your neighbour is only common-sense. If we all loved our neighbours there'd be no wars. Just think of how we all try to do our landlords down, for example, leaving the light on in the stairs so that they have to pay more money. Now if we were as careful of our landlord's property as our own, our landlords might be kinder to us and reduce the rent. And then if we were to try the same thing on an international scale —' Conscious that he had never made such a long speech in front of Baco and Chanu before, Bigou broke off unhappily.

'There'll always be wars,' Bacqueroët said out of his sore sightless eyes. 'There'll always be wars for the same reason as we never learned the truth about Stavisky: human nature. And one of these four mornings there's going to be a very big war indeed.'

'There's the Maginot Line all the same,' Baco said, slodging a great gush of wine over a mouthful of food. 'We're as safe as houses behind that.'

'There are twice as many German babies born every year as there are French babies,' Bacqueroët said.

'There's the Maginot Line, I tell you, and then there's always England,' Baco said.

'I fought in one war and I'm not going to fight in another,' Verneuil said. 'The next time the strafing begins, I'm doing a bunk.'

'Oh, no, you won't,' Bigou said. 'You'll "march, child of the fatherland, that no impure race may feed on the furrows of our fields."'

'All that's stupid,' Chanu said. 'For one thing Hitler hasn't got the mass of the German people behind him, although of course they've got to pretend that they're behind him. And there are too many Germans alive who know what war is.'

'I think war's terrible,' Madame Turbigo said.

'There oughtn't really to be any wars after what Jesus said, ought there?' Odette said.

'What France needs more than anything else is discipline,' Bacqueroët said.

But this was a hard saying and nobody could bear it, so they all scowled a little at Bacqueroët, even although he had been so terribly wounded for France, and shook their heads in commiseration.

> 'Si demain tu vois ma tant-e
> Compliment-e-
> La de ma part,'

Baco sang, to change the subject.

The next course was roast mutton plugged with garlic. Everybody began to smell like acetylene lamps, although as they all smelt together nobody smelt anybody else. Baco ate more noisily than anybody else, pronging great slices of meat onto his fork and ramming them into his mouth with a flourish, and washing them down with gigantic gulps of wine. Everybody talked with his mouth full and nobody listened. Odette alone was silent, picking at her meat with grave endeavour. Bigou wondered if she were wondering what this bibbing and gluttony had to do with loving Him Whose kingdom was not of this world, but when the coffee and the liqueurs were served and she slid silently from the room, he was too imbecilically drunk himself to wonder about anything at all.

Baco ripped open his waistcoat. Through a gap in his shirt his distended belly bulged out like the inside of a football.

'Life's lovely all the same,' he said.

'There's only one thing I need and that's to win the big prize in the lottery,' Verneuil said.

'If I won I'd buy a yacht,' Baco said.

'There's no two ways about it,' Chanu said. 'When one wins one must be discreet. One mustn't be like Bonhoure and run off with one's ticket to the Pavillon de Flore the day the result of the draw's announced. When I win I'll wait five months before I claim my winnings, and then I'll get the bank to cash my ticket for me. Like that I won't have a lot of camels queuing up outside the shop to cadge on me.'

'If I win I'll say "merde" to the managing director of the Société des Transports en Commun de la Région Parisienne,' Verneuil said. 'And I'll never do another stroke of work as long as I live.'

'And if I won I'd send you to Switzerland,' Bigou said, smiling at the familiar tender face of his wife.

'And if I win I'll buy a new wireless set,' Madame Turbigo said. 'Something that makes a noise.'

'That's another thing that's ruining France,' Bacqueroët

said. 'The philosophy of facility. And then to be sure of winning you'd have to live for thirty-six thousand six hundred and sixty-six years and take a ticket in every draw.'

'That's nonsense,' Baco said. 'Monsieur Bonhoure won the first time he took a ticket.'

Bacqueroët didn't answer, but everybody could see that he was annoyed. Bigou began to feel sorry that he had invited him because, although he respected him for his wounds, he really was a gloomy fellow with all his talk of another war. Chanu started boasting that he could still make love to three girls one after another provided they were pretty enough. With the remnants of his new zeal Bigou tried not to listen, but the wine he had drunk was stronger and he was soon laughing as loudly as the rest. Down on the terrace of Baco's café he could hear the guffaws of other parents celebrating their children's union with God. He emptied his liqueur glass and tipped himself out some more brandy. All was for the best in the best of worlds; it was the month of May, the month of Mary.

IV

THE POLITICIANS began to get down to things. It was decided to take sterner steps to suppress tax evasion. It was decided that a family allowance of thirty francs a month per child was insufficient to encourage a higher birth rate. The *Sourire* was published in smaller *format*, but it was just as dirty as ever. Pentecost came and went: on the Saturday morning a string of Renaults and Peugeots and Citroëns

tearing out along the macadam; hard selfish faces behind
hard selfish windscreens; men with plus fours down to their
ankles and women with china faces and glass hair; politicians roaring out of Paris to celebrate the descent of the
Holy Ghost upon the apostles by copulating with their typ-
ists; and on the Monday evening the same string of Renaults
and Peugeots tearing back: 'Behold I will send you a Com-
forter.' And on the sun-baked streets of Italy the writing on
the wall: '*Il secolo xix è stato il secolo della nostra libertanza;
il secolo xx sarà il secolo della nostra potenza,*' which meant:
'*Mene, mene, tekel, upharsin,*' which meant: 'I'm bigger
than you are, you dirty little twirt,' but Pierre Laval knew
that was only Benito Mussolini's way of saying: 'I solemnly
guarantee to respect the interests of France and her empire.'
It was decided to cut the salaries of civil servants by ten per
cent; it was decided that Pierre Laval was a dirty dog. It
was decided that the Abyssinians were savages and that it
was very noble of Mussolini and Badoglio to go to the
trouble of teaching them the uses of poison gas; it was decided that Pierre Laval was a clean dog and that the English
were a nation of hypocrites who were just as bad as Frenchmen after dark. It was decided to draw the winning tickets
of the Loterie Nationale in the principal provincial towns as
well as in Paris. It was decided that Monsieur Deibler had
no right to an increase in salary, even although he had to
pay out of his own pocket the costs of transporting the
guillotine from Paris to Ajaccio.

At Drancy and Saint-Denis and Argenteuil grim angry
men began to gather, violent men from Billancourt and the
Porte de Saint-Ouen, men with eyes like Saint John the Bap-
tist from Ménilmontant and Belleville, earnest little men

with straw hats from the Quartier Latin, Mahatma Gandhis and Saint Francises of Assisi that smelt of sour wine, garlic, machine oil, and stale sweat. They were unhappy because Darwin had told them they couldn't believe. They were angry because their employers wouldn't pay them enough to feed and clothe their families. All over Paris and all over France the cafés were full of men saying 'Nom de Dieu' and 'Merde' and that they had had enough. For they did not know that the men of science as well as the churchmen had gone wrong. They did not know that man should live neither by bread alone nor by every word which proceedeth out of the mouth of God alone, but by both. They did not know that there was an ecstasy of the body and ecstasy of the spirit, but that the purest ecstasy was the ecstasy which was of both the body and the spirit. They did not know that there was a truth to be known about the world when you were quiet about it without a telescope. They did not know that Darwin had seen a long way into reality, but that if he could have got into the soul of Saint John of the Cross he would have seen farther. They did not know that intelligence and goodness were virtues as well as courage and compassion. They knew only that they were hungry and cold and that when died they would die forever.

The angry men were angrier still when Hitler sent his troops into the Rhineland and Albert Sarraut's great bladder of blown-out stupid mean face said, 'Jamais la France ne consentira à traiter tant que Strasbourg restera sous la menace du canon allemand,' because they knew it was all baloney, as indeed it was, or perhaps it wasn't, because, as Hitler never asked France to parley, France never had to consent to parley. Of course it was all the fault of England,

too, but then the English had always been a perfid double-
dealing gang of cut-throats leching and runting and grunt-
ing beneath a blanket of bibles. Louis Marin, Edouard
Herriot, Léon Bailby, Jean Mistler, Camille Chautemps,
Léon Jouhaux, Colonel de la Rocque, and Monsieur Ybarné-
garay all shot the tops off their mouths on the matter and
Monsieur Albert Lebrun mooned through the corridors of
the Elysée. Spring came again, and in the evening in the rue
de Rivoli the sun shone in at the casements of the Tour de
Saint-Jacques and made the panes glow as though candles
had been lighted behind them. It was decided to take
sterner steps to suppress tax evasion and to replace wooden
railway carriages by steel ones. The Popular Front had come
to power, but the tyres of the super-cheats and their whores
still rode smoothly over the bones of one million five hundred thousand Frenchmen. It was the month of May again,
the month of Mary.

V

In June, 1936, the balance sheet as at the previous 31st
December of Entreprises Françaises d'Installation de Chauffage Central looked much the same as it had in February,
1934, except that the profit brought forward from the profit
and loss account was three times as large. In his corner of
the counting-house Bigou was beginning to draw up the
directors' commissions statements. He took two sheets of
paper. On the first he wrote:

Monsieur Gaston Dupont
Net Profit for the year ended 31st December, 1935:
Frs. 12,752,327.75
Commission at 10% thereon   1,275,232.75
Certified correct.   J. G. Bigou.

And on the second he wrote:

Monsieur Emile Théophile Ignace Terrasse
Net Profit for the year ended 31st December, 1935:
Frs. 12,752,327.75
Commission at 5% thereon   637,616.40
Certified correct.   J. G. Bigou.

The staff of the department store on the other side of the torrid June boulevard was having a stay-in strike. With their faces glued to the huge glass windows they looked like fish in a bottle, but the people in the street had grown too used to the spectacle to pay much attention to them. The strike had been going on for some days now. The staff of the Entreprises Françaises d'Installation de Chauffage Central wasn't paying much attention either. They were too busy discussing their own grievances to care about those of other people.

'There's no two ways about it,' Oppilliard said. 'We've got to get a collective contract.'

'Collective contracts aren't French,' a girl who was clacking away at her typewriter said. She was plain and tired and devout and she had photographs of Father Damien and Shirley Temple pinned up above her desk.

'Sweating your employees isn't French either,' another girl said. 'I'm fed up with slaving like a convict and getting nothing for it. I get up every morning at six and make the beds and clean the house before coming to the office. And then at lunch time I've got to rush away home and make my husband's lunch.'

'Blum and Thorez and Jouhaux are going to see that employers pay decent salaries, and then there won't be any need for married women to work,' Oppilliard said. 'That's what's the matter with France: there are too many married women working.'

'And then I've got to hurry back here at two and slave like a convict till six, and then I've got to hurry back home and cook my husband's dinner and wash up afterwards,' the girl went on. 'And then when you're ill they won't pay you your whole salary, but make you claim back first from the Health Insurance people. And then you've got to go and queue up for hours in the Avenue Lowendal and get a raspberry at the end of it.'

Screwing out his figures, Bigou was surprised that he knew exactly what the devout girl was thinking: she was thinking that Jesus Christ had done more unpleasant things than queue up for hours in the Avenue Lowendal and get a raspberry at the end of it. Almost angrily he turned from Christ's sorrows to the sorrows that never got read about. Were not the workers of the world crucified every day? And what had they to look forward to at the end of it all except becoming a heap of manure in a cemetery? More angrily still he turned to his own sorrows; Marie was ill again and Odette was staying away from school to look after her.

'It's a disgrace,' Oppilliard said. 'The whole of the wealth of France is concentrated in the hands of two hundred families. Is that fair? And then here. We work like convicts and Dupont and Terrasse get all the money. Not only do they get whopping big salaries, but they get huge commissions on profits as well.'

Bigou collected his papers and went out of the office before they could start asking him awkward questions. He went into the lavatory to try and screw up courage to ask Monsieur Terrasse for a rise, as he was still earning only two thousand francs a month. Ought he to begin: 'Monsieur Terrasse, my wife is very ill again and through sheer necessity I have to ask you for an increase in salary?' Or ought he to make no mention of his wife at all? After all, he had worked hard and the firm was earning colossal profits. He was still undecided when he came out.

Monsieur Dupont was in Monsieur Terrasse's office when Bigou entered. They went on talking just as though Bigou wasn't there.

'There's no need to worry,' Monsieur Dupont said. 'This agitation is bound to die down. It's only in the industrial districts, after all. And then the peasants of France have too big a stake in the country ever to become communists.'

'It's disquieting all the same,' Monsieur Terrasse said.

'I know,' Monsieur Dupont said. 'But we must be firm. We mustn't give in. And above all we mustn't let any false sentiments of pity get the better of us. And then the common poeple haven't got the same feelings as we have. They're not used to comfort. And they'd make a terrible mess of things if ever they got the whip hand. You know what Horace said: *"Odi profanum vulgus et arceo."* "I loathe common people and I spew upon it." I learned the quotation as an instance of a perfect tense used as a present indicative, but now I remember it for other reasons. So no collective contract and no immediate rise in salary. Of course we may have to give in to the factory workers, but I don't want any trouble with clerical workers. And if they start yelling, just tell them that they've no need of a collective contract as they're paid above standard rates as it is. That's the amusing thing about their demands: they're so hopelessly modest.' He switched round as he became aware of Bigou's presence. 'Well, what the devil do *you* want?' he asked.

'Excuse me, monsieur, but I've brought the commission statements,' Bigou said.

'I hope that you haven't been eavesdropping,' Monsieur Dupont said as he snatched the papers from Bigou.

'Bigou is a very prudent employee,' Monsieur Terrasse purred as he looked at the figures over Monsieur Dupont's shoulder.

'I am glad to learn that. Today more than ever directors have need of prudent employees.' As Monsieur Dupont pursed his lips in appreciation at the figures, Bigou couldn't help wondering how many gallons of champagne they had sucked in during the last fifteen years and how many women they had kissed. 'We'll have to invest this money,' he said. 'What are *you* going to do, Terrasse?'

Monsieur Terrasse smiled a thin knowing smile.

'I certainly wasn't thinking of buying Government bonds,' he said.

'That would be stupid,' Monsieur Dupont said. 'Not with the Popular Front bitching up the whole show. And industrials aren't much good either. To my mind there's only one thing to do and that's to buy English pounds.'

'Or American dollars,' Monsieur Terrasse said. 'I have a friend on the Bourse who says that dollars are an even better investment than pounds because if there's a war America's bound to stay out of it this time.'

'Or gold,' Monsieur Dupont said. 'Gold doesn't bring in any interest, but with all the currencies in the world depreciating right and left the profit on ultimate realization will more than compensate for dividends.'

'I believe you're right,' Monsieur Terrasse said. 'As it is, I've got Swiss francs and dollars and gulden and pounds, so why shouldn't I try gold for a change?'

'Why not?' Monsieur Dupont said. 'In any case you're bound to make a profit because whatever Blum says the franc's certain to go west one of these four mornings.'

'In fact the worse things go in France, the richer we'll be,' Monsieur Terrasse said.

'Precisely,' Monsieur Dupont said. 'After all, every man for himself.'

'There's only one thing that's worrying me and that's that camel Vincent Auriol,' Monsieur Terrasse said. 'According to him all investments abroad and in gold have got to be declared to the Enrégistrement.'

'Don't you worry about that,' Monsieur Dupont said. 'There are far too many deputies in the swim themselves for them ever to dare to put the law into operation. They say that even Blum's got most of his capital invested in Switzerland.'

Both men opened their mouths wide and laughed. Their unspiritual piggy eyes glinted with glee at the rottenness of the world. Bigou felt angry and hurt and humbled because it was for a fairer France that he and millions of his comrades had fought for four long years. Monsieur Dupont must have perceived the misery on his face, for he turned round suddenly.

'I hope that you will have the good sense not to repeat

outside this office what you have just heard,' he said to Bigou.

'Of course not, monsieur,' Bigou said, and despised himself for not saying: 'I'll shout it from the housetops.'

'I assure you Bigou is one of our most trustworthy employees,' Monsieur Terrasse said. 'And if you want a proof it's he who helps me to cook the fiscal accounts. Well, Bigou, what are we going to doctor this year? The bad debts reserve or the depreciation? Or would it be better to leave out half the sales and rewrite the journal?'

Monsieur Dupont laughed loudly at this. Bigou smiled thinly because he was disgusted and ashamed. Each year when he had worked out the true profit on which the directors' commissions were calculated, he had to rearrange the figures so that they showed the profit on which Messieurs Dupont and Terrasse thought the company ought to pay tax. By the time he had finished with this year's accounts, the profit of twelve million would probably have dropped to one of six million or even less; and if there was any rewriting of the books to be done, he might have to work hours of overtime in order to accomplish it. All over France the same sort of thing was happening. While Germany and Italy were rearming, thousands of Duponts and Terrasses and millions of Bacos and Chanus were draining France of her life-blood because they were too selfish and stupid to see that they were the State and not Louis XIV. And there was little chance of their being found out because the tax inspectors were so overworked that even when they were competent, they had not the time to probe firms' accounts. Disgusted and ashamed Bigou stood there, with a large sad look in his eye, because he would have liked to be able to believe in something clean rather than in something dirty.

'We'll have to be giving you a little bonus one of these days, I see,' Monsieur Dupont said, patting Bigou condescendingly on the shoulder. 'Of course not immediately, but one of these days if you stick in and do your work well. And in the meantime you're at liberty to take advantage of any of the little tips as regards investment of your savings you may have gathered from Monsieur Terrasse and myself.' He made a sign and was gone before Bigou had the time to realize that after eighteen years' hard work his total savings amounted to a deposit of fifteen hundred francs in the post-office.

Monsieur Terrasse looked with damp eyes at the door which had just closed on Monsieur Dupont's back.

'What a fine man!' he said, beaming at Bigou. 'Old man, that Maginot Line contract's a gold mine. We'll double our turnover next year. And then, even if there isn't war with Germany, the pipes will wear out one day. And what with the Italian menace I shouldn't be surprised if they built another Maginot Line along the Alps soon. We earn big money, of course, Monsieur Dupont and myself, but we've got to work for it. That's just what a lot of employees don't seem to understand. They think that they should earn as much as their bosses, but that's all nonsense. An employee's only got to do his job well and he knows that his salary's waiting for him at the end of the month. Yourself, for example. Your job's figures and figures it remains, whereas I've got all sorts of other fish to fry. I tell you honestly, Bigou, there are times when I shouldn't mind changing places with a chap like you. Well, what is it?' he asked as a woman clerk entered the office.

'Please, monsieur, it's about Madame Lamballe.'

'And who is Madame Lamballe?'

'She's a char, monsieur, and she didn't come today, but she rang up and said she was ill, monsieur, and she says please can she be paid in full all the same as her husband's out of work and her baby's sick. She comes for an hour each morning, and is paid four francs fifty.'

'Tell her that business is business and that the company can't afford to pay people for lying in their beds doing nothing.'

Bigou was sorry for the charwoman with the husband out of work and the sick baby, because he knew that she, too, looked on a blue and gold and green world out of a window in her face and that Jesus Christ had not meant that business was business when He said: 'And the second is like unto it, namely this, thou shalt love thy neighbour as thyself.' But as the woman left the room and the seconds passed, he knew it less. He also knew that it would be imprudent to ask for a rise in salary for himself. With Monsieur Terrasse sitting so neat and clean and well-dressed at his desk, it looked so easy to be rich that he was almost able to believe that it was through his own fault that Marie was ill and he was unable to send her to a sanatorium.

When Monsieur Terrasse had given him detailed instructions as to how the larger part of that year's profit was to be concealed, Bigou went back into the counting-house. Oppilliard and the other clerks were still arguing the toss about collective contracts and a forty-hour week. As he listened to their inability to agree, Bigou almost despised them for not talking about speculating against the French franc. Was not, he wondered, the present corruption, which was at least elegant, preferable to the tumult which threatened to overthrow it?

At six o'clock the employees all banged their hats on their heads and rushed out of the building. Most of them did not speak to one another as they ran down the stairs in their mean clothes because they had worked so long and so drably together that they hated one another. The secretary with the golden hair was standing in the doorway as Bigou went out. She was wearing a new black frock and it pleased Bigou to think that she smiled at him. Like dirty water gurgling out of a basin the employees swirled through the door into the street.

Outside on the boulevard Paris seemed as though it would go on forever. There were so many people walking on the boulevard that they looked like blackcurrants being shaken about in a basket. A scavenger in rubber boots and a peaked cap marched along the edge of the pavement stirring with a broom the water that was being poured along the gutter to cleanse it. A tramp was washing his face in the stream of toffee papers and used bus tickets. Watching him, Bigou wondered if Christ wouldn't have to do the same thing if He came back again to earth or if the Pope would recognize and invite Him to the Vatican. A bus screeched up the causeway, its platform weighed down with perpendicular men stuck like pencils in a box. A school of early evening whores swam slowly up the pavement. Although it was not yet the fourteenth of July, a tricolor or two hung in a dry drip from an occasional balcony, testifying against communism, but there was also a red flag to be seen flying from the top of the department store. On the Place de la Madeleine there were rows of coloured posters stuck on boards for a municipal bye-election. Bigou crossed to read them. There were seventeen candidates for one seat and everybody was calling everybody else a thief, a liar, a traitor, a taker of bribes, a camel, a calf's head, and a midden. When he had read them all through, the evening was still going on, but the whores had stopped to give money to the tramp.

VI

WHEN he arrived home Bigou found that Marie was so ill that she had sent Odette across the road to ask the tart's mother to come over and cook the dinner. She smiled at him with her mouth as he came into the room, but there was no smile in her eyes which were small and frightened. Bigou took her hand in his; the skin was rough and scored with channels which looked like half-healed cuts and the nails were big and twisted.

'I'm sorry, Jean, for being such a nuisance,' she said. 'I tried not to go to bed, but somehow I hadn't any more strength left.'

'Don't you worry about that, Marie,' Bigou said. 'You ought to have sent Odette for a doctor, that's all.'

'I was frightened it would cost too much money,' Marie said. 'You know what these doctors are. Fifty francs a visit and medicine and all sorts of things. And then I'm not really as ill as I look. I'll be all right again in the morning. I must be, because I've still got the washing and ironing to do.' She fluttered her eyelashes at him as she spoke and tried to smile. 'Jean, promise me you won't let them send me to hospital.'

'Perhaps you'd be happier in hospital, Marie,' Bigou said. 'You'd have people to look after you.'

'But even in hospital it'd cost money, Jean. Thirty francs a day at least. And when people die, they bring the coffin right up the ward and you can hear them hammering the nails in. And then if you haven't enough money to be buried properly, they clamp you in a tin box and throw you in the common ditch. It's terrible to die in hospital, Jean. The doctors and the nurses and the students just don't seem to care. I suppose it's because they see so many. Jean, when I die I don't want to die in front of people who don't know me; I want to die in front of people who've seen me when I was young and wearing pretty clothes.'

'Marie, Marie, of course you're not going to die,' but the hollow in his stomach told him that she was. As he sat on the bed with her poor gouged hand in his, he told himself that the curtains on the window ought to have looked different because Marie was dying, but they looked just the same, and the sky outside was blue and down on the street the traffic was roaring by in a broth of rattling screws, screeching brakes, barking gears, and skidding rubbers. He supposed that he ought to send for a priest, but perhaps that might frighten Marie, and in any case she mightn't like him sending for a priest with the Lacordaires always liable to be peering through the glass door of the loge and see him going upstairs. The traffic ceased for an instant and across the empty evening came the sound of a woman's voice calling. Then the traffic went on again with its harsh and purposeful purposelessness.

'Jean, I never could understand why you fell in love with me and not with Denise.'

'You were much prettier than Denise, Marie, and much kinder.'

'But I wasn't prettier than the girl with red hair standing outside the cathedral in Strasbourg. You told me yourself that you wouldn't have minded making love to her. I remember the way the wind kept blowing out her frock.' She sighed and closed her eyes. 'Jean, do you believe in eternal life?'

'Sometimes when I'm in church I do, but outside afterwards when the pavements are wet I'm not so sure.'

'Jean darling, we've been married for nearly fifteen years and there are so many important things we've never talked about.'

'I suppose that's the same with most people, Marie. Life's such a scurry to get the necessary unimportant things done that nobody's got time to talk about the important unnecessary things.'

'Jean, do you remember that day you said my eyes were the loveliest things you'd ever seen? Jean, tell me again that my eyes are the loveliest thing you've ever seen. Even if it's not true, please tell me.'

'Marie, your eyes are the loveliest thing I've ever seen. They've got such lovely lights in them.'

'If death is just sleep, then I'm not afraid, but if it's Jesus waiting for you, then I suppose I am a little.'

'Listen, Marie, you're not going to die. And even if you were, you'd have nothing to be afraid of; you've never done anybody any harm.'

'Perhaps life's something more than just not doing anybody any harm.' She raised her hands and looked at them, bending her fingers like claws. 'There are some lovely new summer frocks in the Belle Jardinière catalogue,' she said, and then she died.

It took him some time to realize that she was dead because
the curtains and the sky still went on looking the same and
down on the street the traffic still went thundering by. It
did not seem possible that she could go out like that, un-
ceremoniously, like a cigarette. 'Marie, we did so many
things together,' he cried, but her eyes were as empty as
oysters.

When he finally realized that she had gone from him, he
closed her eyes. At first he was afraid to touch the eyelids,
but he managed in the end, looking up at the ceiling while
he did so. Then he knelt and began the Paternoster, but
by the time he had reached 'give us this day our daily bread,'
he realized that he wasn't meaning what he was saying and
gave it up as a bad job. He remained on his knees for a little
longer, but when Baco's wireless began to play *Les Gars
de la Marine,* he rose and went into the kitchen where he
knew there was a broken bit of candle lying about. Marie
was still dead when he came back. He stuck the candle in
the neck of an empty beer bottle and lit it. Then he filled a
toothbrush jar with water and, using an old Palm Sunday
piece of boxhedge as hyssop, sprinkled his wife. As he
sprinkled he said: '*Asperges me, Domine, hyssopo et mun-
dabor,*' but the words didn't sound as fine as when the curé
said them in church. He knelt again by the bed, but no
prayer came to his lips save the longing that she were alive
again, and even of that he wasn't sure, because of the money
her being ill would have cost him. On the other side of the
street Baco's wireless began to play *Parlez-Moi d'Armour.*
As he rose to his feet, Odette and Madame Turbigo came
into the room. 'Your poor mother's dead,' he said as he took
Odette by the hand and led her to the bed.

'Poor mummy, she doesn't look dead,' Odette said. She stood with her hand in Bigou's and her shoulders held taut. Then, still with her hand in Bigou's, she bent forward and kissed the still, shrinking little face in the bed. 'It's funny I'm not at all frightened,' she said.

'She's beautiful,' Madame Turbigo said. 'She reminds me of monsieur my late husband's sister-in-law. She looked beautiful too when she burst.'

'She was always kind,' Bigou said. 'She always loved me even although I couldn't give her pretty clothes and a motor car.' The tears began to pour from his eyes and his mouth fell away from him so that he could not speak.

'We must dress her all the same,' Madame Turbigo said. 'And we must watch her too. Odette, run across the road and tell my daughter to come. She's not going out to see her friend tonight.'

Odette ran out of the room. Madame Turbigo took the boxhedge and dipped it in the toothbrush jar and made a geometry of benediction over the dead woman.

'We must dress her,' she said again.

'But isn't that the undertaker's job?' Bigou asked.

'A shroud costs money and besides it looks far too Catholic,' Madame Turbigo said. 'When my father burst, the curé wanted him buried in a shroud, but my mother insisted on his being buried in his Sunday suit and with his best boots on.' She made for the wardrobe and began rummaging among the shabby dresses hanging there in headless Indian file. 'And stockings, she'll need stockings,' she said.

Odette came back accompanied by Mademoiselle Turbigo and a crowd of persons who clumped into the flat and stood mooning at Marie with half-sad, half-thrilled eyes. Baco,

Chanu, Latérade, Verneuil, and the Lacordaires were all there and Choiseul the policeman and the fishmonger's assistant as well. They all shook hands with Bigou and they all said 'All my condolences,' and they all made the sign of the cross over Marie with the boxwood, and when they went out, they all shook hands with Bigou again and said 'All my condolences' again. Only the yellow tart and her mother and Odette and Baco remained.

'We none of us amount to much,' Baco said, elated behind the gape of his mouth with a sense of personal immortality. Once more the wheel had revolved and once more the ball had not rolled into his number. 'Here today and gone tomorrow,' he said.

'You men will have to get out of here while we wash her,' Madame Turbigo said.

Bigou wondered whether Odette ought not to have come out onto the landing too, but Odette stayed behind with a determined little expression on her face. Out on the landing Bigou stood by the minuterie so that he could press it on again as soon as it went out.

'When you're dead you're finished,' Baco said.

'Not necessarily,' Bigou said.

'The priests can say what they like, but when you're dead you're finished,' Baco said.

'There are possibilities all the same,' Bigou said.

'When you're dead you're finished; the worms eat your arse,' Baco said. The minuterie went out and Baco was blotted out, dirty cap, dicky and all. Bigou pressed the button again; a clock was heard away down in the loge and Baco was sculptured anew, mystically unmystical. 'When I croak I hope I know nothing about it,' he said. 'And then I'd like to croak best after a good meal.'

'Unfortunately we're not allowed the choice,' Bigou said. 'And then even when you're dead there are all sorts of formalities.'

'The undertakers do all that for you,' Baco said. 'I remember when my wife's cousin croaked in Nantes. All her relations were in Paris at the time, but we just sent a wire to the local undertakers and they had the old bitch all packed up and all the bumphs filled in at the mairie and everything when we arrived.'

'Perhaps it would be cheaper to make the declaration at the mairie oneself, see the priests and the cemetery people oneself, and just get in the undertakers to do the actual transporting,' Bigou said.

'Whichever way you go about it you'll be robbed,' Baco said. 'The undertakers are in league with the priests and the priests are in league with the undertakers. Death's just a racket like everything else. France is rotten. That's all.'

'Perhaps things'll be better under the Popular Front,' Bigou said.

'Things'll be even worse under the Popular Front,' Baco said. 'Léon Blum's going to bugger everything up. Tardieu, Chautemps, Laval, Sarraut, Blum, they all bugger everything up.'

'All the same Blum's going to do great things for the worker,' Bigou said. 'Increased wages, forty-hour week, and all that.'

'I'm not a worker,' Baco said. 'I'm a boss. I'll have to pay the waiter I get in on Sundays and holidays more now because the swine have protested against the insult of the tip, but they'll go on taking tips all the same.'

Bigou was silent. He understood that he could no more

realize what Baco felt about having to pay his waiter more than Baco could realize how he felt about Marie's having futted out without his having been able to say goodbye to her properly. It wasn't his fault and it wasn't Baco's fault; he had never had a waiter to pay and Baco had never seen Marie when she was young and giggling in the grass when she was tickled.

The minuterie went out again, but before Bigou had time to relight it the door of the flat had opened and Madame Turbigo stood framed in pink light.

'She's ready,' she said.

Baco excused himself from going back to see Marie again because he said there was sure to be a lot of customers waiting for him in the café. Bigou and Madame Turbigo tiptoed back into the flat. Marie lay on top of the bedclothes with her least shabby frock spread out from her feet like a fan. In her hands she clasped the crucifix which Madame Turbigo had taken down from the wall. Her hair was fluffed out over the pillow and gleamed dark blue where the candlelight fell upon it, but her face, as Bigou looked at it, seemed to be receding. Odette and Mademoiselle Turbigo knelt by the bed, but the yellow tart seemed to be praying more ardently than Odette.

'She's beautiful, isn't she?' Madame Turbigo said.

Bigou touched the dead woman's hands; they were as cold as the Christ on the cross they were grasping.

'She's dead,' he said.

Bigou watched her while Madame Turbigo and her daughter and Odette dined in the kitchen. When they had finished, he went into the kitchen, but he could not eat, so he came back into the bedroom again. Madame Turbigo

had put Odette into the small bed and was sitting beside
her holding her hand. The yellow tart was kneeling beside
the bed with her hands clasped in front of her face. Bigou
sat down in a corner and tried to pray, but he didn't know
quite what to pray about. Marie, Marie, where was she now?
Either in hell or heaven or purgatory, for the soul was judged
as soon as it left the body, so the priests said. The general
judgment didn't come till after the second advent, when the
guilty would be howked up from hell to have their fornica-
tions counted out to the blessèd. Marie wouldn't get her
body back till then. Would she get her tired old body back
or the young one that used to wait for him by the river?
With his riddle unsolved, he fell asleep. When he awoke
again, it was dark. Madame Turbigo was still holding
Odette's hand and the yellow tart was still praying by the
bed, the lovely shadow of her head stamped black and clear
on the wall by the pale flame of the candle.

VII

WHEN THE HEARSE arrived at ten-twenty two mornings later,
Madame Lacordaire stayed in her loge, because she resented
Bigou having done her out of a commission through arrang-
ing the undertaking himself. Monsieur Lacordaire was already at his work, and even if he hadn't been he would
have stayed in the loge, because he was afraid of his wife.
Bigou and Odette were alone in the flat when they heard the
undertakers' assistants' boots coming upstairs. Chanu, Baco,
and the yellow tart and her mother had said that they would

come to the church, but that they couldn't come to the cemetery because it was such a long way out and besides Chanu and Baco had their businesses to attend to and Madame Turbigo and her daughter had promised to take Odette home with them because it wasn't right that she should see her mother thrown into the hole. There were to be no other mourners because Marie's and Bigou's relatives all lived in the country.

When the undertakers' assistants walked into the flat, they smelt of the brandy they had just been knocking back in Baco's café opposite. They wore black uniforms with white numbers sewn on the collars, and peaked caps with shiny leather tops, which they did not remove. Some of them wore strips of linen round their necks instead of collars. They all had different shapes of untidy moustaches, but they all had the same kind of eyes with no light coming from behind them. They had been at two funerals already that morning and they stared at Bigou and Odette with immense disinterest.

'This the place?' one of them asked.

Bigou nodded and turned away and made Odette turn away so that neither of them should see the coffin as the men advanced to take it on their shoulders. They did not turn round again until they heard the end of the coffin bang against the door as the men carried it from the flat. It made a nasty noise and Bigou thought he could hear Marie's body rolling about. There were four men to carry the coffin: two took the front and two took the rear. Bigou stayed behind for a few seconds to shut the door of the flat and Odette stayed with him. When they looked over the banister, the coffin was already one floor down and looked like the coffin of a dead person they didn't know. They ran down after it, but even when they had overtaken it, it still looked unfriendly and wooden as though Marie couldn't really be inside it. The undertakers' assistants moved with the precision of horses descending a slippery slope; their legs looked more reverent than their faces. The curtains of the concierge's loge were drawn as they passed, but Bigou thought he could see Madame Lacordaire's trollopy head moving about behind them.

At the front door the master of ceremonies was talking to the driver of the hearse; he had not bothered to come upstairs because it was only a cheap funeral, but he wore a starched shirt with a tricolour wound round it because he was going to officiate at an expensive funeral afterwards. He flicked off his cockade as the coffin passed, but did not strut out in front of it to the hearse tapping with the point of his cane, and went on talking to the driver instead. The hearse, with the letter 'B' stuck on it, stood drawn up between a dustbin and a tricycle with BLOTTO FRERES painted in white beneath the crossbar. Baco and Chanu and the yellow tart and her mother stood in a group ready to fall in behind the hearse as soon as it should start. All wore black, but Baco and Chanu wore bowler hats with mourning bands round them as well, because they each had had cousins who had died a few months previously. As the coffin was slid into the back of the hearse, Bacqueroët came feeling his way along the pavement and took up his place beside them. He took off his hat and Baco and Chanu took off their hats and then they all clumped them on again. A group of girls in white overalls came out of the shoemaker's shop opposite and stood to stare.

The master of ceremonies finished his conversation and went and stood in front of the hearse with his four assistants. Bigou and Odette stood behind the hearse and Baco and Chanu and Bacqueroët and Madame and Mademoiselle Turbigo came and stood behind them. By now there was quite a crowd of people in front of the café as well as in front of the shoeshop. The driver let in the clutch and the hearse moved slowly forward in first gear because it was a just and a wholesome thing to walk slowly, out of reverence for the dead, from the house to the church, although later they would whiz along on top gear from the church to the cemetery because even reverence could cost too much in time and petrol.

The requiem Mass was to be said at the parish church of the district because the archdiocesan authorities did not allow the clergy of chapels of ease to rake in the shekels by celebrating marriages and funerals. As they passed under the railway bridge and turned up the Boulevard Exelmans, an enamel young woman came walking along behind a pekinese. The wind was plastering her dress so closely against her legs that she looked as though she were wearing trousers. She did not cross herself as the hearse passed, but walked on with her smiling teeth biting out at the wind. Bigou reflected with pleasure that one day she, too, would be dead and that her body would corrupt. In front of the hearse he could hear the master of ceremonies arguing the toss about how the five-day week was going to apply to the undertaking business, and behind him Baco and Chanu discussing whether they should put up their prices right away or wait until the Popular Front had muddled things a little more. Bigou wondered why even one's friends couldn't be silent and circumspect at such a moment, but he drew consolation from Odette, who was walking with a reverent and sad little mien. From now on she and he would have to be everything to each other.

There were no black hangings on the porch when the hearse drew up outside the church, because Bigou had not been able to afford the five hundred francs extra; instead workmen were erecting a pink-and-white canopy, because there was to be a swagger wedding at eleven. The undertakers' assistants whisked the coffin out of the hearse and rushed it into the church because they had been warned that they must have it out again before the wedding began. A priest walked in front of them gabbling the *De Profundis*, but Bacqueroët didn't come into the church with the rest, because he was a free-thinker and knew that the world had made itself.

The third best black frontal was on the lady altar because there had not been time since the previous funeral to change it to the fourth best for Madame Bigou. The undertakers' assistants shot the coffin into the catafalque and went outside to talk communism in the porch while Jesus Christ came again in His Sacrament of Love. The priest who had been reciting the *De Profundis* took off his black stole and hung it over his arm and knelt at a prie-Dieu on the gospel side of the altar. Bigou and Odette knelt in the front row and Baco and Chanu and the yellow tart and her mother crammed in behind. Another priest came bouncing out of the sacristy preceded by two tiny servers who were giggling. In his black vestments the priest went up the steps, lumpety, lump, and laid the chalice and the paten on the altar. He grinned at the other priest as he came down the altar steps again and the other priest grinned back. When he began the Mass he did not say 'In nomine Patris, et Filii, et Spiritus Sancti,' but 'Inomtrisliietspiritancti.'

Bigou could not pray for the yammering and the clammering the priest was making as he rushed non-stop through his Latin trying to get it over before the congregation for the wedding arrived. Propping his paunch on the altar, the priest gargled the lonely words of the gospel as though they were extracts from a railway company's byelaws. He charged through the offertory, preface, and sanctus, raising his great meaty hands to God. Then he bent to turn the elements into Christ's Body and Blood. The Host rose, a thin white moon, but it didn't seem to be Christ's Body at all, because the server forgot to ring the sacring bell; but the chalice seemed to contain Christ's Blood, because the sun was shining on it. The rest of the Mass was galloped through. The celebrant left the altar and the beadle came out with the incense and the holy water which he handed to the servers with a wink. The other priest put on his stole again and approached the catafalque to give the absolutions.

'Libera me, Domine, de morte aeterna,' he began. With loose lips and wandering eyes he spewed forth the Church's magic: 'Tremens factus sum ego, et timeo, dum discussio venerit, atque ventura era. Quando movendi sunt et terra.' The lovely words shot forth like precious ointment poured from a tin mug. 'Kyrie eleison, Christe eleison, Kyrie eleison.' From Latin he passed to Greek and from Greek back to Latin. 'Pater noster,' he invoked and hared round the coffin twice, widdershins, blessing it with holy water and puffs of incense. The witchery was over and the chapel empty in the sunlight. The undertakers' assistants came back and yanked the coffin out of the catafalque and carried it out of the church.

As they passed down the steps, pink and pale green and heliotrope young women were already arriving for the wedding. Marie's coffin looked very lonely as it was carried through their pretty dresses. The priest came scurrying out and spouted the canticle of Zacharias through the open back door of the hearse: *'Benedictus Dominus, Deus Israel, quia visitavit et fecit redemptionem plebis suae,'* because Bigou had not been able to pay enough money for him to go and say them at the cemetery. Then he hurried back under the awning. Bigou kissed Odette who was weeping and shook hands with the others and with Bacqueroët who had waited outside all this time. Then he climbed up in front of the hearse with the driver. Through the open door of the church the tapers burned on the high altar for the wedding, like distant stars. The master of ceremonies and his assistants took off their hats and the hearse started off.

The hearse shot along between two ribbons of pavement. It climbed the rue de Boulainvilliers and rolled along the rue de la Pompe, casting a fleeting flob of exquisite shadow on the pale green blind of a closed shop. Outside the mairie due seizième three policemen stood and gazed with boredom at the drip of history. Outside Saint-Honoré d'Eylau three other hearses were waiting for coffins. At the Etoile children paddled among the pigeons which came flying down from the Arc de Triomphe in a lovely lace. The sky looked like a mirror splashed with shaving-soap.

The hearse rolled along the Boulevard de la Madeleine. The pavements were full of pretty women looking into shop windows. The hearse rolled up the rue Lafayette and the avenue Jean Jaurés. The pavements were filled with hatless women walking to or from market, each with the same expression of unperturbed despair. The hearse rolled past the poor, blessèd because they should see God. The hearse rolled past the mairie de Pantin and on and out and up the route des Petits Ponts which had just been renamed the rue Henri Barbusse.

The hearse could not roll along to the lower part of the cemetery where the cheaper graves were because the path was too narrow. When it could go no farther, undertakers' assistants, who had apparently been awaiting its arrival, took the coffin out of the hearse and carried it along to the grave. There were twenty new graves all in a row; two were being dug and three were being filled in. The gravediggers did not look up as Marie's coffin came along, but went on with their work. The gravedigger who was waiting to fill in Marie's grave stood swilling wine out of a bottle. When he had finished drinking, he wiped his moustache on his elbow and moved the little pot of holy water on to the next grave because there was no priest. Bigou stood hatless while the wind blew streaks of cold hair down onto his forehead. The grave looked very deep while it was empty, but it looked deeper when the coffin had been lowered into it. The undertakers' assistants lounged off. Bigou stood staring down at the coffin. He tried to think about Marie, but all he could think of was that they would be burying somebody else on top of her in five years' time. The gravedigger sighed impatiently. Bigou took one last look and walked away. When he reached the hearse, he found that the driver had already changed the letter 'B' to an 'L.'

VIII

THE ANGRY MEN began to get down to things. It was decided
to make the rich pay. It was decided that, as only two hundred families had had the exclusive privilege of messing
things up for the last fifty years, it was only right that everybody should have a shot now. It was decided to take stern
steps to suppress fiscal fraud and to do away with wooden
railway carriages. It was decided to open the 1937 Exhibition on time. It was decided to work only forty hours a week
and in five days. It was decided to close the banks on Satur-
days and the department stores on Mondays. It was decided not to devalue the franc. It was decided that the
tricolour was the emblem of reaction, although a more pic-
turesque phrase was attributed to Monsieur Edmond Zay.
It was decided that the union of all Frenchmen was necessary. It was decided by the angry men that the burgesses
were seeking to sell France to Germany, Italy, and the Vatican. It was decided by those who were angry with the angry
men that the socialists and the communists were seeking to
sell France to Russia. It was decided that the union of all
Frenchmen was necessary. It was decided that Léon Blum,
Vincent Auriol, Yvon Delbos, Léon Jouhaux, Maurice
Thorez, and Paul Vaillant-Couturier were saints. It was decided that Léon Blum, Vincent Auriol, Yvon Delbos, Léon
Jouhaux, Maurice Thorez, and Paul Vaillant-Couturier were
dirty dogs. It was decided that it was more prudent not to
mention politics in restaurants unless you wanted to get a
sardine in the eye.

It was decided that a prominent cabinet minister owned

the posh new whorehouse in the Boulevard Edgar Quinet.
It was decided to open the 1937 Exhibition on time.
It was decided not to devalue the franc.
It was decided to take stern steps to suppress fiscal fraud and to do away with wooden railway carriages.
It was decided not to devalue the franc.

IX

BIGOU KNEW that it would be no use trying to sleep on the eve of the fourteenth of July, because there was to be dancing all night in the street, so he decided to go to the café and to take Odette with him. Although only thirteen, she was beginning to be a big girl now and her breasts were moulding up in her bodice. Besides, old Terrasse had just given him a rise of one hundred and fifty francs a month and he wanted to celebrate. At least four loud-speakers and two orchestras would be grinding out music and there was to be a procession and fireworks as well.

Madame Lacordaire watched them leave the house with a yellow eye because she had not yet forgiven Bigou for doing her out of a commission on the funeral. She was all prinked and preened in black satin and had washed her feet specially for the occasion. Behind her in the loge her husband sat cleaning his nails with a fork, as his brother-in-law and his wife were coming for dinner.

Night had fallen and the ragtaggle of celebration was already in full swing. The terraces of the principal cafés were festooned with Japanese lanterns and the four loud-speakers

and the two orchestras were blaring out different tunes. Clots
of people were gyrating on the pavement, their feet making
a noise like tissue paper being crumpled. Under the viaduct
in a fume of oil a miniature merry-go-round kept twisting a
palette of pink pigs and blue bicycles and wheezing out *Les
Gars de la Marine*. In the distance a firework rose lugubri-
ously into the sky and squittered into stars.

'What about a smack at the merry-go-round?' Bigou suggested. His extra hundred and fifty francs were beginning
to burn a hole in his pocket and he wanted to spend money
and make Odette happy.

'Silly, that merry-go-round's only for babies,' Odette said.

Bigou said nothing, but he was hurt that Odette should
have refused his suggestion. Sometimes he wondered if he
understood the child properly and if he would not have
done better to accept Madame Turbigo's suggestion that
Odette should go and live with her as her daughter now that
the yellow tart had found a super-wealthy lover who had
rented a luxury flat for her in the Avenue Paul Doumer. The
sound of quick trumpets drew near and a hover of lights
came in sight, advancing from the Porte de Saint-Cloud. The
lights turned into flares and the flares turned into boys in
white trousers blowing their bellies down trumpets and a
soup of gold helmets on top of firemen trolloping along out
of step. Everybody stopped dancing to watch them go by
and as soon as they had passed everybody started dancing
again.

'All the same there are times when one is proud to be
French,' Bigou said, squeezing Odette's arm.

The child nodded listlessly and allowed Bigou to lead her
into the café. Madame Turbigo and Chanu and Bacqueroët

and Latérade were all there, jammed along the counter with a lot of other people Bigou didn't know. Behind the counter Baco was pumping, squirting, and swilling out drinks which the buckshee knock-kneed waiter was rushing out to the terrace. His wife sat enthroned at the cash desk. She had a large slice of vegetable face and eyes as expressionless as marbles. Bigou was pleased to see the way they all smiled at Odette and thought how pretty the child was growing and how like her mother she was and how proud he was to be her father.

'A grenadine, Mademoiselle?' Baco asked.

'No, a vermouth and soda,' Odette said, with intense gravity.

'*Nom de Dieu!*' Baco swore and laughed so much that he showed his gold teeth stuck in the back of his mouth like collar studs.

Bigou paid for drinks for Madame Turbigo and Chanu and Bacqueroët and Latérade also because his extra hundred and fifty francs was making him feel so wealthy, and besides there would be another hundred and fifty francs next month too, although the cost of living would probably have gone up again by then. He would have stood Baco a drink as well, only he knew that Baco wouldn't have drunk it, but would have charged him for it just the same.

'Life's lovely all the same,' Bigou said as he clinked glasses with Chanu, Bacqueroët, Latérade, Odette, and the yellow tart's mother. 'And then that torchlight procession. People can say what they like about France, but there's life in the old dog yet.'

'Have you ever seen the Nuremberg Congress on the cinema?' Latérade asked. 'Things are going badly. There's no two ways about it. Hitler wants war.'

'That's bosh,' Baco said. 'Hitler's a nuisance, but he's got no guts. I know because I've a customer who's just come back from Germany and he says that the Germans don't want war. And then there's the Maginot Line. We're as safe as houses behind that.'

'Hitler's just a false alarm,' Chanu said. 'Besides, he's an ex-soldier and he knows what war's like. When he was at the front and the strafing was on, I bet he was as frightened as anybody else.'

'That's just what Hitler's counting on,' Bacqueroët said. 'That's why Hitler and Mussolini are always crying that the democracies are played out; because they think that the mere thought of war makes them frightened. To my mind there's only one way that the democracies can ever hope to get the better of the dictators and that's by temporarily adopting their methods.'

'That's nothing more or less than fascism and fascism will never go down in France,' Chanu said.

'You mean it's nothing more or less than discipline,' Bacqueroët said. 'And discipline is what France needs.'

'*Je m'en fous de la discipline comme de l'an quarante*' Chanu said, but not too rudely. Nobody was ever rude to Bacqueroët because he had been wounded so badly in the war.

'You can say what you like, but there is something wrong in France, all the same,' Bacqueroët said, switching his sore sightless face gloomily over them all. 'Not only are we no longer shocked by our own faults, but we are no longer shocked by other people's. We accept it as only natural that politicians should line their pockets when they are in office. We shrug our shoulders when we hear that the Italians have used poison gas against ignorant savages in Abyssinia. We cheat in order not to pay our proper taxes and we are neither surprised nor horrified when we learn that everybody else cheats too. We are communists and fascists and lechers and thieves and liars and cowards before we are Frenchmen. And now we are all going to earn more money by working less and *Paris-Soir* tells us that France has a new problem: the problem of how Frenchmen shall employ their new two days of leisure a week. And in Germany and Italy the munitions factories are working all day and all night. There is no new problem in Germany and Italy, but only an old one: that of preparing to take by force what they want. And that is why I say that discipline matters in France, and if to want discipline for one's country is to be a fascist, then I am a fascist.'

Bacqueroët's little speech frightened them all so much that for a second or two nobody said anything. The ring of glasses and saucers clinked out across the churn of the loudspeakers and the merry-go-round. In their pink cavern of lighted scooped-out world Baco and Chanu and Latérade and Odette and the yellow tart's mother stood painted against the invisible sliding tapestry of time. A workingman with a lean ascetic face standing away down the counter broke the silence.

'The communists are right and the fascists are wrong,' he said.

'What's the difference, anyway?' Chanu asked.

'Hitler and Stalin,' Latérade said.

'That's easy,' Baco said. 'The rich are fascists and the poor are communists, and as I'm neither rich nor poor, I'm neither one nor the other.'

'Fascists salute with the open palm and communists with the closed fist,' Madame Turbigo said.

'Communists are right and fascists are wrong,' the man with the lean ascetic face said.

Although deep down beneath his waistcoat Bigou knew that Bacqueroët was right and that France wanted discipline, he was glad when Baco changed the subject. After all, tomorrow was the fourteenth of July, and it wasn't every day of the week a fellow got a hundred and fifty francs rise, and even if Bacqueroët had got badly messed up in the war, he had no right to go about trying to make other people miserable.

'That zebra on the other side of the road gets me down all the same,' Baco said. 'He's doing up his café from top to bottom and putting in new tables and chairs and a sit-down lavatory, so I suppose I'll have to do the same thing here.'

'There are no sit-down lavatories in Russia,' the working-man with the ascetic face said. 'Sit-down lavatories are for fascists and the two hundred families.'

Verneuil, who had just garaged his bus at the dépôt in the Avenue Mozart, came into the café. He was in uniform and carried his lunch-box under his arm.

' "*Merde*" to the lot of you!' he greeted, saluting their serious faces. 'Why the long faces? This isn't Good Friday; it's the eve of the fourteenth of July.' He playfully pinched Odette's cheek. 'How's tricks?' he asked.

'We were just discussing politics,' Baco explained.

'*Nom de Dieu!*' Verneuil exclaimed. 'There are no longer any politics to discuss. France is in a state of revolution. We're going to guillotine the rich and string the priests to the lamp-posts.'

'It's all going to end badly,' Latérade said. 'That's what I always say to Madame Latérade. "Darling," I say, "it's all going to end badly."'

'Nonsense,' Verneuil said. 'After all, there's Blum and Cachin and Clamamus and Thorez and Jouhaux!'

He was interrupted by the entrance of Gudule Flotte, the old woman of eighty who touted *Paris-Soir* and *L'Intransigeant* from café to café. She made five centimes on every copy she sold. She had a face as wise as an old shoe.

'*Soir, m'sieurs et dames,*' she greeted. '*La der des ders. Paris-Soir, L'Intran', dernière édition.* The latest news from Spain.'

'*Nous nous en foutons pas mal de l'Espagne,*' Chanu said, who always got a bit nasty when he was drunk. 'We live in France, after all.'

Both Madame Turbigo and Bigou bought a copy, not because they were interested in Spain, but because they were sorry for Gudule with her poor bulged out empty belly beneath her torn frock. Apart from a headline, MADRID NE RÉPOND PLUS, there was, as far as Bigou could see, no news about Spain except that a man called Carlos Sotelo had been murdered; the front page also said that 1,881,763 Germans were born each year as against 742,722 Frenchmen and that Maurice Chevalier would sing in the Place de Belleville that evening; inside there was news about Marlene Dietrich, Father Divine, and the Swedish minister for agriculture visiting Rumania; on the back page there were photographs of a Negro being hanged in Alabama, a man seeing his wife run over by a taxi, Cardinal Verdier on holiday in Brittany, and celebrated heiresses on the Lido.

Odette gave Bigou a nudge with her elbow. Bigou realized

that the child was bored. They finished their drinks and
went and sat on the terrace. The night was so sultry that
it tasted like carpet. On the Eiffel Tower they were flashing
electric advertisements for Citroen: C-I-T-R-O-E-N down
and N-E-O-R-T-I-C up. Bigou squeezed Odette's hand.

'Happy?' he asked.

She nodded without enthusiasm.

'If you don't mind, I'd like to dance,' she said.

The noise of the loud-speakers sounded like sheets of cor-
rugated iron being thrown about. Bigou was still looking
for a vacant table on the terrace when a long gleaming white
car drew up along the kerb and Mademoiselle Turbigo got
out. She was wearing a big black hat and a white dress and
was followed by a man with a face like a foundation stone
carrying a miniature fluffy dog. Baco came out of the café
and began to fawn over them.

Odette stared with solemn interest.

'That's the yellow tart's new lover, isn't it?' she asked at
length.

Bigou was shocked that she should know about such
things.

'That's not for you to talk about,' he said. 'And the lady's
proper name is Mademoiselle Turbigo.'

'Everybody calls her the yellow tart,' Odette said. 'When
I'm grown up, I'm going to have a lover with a big car too.
Tell me, why do women get prettier dresses and things by
being tarts than by getting married?'

Bigou was about to expostulate again when Latérade
came out of the café and jocularly asked the child to dance.
With a sad eye Bigou watched them twirl away in the rout.
He was walking back along the terrace to look for a vacant

table when he came face to face with the abbé Pécher hurrying through the night.

'Good-evening, monsieur l'abbé,' he greeted. 'You're out late.'

'You're right,' the priest said. 'I've been to a deathbed. An old man. Not a very good old man, I'm afraid. And how is Odette? I haven't seen her at Mass for some time. She must be more than ever careful to attend to her religious duties regularly now that her poor mother's dead. So many begin, but so few persevere.'

Bigou knew that Odette hadn't been to Mass for months now, but he didn't want to tell the priest for fear of hurting his feelings.

'You can rely on me to give the matter my strictest attention, monsieur l'abbé,' he said, unconsciously falling into step with the priest. At every café they passed, the same racket and rumpus was going on; everybody was dancing, but nobody looked as though he were thinking about the Bastille or what its fall had meant to life and letters.

'One must not be too hard on the people,' the priest said through his twisted unhappy lips. 'They've had their religion taken from them by state education. And yet there's more good done in Paris than one imagines. Even in the Point-due-Jour you've no idea of the number of people who come to Holy Communion every day. God has permitted great sinners to live in France, but He has also raised up great saints.'

Bigou did not know quite what to say; it was not the sort of conversation to which he was accustomed.

'What the poor don't understand, monsieur l'abbé, is why the priests always seem to be on the side of the rich,' he said.

'Unfortunately the criticism is not without foundation,' the priest said as they turned up the Boulevard Exelmans. 'But there are signs that the voices of Maritain, Bernanos, and Mauriac are beginning to be heard. And then it's not the Church that's wrong, Monsieur Bigou, but churchmen. That is what is so sad; our religion is so true, but the way we live it makes it seem so false.'

'It's like this, monsieur l'abbé,' Bigou said, encouraged by the priest's candour. 'The workingman feels that there is something of a fraud in pretending that fornication and adultery are the only sins when there are so obviously so many others, if you'll pardon the word, monsieur l'abbé.'

'That is because the clergy have not taught morality implicit in the gospel of Christ,' the priest said. 'There's been too much fuss made about women showing their knees in church and far too little about armaments and cruelty and oppression and employers underpaying their employees and sickness and unhappiness and false national ideals. And in France the burgesses, who in the towns represent the practising Catholics, have been stupid and selfish. They have underpaid labour disgracefully and flaunted in high living and pleasure the wealth they have wrung from the work of others; and, what is worse, they have alienated the poor from religion and taken from them the God-given right to kneel and be humble. You are right, Monsieur Bigou; churchmen must attack sin with canon as well as with revolvers; for not only do we want our young men and young women to be pure, but we also want them to be kind and compassionate to distant as well as to near unhappinesses.'

'You are right, monsieur l'abbé,' Bigou said, feeling once again as he had felt when watching Odette make her first communion. 'The whole world's waiting to believe in something good and clean and pure and holy, but it's not going to be able to do so as long as churchmen are afraid openly to condemn evil where it lies.'

'You are right and you are wrong,' the priest said. 'You are right because, when people think about the stars, they can have no difficulty in believing that the Body and Blood of Christ are really and truly present in the Eucharist. And you are wrong because the Popes have condemned evil openly where it lies in their encyclicals; Leo XIII in *Rerum Novarum*, Pius XI in *Mit Brennender Sorge* and *Non Abbiamo Bisogno.*'

'But nobody listens to encyclicals,' Bigou said. 'And besides, they want to listen to the small voices as well as the big voices: to the parish priest telling them that the encyclical is not just another official utterance.'

'Péguy was a small voice and he wasn't listened to either,' the priest said. 'When he said that work well done was its own reward, he enunciated a great truth; and when he said that the true craftsman took as great pains over work which would never be seen as over that which would, he enunciated another. Both truths have been forgotten in the meretricious France of today.' They left the noisy scatter of the boulevard with heads bobbing about under the lanterns and stood outside the dilapidated house in which the priest had his lodging on the seventh floor under the slates. 'Eh, oui, Monsieur Bigou. Intelligence, compassion, and goodness, these are the virtues.'

'And courage, monsieur l'abbé.'

'And courage, Monsieur Bigou. There's going to be need for that, too.'

They stood there smiling at each other in the pale green glow of the lamp-post, Bigou and the humble apostolic priest who ate meat once a week and did his own cooking and laundry and was despised by the poor whom he served because they thought he had become a priest because it was an easier job than clerking in an office.

'Well, good-evening and good-night, Monsieur Bigou,' the priest said, holding out his hand.

'Good-evening and good-night, monsieur l'abbé,' Bigou said.

Odette was dancing with a pale washed-out long-haired young man when Bigou arrived back at the café. There were still no vacant tables, but there was an empty chair at the table at which Bacqueroët was sitting alone, so he asked Bacqueroët if he minded his sitting beside him and Bacqueroët said that he didn't. All the loud-speakers were playing different tunes, but that didn't seem to worry the dancers, who, believing in neither God nor Napoleon nor Monsieur Albert Lebrun, shuffled round and round with bored abandon. With his stick gripped between his knees, Bacqueroët held his hacked face up to the stars he couldn't see.

'I remember in 1913,' he said. 'She had golden hair and her parents were away in Rouen. She had lovely legs too. Tell me; what are women's legs like these days? Tell me a little about their legs.'

But Bigou wasn't listening because what the abbé Pécher had just said to him was making him feel preoccupied and holy; but when he had had a few more drinks he didn't feel preoccupied and holy any longer, but Bacqueroët had gone home by then.

X

THE ANGRY MEN went on getting down to things, and those who were angry with them went on getting down to things too. It was decided not to intervene in Spain, but only to let ammunition and guns and volunteers over the frontier at Port Bou. It was decided that Monsieur Roger Salengro, Minister of the Interior, had deserted on his bicycle to the enemy in 1914 and directed their artillery fire on the trench occupied by his battalion. It was decided that Monsieur Roger Salengro, Minister of the Interior, had not deserted on his bicycle to the enemy in 1914 and directed their artillery fire on the trench occupied by his battalion. It was decided to devalue the franc, although it wasn't really a devaluation, but a levelling down to the dollar and the pound in agreement with New York and London, and, besides, the franc was going to float anyway between 110 and 105 to the pound and if you wanted to work it out in dollars you had only to divide by 4.87. It was decided to open the 1937 Exhibition on time. It was decided to tax at two per cent the unallocated reserves as at thirty-first December, 1935, of limited companies, and that was a suck to the fifty-seven thousand two hundred families who had seen the law coming and had been wrangling away their reserves during the current year. It was decided that His Eminence Jean Cardinal Verdier was a great Frenchman because he had told a workman on the site of the Pontifical Pavilion at the Exhibition that it was less sinful to say 'merde' than to say 'Nom de Dieu.' And the great big presses of the Journal Officiel kept turning and Monsieur Albert Lebrun kept signing, in the land of his dreams.

It was decided not to devalue the franc any more.

It was decided that the union of all Frenchmen was necessary.

It was decided to increase the birth rate.

It was decided that 'eau, gaz, électricité,' did not necessarily mean 'Liberté, Egalité, Fraternité.'

It was decided that there was nothing really to fear from Hitler because Madame Geneviève Tabouis knew exactly what he had up his sleeve because she was not the niece of Jules Cambon for nothing.

It was decided that the new whoreshop in the Boulevard Edgar Quinet must be doing really well, at least so the cashier at the bank said, because every morning the headmistress handed in great wads of francs, pounds, dollars, pesetas, lire, pengoes, kröner, and zlotys.

It was decided to take sterner steps to suppress tax evasion and to do away with wooden railway carriages.

It was decided not to intervene in Spain.

XI

ODETTE said that she didn't want to start going to Mass again when Bigou told her what the abbé Pécher had said, but Bigou said that she must go to confession and communion as well. Whereupon the child said that she wasn't going to confession and communion unless Bigou went to confession and communion too. Bigou said that, of course, he would go, and that, *bon sang*, he wasn't afraid to confess his sins to any priest, and that, *Nom de Dieu*, he wasn't afraid to try to lead a better life either. All the same he didn't like the idea of confessing his sins to the abbé Pécher or to any of the priests in the district whom he knew by sight and still less did he like the idea of Baco or Chanu or Latérade or Verneuil seeing him snooping into the church on a Saturday afternoon, so they took the underground to Saint-Eustache.

Inside, the church was full of the dust of centuries of dead prayer and sermons. Great bars of sunlight stretched in front of the windows propping the walls like buttresses. A few black figures knelt in the nave squeaking their chairs as they prayed. In front of a side altar a fuddle of candles burned in a golden blob where a blue-and-white nun was giving a lesson in the catechism to a tatter of bored children. Her querulous voice creaked out over the ghost of the baptism of the infant Talleyrand: *'La Troisième Personne de la Sainte Trinité est le Saint Esprit qu'il faut beaucoup prier pour qu'il nous donne la lumière et l'inspiration.'* Through the crimson robes of *Saint Denis* carrying his stained glass head sang the voice of a message-boy:

> *'Nous avons bien rigolé;*
> *Tout le village a flambé,*
> *Avec les pom-pom —*
> *Avec les pom-pom —*
> *Avec les pompiers!'*

'Who is the Third Person of the Holy and Indivisible Trinity?' the nun asked.

'The Holy and Indivisible Virgin Mary,' a small boy answered.

Odette giggled and would have lingered in the hope of hearing more, but Bigou led her on to the hamlet of dusty confessionals behind the high altar. There was only one priest hearing confessions. The bulge of his freshly starched surplice stuck out of the open framework of the door and a pair of repentent soles and heels peeked out from under a green curtain. Lined along a stool sat the mean thin file of the next for shaving: blotched old women with screwy noses, grey little men in humble suits, pimply young men and dank depressed young girls, striving to abandon their greeds and their unkindnesses for love of the Saviour. Odette and Bigou went and sat at the end of the stool. From the confessional came the sound of muttering: ssh, ssh, ssh from the penitent, ssh, ssh, ssh, from the priest. 'France is still a Catholic nation,' Bigou thought as a cod-faced woman backed out from under the green curtain and minced off to say her Hail Marys. He found a blur of unexpected pleasure in picturing unseen swarms of saints going out in the small mornings to receive the Body of God at early altars. Perhaps Baco and Chanu and Latérade and Verneuil were wrong when they laughed at priests and what they taught. Odette tugged at his sleeve.

'Well, what must one do now?' she asked.

'*Dame*, one must pray.'

'You mean make an act of contrition?'

'They must have taught you that at catechism.'

'But supposing one isn't sorry for one's sins? Supposing one knows one will sin again? Supposing one *wants* to sin again?'

'One must pray.' It was all he could think of to tell her, although he thought there must be something else. Odette stared in front of her with her hands clasped in her lap and a fixed little smile on her lips which he couldn't quite interpret. *Bon sang,* how like her mother, she was and what good friends they were going to be! Baco and Chanu and Latérade and Verneuil were all very well in their way, but there was no friendship like that which could sweeten between a father and his daughter. Words that he hadn't repeated for years came whispering to his lips: 'O, my God, Who art infinitely Good in Thyself and infinitely good to me . . .'; but when he racked his brain for the rest, they wouldn't come, and the heat from the sun shone in through the window and burned the back of his neck. A young man in great pumped-out plus fours left the far side of the confessional and marched away with righteousness in his hair. Everybody moved up along the stool and a large unhappy man with a carbuncle on the end of his nose came and sat down next Bigou. He was shabbily dressed and hitched a rosary out of his pocket. A bunch of keys was entangled in the rosary and it took the man some time to separate them, but his lips kept praying all the time. Bigou tried not to look at his carbuncle, but he kept on looking just the same.

Inside the confessional the priest began to hurry through the penitents. Soon Bigou and Odette and the man with the carbuncle on the end of his nose were the only three waiting to be shriven. When it came to be Odette's turn to go and kneel behind the curtain, she hung back and said that she wouldn't go at all unless Bigou went first. The grill was closed when Bigou knelt in front of it. He fixed his eyes on the metal twist of Christ above his head and tried to think of what he was going to say, but he was distracted by the lurch of the woman penitent's voice on the other side of the grill and by the priest's. '*Oui, oui, oui,*' said the priest. '*Et puis alors je me suis mise en colère avec ma bonne quand*

*elle m'a cassé de la vaisselle que j'avais payée trente francs
la pièce au Printemps.'* 'Oui, oui, oui,' said the priest. *'Et
puis alors un soir quand mon mari est rentré légèrement en
retard . . .'* When the little wooden door behind the grill
on his side of the confessional shot back, Bigou still didn't
know what he was going to say to the priest.

'Bless me, father, for I have sinned,' he began when the
priest had blessed him. 'It's at least ten years since my last
confession.'

'Yes, my son,' the priest said. 'And what sins can you remember having committed?'

'A bit of everything, I suppose,' Bigou said, and then it all
came blurting out. One moment he hadn't known what he
was going to say and the next the great vomit of self-accusa-
tion came of its own accord. He had lied, he had looked
upon women with lewd desire, he had been prideful, he had
hated others most when he had seen that they were moved
by desires as mean as his own, he had ruled his life from
motives of human respect, for weeks and months he had not
thought of God at all, he would probably have been unfaithful to his wife if he had been rich enough to afford mistresses, just as he would probably have gone to Mass occa-
sionally had he not been afraid of the criticism of his friends,
he had lied, he had looked upon women with lewd desire.
When he caught himself beginning the catalogue over again,
he stopped.

'My son, you must pray to Almighty God to give you the
grace of perseverance,' the priest said. 'You must try to love
God more and you must realize that our holy religion is
true. Even if nobody believed or practised the Catholic
religion, even if there were no Pope in Rome, the mathe-

matics of Christian doctrine would still be true just as the natural laws were true before scientists were able to measure their workings. Realize this and you will fear less to serve God openly, because you will understand that it is the worldlings who are foolish and not Christians. *Qui ne vit pas comme un saint vit comme un insensé.* You must also try to love your neighbour, even when you have seen him, heard him, and smelt him. Saint John tells us that a man is a liar if he says that he loves God Whom he hath not seen and hates his neighbour whom he hath seen. At the risk of heresy, I would say that I do not altogether agree with Saint John, for it is often precisely because we have seen our neighbour that we find it so difficult to love him. In the street, in the bus, in the underground train, we feel forced to hate him; we hate his ugliness, his air of importance, his empty eyes, his fatty lips, his umbrella, the way he unfolds his newspaper all over our knees, but chiefly, I think, we hate the hostile indifference with which he regards us. It is this sin of hatred, which is at the root of most of the world's troubles, which we must try to conquer. We can conquer it in three ways: by remembering that we must often appear as hateful to our neighbour as he does to us; by remembering that Christ died for him as well as for us; and by frequent communion. There is no easy way to salvation, my son. Saint Augustine, Saint Ignatius, Saint Jean Vianney didn't find the practice of perfection any easier than you or I. Perhaps they loved our Lord more and perhaps they were more persevering, that is all. For your penance you will say one decade of the rosary.' He turned away from Bigou, mumbled away, made the sign of the cross: ' . . . *sint tibi in remissionem peccatorum, augmentum gratiae et praemium*

vitae aeternae. Amen. Go in peace, my son, and pray for
me.'

Bigou was touched that so holy a man as the priest had
asked such a sinner as himself to pray for him. He went and
knelt in front of the high altar and began his penance, counting the petitions off on his fingers as he had no beads. A
peace and a content such as he had not known for years
surged up within him. A few minutes later Odette came and
knelt beside him. Together they knelt until footsteps and
clanking keys came down the church and the voice of the
sacristan shouting: *'On ferme.'* They rose and walked out
into the street which still looked as worldly as when they
had left it.

Bigou's heart was so full that he wanted to tell Odette
how happy he was, but he could find no words to match the
great golden glow within him. The priest who had heard
their confessions came out of the church behind them and
walked away down the hot pavement with the sun lighting
the shine on the back of his cassock. He looked very ordinary and humble and unimportant out in the open air with
the rush of buses all about him. The pavements smelt of the
vegetables which had lain there in the early morning when
the market had been on. Bigou pulled Odette's arm through
his.

'So we're pals?' he asked.

'If you like,' she said.

He could have wished that she had replied with more
enthusiasm, but supposed that at Odette's age children found
it difficult to be friendly with their parents. They walked up
the rue du Pont Neuf together and turned into the rue de
Rivoli. Odette kept stopping to gaze into shop windows

where women's hats and dresses were displayed and Bigou laughed and gazed with her, thinking how like her mother she was. They sat at length on the terrace of a café next a tailor's shop in whose window a small mechanical dwarf dressed in a straw hat and green suit kept twirling from right to left and from left to right and tapping on the glass with the point of his cane. Across the Seine came the bells of Sainte Clothilde ringing the angelus. In the distance the sun shone into the windows of the Tour Saint Jacques and made the panes look as though candles had been lighted behind them. Year after year at this time and in this place Bigou had seen them thus and had derived from their contemplation a sense of the permanence of France and himself.

'We're lucky to be French,' he told Odette.

'Perhaps the Italians think the same about being Italian,' Odette said.

'Perhaps they do, but it's not quite the same,' Bigou said. 'There's a balance about France that there is about no other nation in the world. Great things have come out of France and even greater things are going to come. This Popular Front movement is going to do an enormous amount of good.'

'Does that mean that even poor people will have pretty dresses and motor cars?' Odette asked.

'Perhaps not right away, but it means that slowly and surely there will be a greater measure of social justice,' Bigou said.

'In that case I'm a communist,' Odette said. 'I don't want to wait until I'm seventy before I have pretty clothes and a motor car. Monsieur Verneuil says that the communists have only to slit the throats of the rich and then everybody'll have everything they want.'

'Perhaps it's not good for people to have everything they want,' Bigou said. 'Perhaps it's better for people to do their duty.'

'I don't want to do my duty,' Odette said. 'I want to be rich and have pretty dresses.'

Bigou saw that it was no use arguing with the child. He sat loving her silently while she brooded with great sullen eyes. When he called the waiter and ordered a grenadine for her, he let her have the vermouth she preferred. On the other side of the street employees of the Samaritaine began to push inside the shop the wheeled counters piled with tennis shoes, bathing-dresses, and children's frocks. From the invisible sickle of the Seine came the hoot of a *bateau mouche* as it edged away round Notre Dame. On the tailor's window next door the mechanical dwarf went on tapping with his stick, but on the panes of the Tour Saint Jacques there were now blue lights as well as gold. Odette sat on in her distemper and a thundery little wind came chasing up the pavement and fluttered out the sleeves of her blouse.

XII

ON A SUNDAY MORNING in October, Bigou lay dreaming that he was about to be guillotined. The Procurator of the Republic had just entered his cell and awakened him with the traditional words: 'Be brave; your appeal has been rejected.' The counsel for the defence was there as well and Monsieur Deibler's assistants and a clutter of policemen and the prison chaplain. The priest heard his confession and said Mass at a portable altar. Never had a Mass seemed to Bigou so short: God was down in the Host and gone again in no time. Then he was handed over to Monsieur Deibler's assistants who bound his feet together and tied his hands behind his back and cut away the collar of his shirt and shaved the back of his head. Their faces were hard and hating as they bound and cut and shaved.

Bigou tried to make them talk to him, so that he might win from them a flickering recognition of his humanity. 'You'll not be rough with me, will you,' he said. 'I mean you won't push me and shove me and pull me. Especially my hair. I don't want to be yanked onto the plank by my hair. I promise you I'll go quietly.' But they did not answer him, and their eyes were as hard and tiny and unkind as boot-buttons as they went on with their binding and their cutting and their shaving. As they took hold of him and began to march him towards the door, it suddenly occurred to him that he did not know what he was being guillotined for, but it was already too late to ask anybody. The fresh new day was upon his cheeks and the sky like a fish's belly and the guillotine before his eyes with Monsieur Deibler standing dumpily beside it with his hands in his overcoat pockets. In a few seconds it would be all over, and he would know all or nothing, but that night the little dwarf in the tailor's shop in the rue de Rivoli would go on turning and tapping with his stick, as usual, and on the panes of the Tour Saint Jacques the sun would shine in blinding asterisks of gold as though candles had been lighted behind them and girls' frocks would blow out over the Seine in the wind. The open basket lined with sawdust was there for his trunk and the little square box for his head and the black van with the single horse which would clop-clop-clop away over the cobbles carrying another extinguished reflection of the earth and the trees and the sky.

Then, just as he was preparing to feel his hair pulled, he woke up. Odette in her bed was still asleep. The lipstick which she had put on for fun the night before was smeared over the bedclothes like rust. Although he had been angry with her about the lipstick, Bigou found it impossible to be angry with her now. She looked so entirely at God's mercy with her face pudgy and tender in repose. Perhaps even Hitler and Mussolini looked weak and lovable when they were sleeping. Perhaps the world's chances of happiness might increase tremendously if the leading politicians of different nations were to see one another sleeping. From Baco's wireless set in the café opposite came the sound of the world's inability to watch for one hour with Him:

'Ça vaut mieux que d'attraper la scarlatin-e,
Ça vaut mieux que de bouffer la mort aux rats,
Ça vaut mieux que de trouver des punaises dans la vaselin-e,
Ça vaut mieux que de faire le zouave au Pont d'Alma.'

The wireless suddenly stopped. Bigou could hear the birds singing and the steps of people hurrying along the street to early Mass. There must be quite a lot of people in Paris who went to early Mass on Sundays, but there didn't seem to be any of them left on Mondays.

Odette awoke. When she had lain for a little while with her eyes open, she got up and began to dress.

'Are you going to Mass?' Bigou asked.

'Of course not. I'm going to Fontainebleau for the day with Madame Turbigo. You've no objections, have you?'

Bigou had plenty: he objected to her not going to Mass; he objected to her going out with a woman who had a daughter who was a tart; and he objected to Madame Turbigo being able to spend money on Odette when he couldn't. He couldn't, however, say so, because he had given up going to Mass himself for fear of what Baco and Chanu and Verneuil would say and because Madame Turbigo had been so kind when Marie died. Besides his rise of a hundred and fifty francs a month had long ago been absorbed by the increase in the cost of living and it would be unfair to deprive Odette of an outing which he himself was too poor to afford. As he watched her pulling on her clothes, he realized that her body was ceasing to be the body of a child and that he was beginning to be a little afraid of her.

When the child was dressed, she was going to leave the flat without kissing him, but Bigou called her back.

'That's a nice way to leave your father,' he said.

'Pardon, I forgot,' she said as she bent and kissed his brow with formal lips.

'Don't you want any breakfast, cabbage?'

'I'll get some from Madame Turbigo.'

'You're very fond of Madame Turbigo, aren't you?'

'Of course. Madame Turbigo's very kind to me.'

'And I'm not, is that it?'

'I didn't say that.'

'But that's what you were thinking, eh? Listen, cabbage, I'd be kind to you, too, if I had the money, but I haven't. That's all there is about it.'

'I know you do your best,' Odette said. She kissed him again, staring past his tired face with empty young eyes, and left the flat.

Bigou lay thinking about her for a little after she had gone. Then he, too, got up and dressed. He went across to the café for breakfast because he couldn't be bothered heating his own coffee and there was no bread in the house anyway. Baco was shuttlecocking up and down behind the zinc counter dolloping out cups of coffee and cocoa and glasses of red and white wine. Behind him stood two enormous brass urns which hissed whenever he turned a handle and gave out tremendous clouds of steam. On the counter itself there were two small baskets full of hot croissants. There was also a sugar bowl out of which Bigou took a lump and popped it into his mouth while Baco's shiny back of waist-coat was turned to pour out his coffee. Chanu winked a condoning eye and went on soaking his croissant in his coffee. Choiseul the policeman was there too. He had just come off duty and was wearing a sweater instead of his tunic, although he still had on his blue trousers. His hostile little eyes were screwed deep down into their sockets like shell-fish.

'Things rolling?' he asked Bigou.

'On little wheels,' Bigou answered.

Both men laughed mirthlessly. Bigou did not like Choiseul and Choiseul did not like Bigou, but neither quite dared to show him hatred. Bigou knew that Choiseul beat up his prisoners when he got them in a cell and that he had blinded the old mangy tom-cat from the laboratory; and Choiseul knew that Bigou had twice gone to Mass on a Sunday.

'There's going to be trouble at the Parc des Princes this afternoon,' Choiseul said. 'The Croix de Feu are going to try to prevent the communist meeting from taking place.'

'*Ils sont embêtants comme la pluie,*' Baco said. 'Here I

have to have my café done up because that fellow opposite is having his café done up and all the time costs are going up because of their eight-hour days and their collective contracts and I don't know all what. *Ce n'est pas gai, la vie d'artiste.*'

'I used to think I was a fascist, but now I think I'm a communist,' Bigou said. 'I'm a communist because my rise of a hundred and fifty francs has been swallowed up by the increased cost of living. *Bon sang,* I'm poorer than I was before.'

'I'm a fascist because I dislike having to pay through the nose,' Baco said.

'*Je m'en fous de la politique comme de l'an quarante,*' Chanu said. 'What I want to do is to win the big prize in the lottery. And when I've won I'm not even going to tell the missus. I'll wait for five months and then I'll have the bank cash the ticket for me and like that nobody'll ever know I've won.'

'*Espèce de con, va,*' Baco said. 'How'll you prevent the bank manager saying the ticket's his and cashing it on his own account?'

'I'll get his receipt, of course,' Chanu said.

'And how'll you prevent his telling everybody it's you that's won?' Choiseul asked.

Bigou drank up his coffee and left them arguing. Outside on the Boulevard Exelmans a fresh strip of eternity was being pulled by, behind the roofs of the long dreary houses. An empty horse-drawn hearse came rattling down over the cobbles, but nobody paid any attention to it. Baco shouted through the open door of the café after Bigou.

'Your boss has just telephoned. He says you're to go and meet him at the office at once.'

At first Bigou was inclined to disobey. *'Il pent courir,'* he called out to Baco, but the habit of submission was too en-grained in him for him to rebel for long. Instead he compro-mised by deciding to go by a roundabout way instead of tak-ing the AS bus direct to the grands boulevards. With a delicious defiance which was enhanced by the knowledge that he wouldn't have to pay for it afterwards, he sauntered along the rue Chardon Lagache feeling the new free morn-ing on his face. Outside the pale green blistered paint of the police station a group of policemen stood twirling their bâtons and yawning. Housewives with net baskets on their arms stumped along the pavements on their way to market, but the better-dressed women were on their way to Mass with their husbands and children. Almost all the girls were pretty and smiling and almost all the boys were slovenly and furtive. It looked as though the wives and mothers of 1946 were going to be more efficient than the soldiers. Was this the cause of France's weakness: the simultaneous pro-duction of exquisite women and effeminate men? But had the men who fought from 1914 to 1918 been effeminate? Had they looked slovenly and furtive when they went to school? His question was still unanswered as he turned up the rue Ribéra. In the rue de la Source a group of Benedictine nuns looked like penguins as they came hurrying late down the street for the conventual High Mass in the Abbaye de Sainte Marie. The sound of the organ came across the warm trees as the monks began to sing the *Gloria*. A young woman in a tight black satin frock walked in front of Bigou, the loaves of her loins revolving like turbines, and the sound of the *Gloria* fell across her too.

In the Avenue Mozart there were plenty of number 16

buses: big, shining, and new and bound for the Madeleine,
but Bigou decided to take a number 12, because it followed
a circuitous route. The avenue was full of cool women in
coloured frocks on their way to or from their devotions.
Nurses were out with flutters of well-fed children. Poverty
seemed a long way off, but Bigou knew it was only a kilo-
metre away, down by Convention and the Quai de Javel. A
young man in worn clothes and an angry face passed up the
street bawling out, 'L'Humanité' but the cool women only
held their chins a little higher.

The number 12 bus was so crowded that Bigou had to
stand on the platform, wedged in between a fat woman and
an elderly man with the red rosette of the Legion of Honour
in his buttonhole. The fat woman smiled at Bigou as they
lurched against each other and said, 'Faut avoir le pied
marin.' Bigou raised his hat and smiled back. Inside, in the
dark cathedral of seats, everybody looked morose, aggressive,
and glum. Bigou thought how much jollier buses would be
if the passengers could indulge in a little community singing, like in a René Clair film, but when he himself began to
whistle, the man with the red rosette glared. Nobody spoke
as the bus panted up the rue Franklin. The conductor kept
diving inside to collect the fares and out again to ring the
bell. The Trocadéro was a mess of half-pulled-down old
building and half-erected new building.

'They'll never finish it in time,' the man with the red
rosette said.

'You mean you hope they'll never finish it in time,' a man
wearing a straw hat said.

The two men glowered at each other, but neither dared
to pursue the quarrel. The bus rolled on down the Avenue

du Président Wilson. Above the titanic wooden gates on the site of the entrance to the Exhibition the red flag with the hammer and sickle and the black flag with skull and cross-bones floated, but nobody looked much because they had all seen it before. The bus tumbled across the bridge and along the quays. The new spire of Saint Pierre de Chaillot piled away up to heaven like a monster wagon-restaurant ice. Far away on the hill the Sacré Coeur lay in trembling white beauty, with the sun turning its shine to snow. Below the sash of the Seine lay spread in blue and silver ruffles. Outside the Chambre des Députés two sullen policemen stood argu-ing the toss. At the Gare d'Orsay Englishwomen with teeth like tigers handed their travelling rugs to porters and yawned on their way to Cannes. Outside the offices of the *Journal Officiel* there was no queue of clerks for the latest batch of new financial laws because it was Sunday. The bus rolled through the green history of the Tuileries with their scarlet and yellow platoons of flowers. Dunlop flattened the knee-breeches of Louis XIV and Shell Mex bit across the incense of phantom Corpus Christi processions. Where Richelieu had read his breviary a pleb in patched pants stuck his beard into the Canard Enchaîné. Out on the rue de Rivoli, Boileau and Mazarin and Mirabeau stood benignly in their niches, each with a pocket handkerchief of birds' droppings on his pate. Bigou got off the bus and walked back and down the rue Royale to the Madeleine, outside which the *camelots du roi* were crying '*Demandez L'Action Française*,' because ten years previously the Pope had put the paper on the Index.

Monsieur Dupont and Monsieur Terrasse were waiting for Bigou in Monsieur Terrasse's room when he reached the office of the Entreprises Françaises d'Installation de Chauffage Central. Mireille Arzelle, the pretty secretary, was there too, sitting on a sofa in a new fur coat. Once again Bigou thought that her smile was less chilling than usual, but it was evident that both the directors were displeased.

'You've taken a long time,' Monsieur Dupont said. 'You must have got my message at least an hour ago.'

'It is such a lovely morning I came a roundabout way,' Bigou said, and stared defiantly at them both as though daring them to reprimand him.

'Bigou's all right,' Monsieur Terrasse said hurriedly to Monsieur Dupont with an indulgent smile at Bigou. 'A bit hot-headed at times, but absolutely loyal and sound.'

Bigou wanted to tell them that he wasn't loyal and sound at all, but a communist and an anarchist and a hater of rich men like themselves who couldn't boil an egg or change a tyre or sole a boot or plough a field or fight a battle or write a poem, but who sucked the wealth from Frenchmen who could. He also wanted to tell them that his rise of a hundred and fifty francs a month had long ago been absorbed by the increased cost of living and that it cost him as much to live without his wife as with her because he had to send most of his and Odette's washing to the laundry and to have a woman in to clean up twice a week; but he didn't, partly because he was afraid, partly because Mireille was smiling at him quite openly now and showing the enticing cavern of her mouth and making him want to put his hand under her coat and touch her long slim exciting body.

'I want you to understand that what I am about to say to you is strictly confidential,' Monsieur Dupont said. 'Monsieur Terrasse assures me that I can rely absolutely on your discretion.'

Bigou would have liked to say, 'I've never blown the gaff about your underdeclaring the firm's profits,' but instead he said: 'Of course, Monsieur Dupont.'

'Good,' Monsieur Dupont said. 'Bigou, France is going to the dogs and the franc's going with it and the company's got to protect itself. Briefly, this is what Monsieur Terrasse and myself propose to do. We propose to form a Swiss Company with registered offices in Geneva and to transfer a large portion of the firm's liquid assets to it. We've got at least twelve million free reserves, haven't we? Less two per cent for that swine Blum's tax, of course. Well, we call our company the Société Génevoise de Commerce et d'Exploitation, and we transfer say ten million to it. With that ten million the Société Génevoise buys gold in Switzerland which it exports to New York and deposits in an American bank in the Swiss Company's name. You see the point, don't you? First of all, we protect the French company's assets against a further depreciation of the franc, and, secondly, we protect the gold itself because it will not be registered in France as the property of a French company and because, even if in the event of war the United States pass a law obliging their nationals to sell their gold, they can't force a Swiss company to sell theirs. It's as easy as pie, really. What I want to know is if there are any objections from a bookkeeping point of view.'

'Credit bank, debit investment in subsidiary company.' Automatically Bigou began to think aloud, as he almost invariably did when solving accounting problems. 'No, there is no difficulty as regards the mechanics of bookkeeping, but the tax people might ask awkward questions. You see, the money the French company advanced to the Swiss company would represent an investment in a foreign subsidiary and

as such would be declarable to the Bureau de l'Enrégistrement.' He spoke with professional enthusiasm, but broke off
when he saw Mireille's half-mocking, half-amused smile.

'That is surely a minor difficulty,' Monsieur Dupont said.
'What I'm concerned with is protecting the company's
money. The franc is at one hundred and ten to the pound
sterling today, but Heaven alone knows what it will be standing at in a year's time. And to my mind there's no need at
all to show the advance to the Swiss company as an investment. It could surely be worked in with the trade debtors
or hidden in the stock or the fixed assets, couldn't it?'

'The inspector might want to probe into any increases
over the preceding year's figures if they were too marked,'
Bigou said, trying not to look at Mireille. 'Of course we could
always spread the increases over: so much to trade debtors,
so much to stock, so much to fixed assets. After all, as business is good, it is only natural that the company's non-liquid
assets should increase. And then we could always say that
we had bought more raw materials because prices were going up so fast. And then all the money needn't come from
the official bank accounts, but from the secret bank funds as
well.' He looked to see how much his employer was going
to smile at him for helping him to betray France, but Monsieur Dupont wasn't smiling at him at all, but was nodding
Mireille to her feet.

'Well, I'm sure that Monsieur Terrasse and I can safely
leave the details to you. Let me have a comprehensive plan
first thing tomorrow morning. Things are going from bad to
worse and there's no time to lose. So long, Terrasse.'

Mireille's fur coat went out of the room and Monsieur
Dupont went out after it.

'What a man!' Monsieur Terrasse exclaimed. 'Such energy, such fire, such determination! What an honour it is for us to work for him, but I expect you'll get another rise as well if you produce a good plan. Not immediately, of course, but sooner or later. And then you'll almost certainly get a trip or two to Switzerland, all expenses paid. Aren't you a lucky man, Bigou?'

Bigou hadn't time to pluck up the courage to say that he was nothing of the sort when Monsieur Terrasse's wife and son and daughter walked into the office to take him home for lunch. They all had ugly squashed faces and chill protuberant eyes and they all looked at Bigou's worn clothes with contempt.

'Monsieur Bigou is our worthy and exceedingly capable bookkeeper,' Monsieur Terrasse introduced. 'He's going to work out a plan for getting the firm's money safely out of France.'

'How clever of him,' Madame Terrasse said. 'And can he get mine out too?'

'Perhaps if you asked him nicely,' Monsieur Terrasse said.

Bigou wanted to tell her that she was seventeen kinds of a disloyal selfish revolting old cow, but instead he smarmed: 'All madame has to do is to deposit her money with the firm, and I'll do the rest for her.'

'That is indeed kind of you, Monsieur — Monsieur Pigou.'

'Bigou,' Monsieur Terrasse corrected.

'Bigou,' Madame Terrasse said. 'I think that Cardinal Baudrillart's so right, don't you? Religion's the only thing that can save France. And that's why we must all support General Franco. Some of our friends are presenting a gold sword to his representative this afternoon and a bishop is going to be there to bless it.'

'France needs a Franco too,' her son said. 'Once and for all we've got to get rid of the vast nonsense of universal suffrage which is only an illusion of government.'

Nobody else spoke, and for a few seconds they stood about showing their teeth to one another. Behind the windows the trees were spread out like veins over Paris, but Bigou wasn't looking at them because he was too busy thinking about the gold sword for Franco. Was it possible that a sword could spread the gospel? Could shells tear Christ into men's entrails or splinter Jesus into their eyes? Outside, the Boulevard de la Madeleine stretched as it had stretched yesterday and when Président Sidi Carnot had driven along it.

'Come, Emile, or we'll be late for lunch,' Madame Terrasse said to her husband.

Bigou waited in the office until they had gone because he did not want to have to walk down the stairs with them feeling so very much poorer than they. When at last he went out into the street, the congregation was coming down the steps of the Madeleine from the last Mass, but there was no kindness or happiness or humility in their expressions. Even the gaiety of the itchy young bitches from the Argentine was hard and divorced from God. Did, Bigou wondered, the rich go to Mass solely as a class gesture? If so the demonstration was a failure because of the way they passed one another in the street with hostile unseeing eyes as though they were not all on the same sofa together, at the mercy of the patience of the poor.

This time he took the AS bus home because he was hungry and in a hurry to eat. In his hole under the Arc de Triomphe the unknown soldier lay beneath a faded wreath, and a girl from Clermont-Farrand was being photographed by her lover. The banner of flame burned palely, but the girl's frock frisked out bravely against Iéna and Sebastopol and Toledo. In the sky a pale blue sun shone like a coin with the rim of another sun peeping out underneath.

XIII

As HE WASHED UP in the flat after his lonely lunch, Bigou became angrier and angrier. What right had Dupont and Terrasse to pay him such a small salary for doing so much work? What right had they to swindle the government? What right had they to expect him to work overtime to help them to swindle the government? And above all what right had they to expect him to work overtime for nothing to help them to swindle the Government? Because he was not face to face with his oppressors, he also grew braver and braver making faces at his own reflection in the cracked mirror and pretending that his face was theirs. He determined that unless he were paid for it, he would not work overtime then or any other daytime to help them to swindle the Government.

Down in the street the pavements were crowded with new clothes walking. In their square black suits the squat fathers of families strolled with their wives and pink and pale blue children. Somewhere a bell was ringing for vespers, but nobody took any notice because in France the poor no longer prayed. As Bigou crossed to the café, taxis crammed with yelling hooligans went shooting out along the avenue to the communist rally at the Parc des Princes, but nobody paid much attention to them either, because somebody was always demonstrating about something these days. In the café Baco in his best black waistcoat and trousers was sloshing out the drinks behind the counter, and Chanu, Latérade, and Verneuil were knocking them back in front of the counter. Bacqueroët stood a little apart with his sore slab of face held away from them all. Verneuil, who was in plain clothes because he had the day off, was laying down the law with vehemence.

'*Et puis merde,*' he said. 'We've had enough. The communists are right. Everything in France is a racket. Take the Stavisky scandal. It's more than two years old already and nobody knows the truth about it yet.'

'It's a disgrace,' Baco said.

'There's no two ways about it,' Verneuil said. 'The people must seize power by force.'

'All this is going to finish badly,' Latérade said. 'That's what I always say to Madame Latérade. "Darling," I say, "all this is going to finish badly," I say.'

'Of course it's going to finish badly,' Bacqueroët said. 'It's going to finish badly for the simple reason that Frenchmen are fascists and communists and free-thinkers and Catholics before they are Frenchmen.'

'I know that it is generally agreed that people ought to be patriotic before they are anything else, but if everybody put their creed before their country, it seems to me there might be more prospect of ending wars,' Bigou said.

'That would be true if everybody in the whole world could be persuaded of the truth of one religion or one politic, but they can't,' Bacqueroët said. 'And then in France people are their own miserable mean selves before they adhere to a politic or a religion. Take ourselves here, for example.

Baco and Chanu aren't communists because they aren't poor enough. Chanu knows perfectly well that he would have to charge less for his meat if ever the communists got properly into power.'

There was laughter at this all along the counter, because quite a few people didn't like Chanu, who had put up his prices when the franc went west in 1926 and again when the pound went west in 1931, and was putting them up again now that the franc had gone west once more.

'They're not fascists either because they're not rich enough and because they might be expected to go to Mass on Sundays if they were and show a certain class spirit which might not always concord with their personal advantage, but when the terror is on France and Germany is at her bowels, they'll be fascists quickly enough. Verneuil's a communist because he's poor and wants to have a big car and a pretty mistress. I don't know what Bigou is, and I don't believe he knows himself; I expect he's a fascist when he's being polite to his boss and a communist when he feels that the dirty swine ought to pay him more and a Catholic when he's taking off his hat to the abbé Pécher and a free-thinker when he's ogling the pretty women in the underground. And I'm a patriot because I've been gashed and hacked about for France and apparently in vain. Gentlemen, I tell you in all seriousness that only one thing matters: Germany is rearming. At this very moment she is trying out in Spain the weapons with which she hopes to annihilate us. There is only one thing for Frenchmen to do: sink their political differences, forget their two hundred families and the Stavisky scandal and their forty-hour weeks and their paid holidays and their privileges and work and rearm and stand ready to fight.

What France wants is not a Blum or a Thorez or a Caillaux or a de la Rocque, but a Clemenceau, and unfortunately she's not going to find one. She's not going to find one because deep down in our dirty hearts we none of us care what matters to anybody else so long as we personally are all right. *On s'en fout de la gueule de la vraie France* because the present decadence is profitable to our pockets.' He finished his drink and raised his empty glass in the air. *'Messieurs, je vous dis "merde" et je vous dis "bonjour,"'* he said as he left the café.

Everybody felt that, badly wounded though he was, Bacqueroët had for once gone too far. They stood shaking their heads after him disapprovingly.

'Mince alors,' Baco said.

'He's got war on the brain,' Chanu said. 'Hitler'd never dare to make war on France. And then there are the English. They're not much good as soldiers, but they have a navy all the same.'

'And then there's the Maginot Line,' Baco said. 'We're as safe as houses behind that.'

'Bien sûr,' Latérade said.

'Perhaps if we only knew the truth, the Germans are as afraid of Albert Lebrun as we are of Adolf Hitler,' Bigou said.

Everybody laughed at this; and they had a few more quick ones to make them go on laughing. When they had drunk four more each, they were quite certain that there was going to be no more war and that the lion was going to lie down with the lamb and the weaned child put his hand on the cockatrice's den.

'It was funny all the same what Bacqueroët said about

you and Chanu,' Verneuil said to Baco, winking at Bigou as he spoke.

'No funnier than what he said about you,' Baco said.

'Or about Bigou,' Chanu said.

'Oh, yes, it was,' Verneuil said. 'The communists have guts and perhaps even the fascists have guts, but those who are neither one nor the other have only stained-glass tripes.' He thought this a great joke and laughed till the booze began to come down his nose.

'I tell you all this is going to finish badly,' Latérade said.

'Then what kind of tripe has Bigou got when he's a communist one moment and a fascist the next?' Chanu asked. 'That's what Bacqueroët said, isn't it?' he asked Baco.

'*Tout simplement ça*,' Baco said.

'I'm a communist forever now and so would you be if you'd heard what I heard this morning,' Bigou said. The Swiss subsidiary and the gold sword for Franco and the rise in the cost of living were all mixed in his anger which he knew would last forever. 'The rich must pay and if they won't we must find means of making them.'

'I notice that neither of you is at the Parc des Princes this afternoon,' Chanu sneered. 'Thorez is speaking, but perhaps you didn't know or perhaps you heard that the Croix de Feu have sworn to break up the meeting.'

'Who's got stained-glass tripes now?' Baco asked.

'*Nom de Dieu!*' Verneuil swore. 'You don't believe that it's because I'm frightened that I'm not at the Parc des Princes. I'm not at the Parc des Princes because I know the communist creed well enough not to need to hear it preached over again every half-hour: nationalization of industry, hang the rich and the priests and disembowel all butchers and café proprietors. And Bigou's not frightened either, *nom de Dieu, merde. Vous me faites chier tous les deux.*'

'Of course I'm not frightened,' Bigou said. 'And now I come to think of it I'd rather like to hear what Thorez has got to say and if any Croix de Feu get in my way I'll gouge out their eyes for them.'

'Let's go then,' Verneuil said.

Arm-in-arm Bigou and Verneuil went bouncing out into the sunlight and stood on the pavement telling each other that they had always known that Baco and Chanu were twisters, robbers of the poor, liars, capitalists, cheats, cowards, and violators of virgins, and that Bacqueroët had been quite right in what he had said about them, but quite wrong in what he had said about themselves. Verneuil also told Bigou that he had always been unable to understand why a fellow possessing such clarity of vision as Bigou had should consort with money-grubbing scum like Baco and Chanu, and Bigou said that it was funny, but he had always felt exactly the same about Verneuil. Then, because they didn't like to go into the café, they went and joined the queue of sad reflective men formed up outside the tin urinal on the other side of the avenue. It took them five minutes to get inside because it was the interval at two near-by cinemas, and then as soon as they got out Verneuil decided that as he was going to a meeting and had drunk a lot, it would be safer for him to make quite sure, so he queued up all over again. As he came out stuffing and buttoning himself for the second time, he began to tell Bigou why he wanted to kill all rich men.

'There's no two ways about it,' he said. 'We've got to destroy before we can construct. The rich won't give up their possessions without a struggle. Even after they've signed an agreement that they'll pay certain wages and grant certain privileges, they'll start to hedge. That's why we've got to slit their throats. And that's what the communist party intends to do. The people of Paris will rise. One night the burgesses of Passy and Auteuil and Neuilly will go to bed behind their velvet curtains and next morning they'll wake up with their throats cut. It'll all be over in twenty-four hours. Then there'll be a government by the people for the people.'

'The rich are cunning,' Bigou said. 'They'll always manage to escape. And what's more they'll manage to make their money escape too. Take my bosses, for example. Only this morning they were telling me of a plan they had to get all their wealth safely out of France. Of course, I told them exactly what I thought of them.'

'Of course,' Verneuil said.

'And then they asked me to help them to work out a scheme so as they wouldn't be caught and of course I told them I'd cut my right hand off first,' Bigou said.

'Of course,' Verneuil said.

'As a matter of fact I'm supposed to be working on the scheme now, but of course I'm not,' Bigou said.

'Of course,' Verneuil said.

Bigou saw that Verneuil didn't believe him and was hurt and resentful until he realized that even his last statement was only partially true, since he would probably be working all out on the scheme by tomorrow morning at latest.

Taxi-cabs piled with hooligans kept bowling along the avenue and Verneuil raised his clenched fist to the toughs and yelled 'C'est la lutte!' and the toughs raised their clenched fists and yelled 'C'est la lutte!' back. On the far pavement groups of well-dressed men carrying walking sticks moved resolutely in the direction of the Porte de Saint-Cloud.

'There go the dirty fascists,' Verneuil said. 'Baco and Chanu are wrong if they think I'm afraid of swine like that. And even if I were afraid, I'd only have to think a little of the people I see in the first-class compartment on the AS bus not to be afraid any longer. You've no idea of the dodges they try so as to get off without paying their fares. And then it's so boring: Porte de Saint-Cloud, Passy, Etoile, Madeleine, Bourse, and then Bourse, Madeleine, Etoile, Passy, Porte de Saint-Cloud. Sixteen journeys a day and shrieking all the time at the dirty swine not to stand in the passage. And then they don't pay you properly. Fourteen hundred francs a month. And then on my day off I've got to wash out the flat for the missus. *Ce n'est pas gai, la vie d'artiste.* I think I'd rather like to kill a few rich men for a change.'

'Bookkeeping's boring and underpaid too,' Bigou said. 'Life's altogether unjust. All the world over, the poor are starving, and yet in Brazil they burn coffee to keep the price up so that the rich don't lose their profits.'

'When the communist party gets into power we'll change all that,' Verneuil said. 'Everybody'll have a big house and a car and a yacht and as much coffee as they want.'

'Perhaps it's because gold is an outworn medium of exchange,' Bigou said. 'The big houses and cars and yachts and decent clothes and coffee are there for everybody to have. I read in the paper the other day that it is the means of distribution that are wrong.'

'You're probably right, but it would be simpler to slit the

throats of the rich,' Verneuil said. 'Why should we be poor
when other men who couldn't do our jobs are rich and
despise us?'

'Hell, yes! Why should we?' Bigou said.

Aided by the alcohol they had drunk, they soon worked
themselves up into a state of extreme indignation. By the
time that they reached the Porte de Saint-Cloud they knew
that they were going to love each other forever and that they
were afraid of nobody and that they were going to listen to
Maurice Thorez in the Parc des Princes however many Croix
de Feu tried to keep them out.

At the entrance to the Parc des Princes a phalanx of well-
dressed young men was drawn up and coming to meet them
was another phalanx of men in collarless open shirts and
jerseys. The toughs charged the gentry and the gentry drove
back the toughs who, reinforced by constant new arrivals,
charged and charged again. Then reinforcements of the
gentry attacked the toughs from the rear and the police
charged from the Boulevard Murat. The battle became a
heavy maul bulging right out over the Place and away along
into the Avenue de la Reine. Yelling at the tops of their
voices, Verneuil and Bigou rushed into the brawl, lunging
out wildly at anybody who looked well dressed. For a little
they fought side by side, but soon they became separated in
the vast porridge of conflict. Bigou found himself windmill-
ing on alone. He knew that he was being hit as well as hitting, but he didn't feel sore and his rage carried him forward. When a young man with a yellow mane struck him
on the nose, Bigou licked with delight at the blood, and
thought how salt it tasted and socked the young man a
mighty blow back. 'And there's for your gold sword for

Franco!' he said as he lammed on. 'And there's for your Swiss subsidiary! And there's for your hundred and fifty francs a month! And there's for your killing Marie!' But soon the phrases became too long for him to say, so he swore instead, and soon he gave that up too because his breath was giving out and he required all his energy for fighting. Then somebody gave him a crack on the ear which nearly sent him to the ground. '*Nom de Dieu*, I am going to hear Thorez all the same,' he muttered as he steadied himself. Suddenly there seemed to be fewer well-dressed young men to hit and he was carried forward by the surge of toughs coming from behind. '*Camarade, va falloir foutre le camp d'ici!*' a big man in a red jersey shouted at him. 'The dirty swine are going to get the garde mobile to fire on us. It'll be another sixth of February.'

As he steered his fighting towards one of the entrances to the underground, Bigou saw Choiseul, brandishing his bâton and hitting out indiscriminately. He hated him again for beating up prisoners in their cells and for blinding the mangy tom-cat from the laboratory, but chiefly he hated him for earning money from his wife's wine agency as well as from his policeman's job and for having a house in the country. Creeping up behind the policeman he caught him a great root with his boot on the backside and crammed his pork pie hat down over his eyes. Then he ducked and barged and pushed and shoved back into the crowd.

Soon, however, he didn't require to barge any more because the crowd sucked him along with it. Gentry and toughs, fascists and communists, they all sludged in a great turgid soup towards the entrance to the underground. Bigou stumbled, fell, and shot down the steps with the rest. With the rest he bought himself a ticket and drooped down onto the platform and stood waiting in the great battered, bleeding, sweating herd until a train came in.

The second-class compartment into which he was forced filled up with men who soon became angry again now that they knew there was no longer any danger of their being fired on. Bigou was wedged in between a postman and a man in a shiny brown suit who discussed across him the events of the afternoon, but when the postman had said 'Nom de Dieu, merde,' seven times Bigou gave up listening. The train lurched on down its ritual rail stringing rue de la Pompe to Trocadéro and Trocadéro to Iéna. At Rond Point des Champs-Elysées a man and his wife got in and stood near Bigou. The woman wore a cheap bright pink blouse and carried a plump baby girl in her arms, but nobody rose to offer her a seat. Bigou tried to make the child smile, but the round eyes remained round and disinterested. The father didn't smile either when Bigou tried to draw him into the game, but went on sticking his tongue into his cheek and pulling it out again. The act of paternity, Bigou reflected, was a casual and easily forgotten benevolence, like helping a blind man across the street. The train rattled on and the postman went on saying 'Nom de Dieu, merde,' across the little girl's face. At Miromesnil the bored little family got out and were blotted out by the Magasins du Louvre's advertisement of hoity-toity harlots stooging around in colossal turfs of winter furs. A young girl got in carrying a bunch of carnations. The carnations smelt of Alfred de Musset, but the postman went on saying 'Nom de Dieu, merde,' across them just the same.

At Strasbourg-Saint-Denis, Bigou got out and crossed to

the Porte de Clignancourt-Porte d'Orléans line, although he had not yet made up his mind where he was going. He sat down on the seat beside the *portillon automatique* to watch the lighted rosaries of the trains rush in, stop and rush out again. Then he mounted one of the trains and was carried to Les Halles where he got out again.

Under the bulk of Saint Eustache at the mouth of the underground an old woman was selling *Paris-Soir* and *L'Intransigeant* and another old woman was selling remaindered copies of *Mein Kampf* by Adolf Hitler. A lot of people were buying evening papers, but nobody seemed to be buying *Mein Kampf*. 'Sensational,' the second woman cried under Bigou's cold nose, 'the absolute proof that Hitler desires to conquer the world. Only three francs a copy. Spend three francs and learn history before it happens. Buy, monsieur, buy.' Bigou shook his head and the old woman put out her tongue at him. 'I'm not like the horses on the merry-go-rounds who can gallop for a year without eating,' she said. Bigou shook his head again and, drawn by the memory of his recent confession, entered the church.

Vespers had just been sung and a pillow of incense from the *Magnificat* floated in a blur before the high altar. In the pulpit a doddering priest was preaching a weary dither on sin to a sparse congregation of old women scattered over the church. *'Ce que constitue le péché grave c'est vouloir désobéir au Bon Dieu,'* the tired voice creaked on. Bigou looked to see if any of the old women were listening, but most of them seemed to be sleeping or praying. *'Donc pour commettre un péché mortel il faut non seulement désobéir au Bon Dieu mais il faut aussi vouloir Lui désobéir.'* In silent rage Bigou stood listening to the voice of the Absolute speaking with the dreary tongue of a finite old man. If the Church was really the Church of God, why didn't the preacher shout with at least the conviction of the blaspheming postman in the underground: '*Nom de Dieu, merde,* the only way for humanity to save itself is to do the easy thing instead of the difficult thing, to tell the truth instead of to lie, to sweat instead of to loll, to walk instead of to ride, to obey Christ because He was Humble and Pure and Good?' Perhaps then the young people of France would come in and listen. He did not wait for the Benediction, but walked back out into the cold slab of night with the stars in a high flurry across the sky. He had not gone ten yards up the street when he met Verneuil.

'*Ça par exemple,*' Verneuil said. 'I'd been looking for you everywhere.'

'I lost you in the crowd,' Bigou said. 'I hit quite a few fellows and then somebody said the gardes mobiles were going to fire, so I got in the underground and came on here.'

'I hit so many people, too, that I thought it would be safer if I left the district for a bit in case the cops came to look for me,' Verneuil said.

'It was a pity that we didn't hear Thorez,' Bigou said.

'There's a Spanish woman speaking at the Vel d'Hiver tonight,' Verneuil said. 'We can go and hear her, but let's go and have a quick one first.'

'That's a good idea,' Bigou said.

They walked away up the street together. In a café opposite the house built on the site of that in which Molière had been born, they stopped to have their quick one. The café was full of men running France and Spain and Great Britain and America and saying '*merde.*' After his second drink

Bigou felt that he, too, could order the world. Confidence flowed through him in a golden gush as he left the café and walked with Verneuil in the direction of Grenelle. Deep in the crystal chasm of the river the amber casements glowed. Above, the lighted windows of the city were stuck like pink postage stamps on the sky. The towers of the cathedral came riding up from Clovis and Rémy and Marie Antoinette.

'The burgesses are swine in their souls,' Verneuil said.

Inside the Vélodrome d'Hiver the tiers were packed with angry men and prophets. All their lives they had stood in queues in a press of patient anonymity: in their mothers' wombs, in undergrounds during rush hours, in factories on paydays, in railway termini on holidays; but now they were patient no longer. The track where Archimbaud, Magne, Speicher, and Maës and other brick-faced professional cyclists twirled once a year for six days and six nights on end was hung with purple, red, and gold flags and banners: 'RIFLES, CANNONS AND AEROPLANES FOR SPAIN'; 'AID THE SPANISH PEOPLE TO CONQUER THE TYRANNY OF THE PRIESTS AND THE BURGESSES.' On a platform sat a group of baggy-trousered men. A dumpy little woman dressed in black was standing in the foreground and screeching in muggy French at the advertisements for Byrrh which belted each tray of her audience:

'Comrades, you have heard that the priests do not please me. *Eso es verdadero.* That is true. You have also heard that one day in Oviedo I threw myself upon a priest who was *paseándose*, who was taking a walk with a big *cigarro* in his mouth and that I bit out half his throat. *Tambien es verdadero.* That also is true. *Y lo haría otra vez si se presentaba la misma ocasión.* And I should do it again if I had the same opportunity. *Camaradas*, do you know what the priests have done to us in Spain? They have done to us, the poor, what the Jews did to Jesús Cristo: they have crucified us. *Además*, it is not upon a cross of wood that they have crucified us; it is upon a cross of gold: the gold that they have kept in their own pockets, the gold they have beaten out of the pockets of the rich into patens and chalices and monstrances, the gold for which they have sold again their own Jesús Cristo *el primer anarchista y comunista del mundo*, the first anarchist and communist in the world. If still you do not believe me, there is another thing. In the cathedral of Sevilla there are two chapters, each of sixty *canónigos*: one to sing the office and Mass for the repose of the soul of Isabella la Católica (who ought to have been saved long ago if she was as good as the priests say she was) and to smoke the big *cigarro*; and the other to sing the office and Mass of the season and to smoke the big *cigarro*. To look after a parish of thirty thousand souls, to baptize them, to marry them, to stuff them with *sagramentos*, there is one little curate, and he is lucky if he finds the time or the money to smoke the quite little *cigarrillo*. When the *Santa Iglesia Católica* does not seem to believe in her own *sagramentos*, how can she expect her children to do so? *Además*, it is not *sagramentos* that her children want, but unconsecrated bread and wine to fill their *estómagos*. And after what I have just said to you is it any wonder that the Spanish phrase for to lead a life of luxury is *vivir à lo canónigo*, to live like a canon?

'*Camaradas*, I am come here to beg, not only for money for the sacred cause of freedom, but also for men who will dare to risk life and limb and win undying fame in the as yet unwritten scrolls of history. Frenchmen have always rallied to the sacred cause of liberty. I am certain, therefore, that I shall not ask in vain. Latin Spain calls to Latin France to help her in her hour of need. Come, then, comrades, and let us be brothers in arms and crush the foul tyrant.' The bombasities of false rhetoric rode grandly on her twisted lips. 'Future soldiers of the new liberty, I kiss your feet.' She sat down amid a blast of applause.

Almost immediately a tall grey-headed old man left his seat in one of the back galleries and made his way down to the platform, where he and the speaker shook hands and clenched their fists at each other amid more applause. The old man was tall and poorly dressed and had a thin tortured face like Mahatma Gandhi or a Dominican friar. He was followed by a trickle of others. Most of them wore neither collar nor tie and some of them had sand-shoes on their feet. When the applause died down, they stood on the platform looking self-conscious and silly. Verneuil tugged at Bigou's sleeve.

'It's a disgrace,' he said. 'Seven volunteers out of a huge assembly like this. I always thought Frenchmen had guts in their belly, but I see I was mistaken.'

'Ssh, ssh,' Bigou said as those around them turned to glare.

'I won't shut up,' Verneuil said at the top of his voice. 'Oh, I know what you're thinking; you're thinking that I'm afraid. Well, I'm not afraid. And then, after all, civil war's the only kind of war that's worth fighting for. It's no fun killing people you don't know, but it's great fun killing people you do know. That's why I'd like there to be civil war in France: so that I could kill a few priests and big businessmen. That's why I didn't like fighting against the

Germans: because I couldn't be sure what sort of Germans I was killing. And that's why I'll like fighting in Spain: because I'll know what sort of Spaniards I'll be killing. And then they say the señoritas are not unkind. Goodbye, Bigou, old man. Tell Baco and Chanu from me that I'm not afraid *et que je les emmerde tous les deux.*'

Bigou ran after Verneuil to try to stop him, but Verneuil ran faster than he did. By the time that Bigou had reached the top of the stairs, Verneuil was already on the platform bowing to a quickly petering-out applause. Bigou did not dare to follow him any further in case the audience should imagine that he wanted to enlist too. He stood at the back of the circus until he saw the file of volunteers shuffle off the platform. Then he went out into the passage and buttonholed an official.

'Is there no means of speaking to the volunteers?' he asked.

The official shook his head.

'I'm afraid not,' he said. 'You see, they're already taking the oath.'

'But when they have taken the oath, will it not be possible to speak to them?'

The official shook his head again.

'I'm afraid not. When they have taken the oath, they will be allowed to see nobody. The Spanish Government does not wish them to be dissuaded by their friends and the French Government does not wish them to be able to tell people that they have been able to volunteer on French soil. They will be sent to Spain at once.'

Bigou nodded dejectedly. A communist deputy was already making another speech at all the faces, but Bigou did not stay to listen. His wretchedness remained with him as he walked back to the Point du Jour.

Although it was Sunday evening and the café was crowded, the only customer Bigou knew was Chanu who was
standing drinking with a stranger. Baco and the knock-
kneed waiter were flying about with cups and saucers and
bottles and tumblers. Crammed against each other in a
corner a young couple sat holding hands; the man's face was
pale and pimply, but the young girl's eyes were filled with
stars. In the opposite corner another couple sat holding
hands; the man was grey and old and the woman fat with a
thick black veil over her face. When Baco and the waiter
arrived back behind the counter, Baco began to slang the
waiter.

'So the tip's an insult, is it?' he said. '*Nom de Dieu*, but
it's the first time I've heard it called that. And then you
won't refuse to take a tip after I've raised your wages. And
then I'm not going to raise your wages. And then you talk
too much. You have all the same got a cheek to go telling
all my customers that I'm paying sixty thousand to have the
place done up. If I want to tell them anything, I'll tell them
myself. *Foutez-moi le camp d'ici* and look after those fellows on the terrace, and if you can't keep your mouth shut,
you can go and tell the grocer I've got the squitters.' He
looked up and pretended to see Bigou for the first time. 'Talk
of the wolf and you see his tail,' he said. 'Well, did you go
to your meeting?'

'Verneuil's enlisted in the army of Republican Spain,'
Bigou said. 'He told me to tell you that he wasn't afraid
et qu'il vous emmerdait tous les deux.'

'Do you hear that, Chanu?' Baco shouted. 'Verneuil's going to Spain to fight for the republicans.'

Chanu merely nodded and went on with his conversation,

because it was dangerous to talk in public about people going to fight in Spain in case those who overheard held other
views. Bigou stayed on and ordered a drink for himself because he didn't want Baco to think that he was afraid after
having told him what Verneuil had said.

'One cannot do the impossible,' the stranger drinking with
Chanu said. 'I admit I'm an inspector of taxes, but that
doesn't rhyme with anything. Every year I've got seven
hundred and fifty sets of accounts to examine for a back
period of three years. Say I work two hundred and fifty
days a year. That makes three sets of accounts each for three
years to be examined each day. You can't do it. And that's
only Profits Tax. How can the Government expect people to
be honest when they know that accounts aren't going to be
examined properly?'

'Profits Tax?' Although he was as drunk as a Pole, Chanu
wasn't going to lose sight of the main chance. 'Do you mean
to say that you can cheat on that tax too?'

'There are thirty-six ways of cheating on every tax just as
there are thirty-six ways of making love,' the stranger said.

'I always thought it was only thirty-two,' Baco said, winking heavily at the couple in the corner. 'They're supposed
to wait another three years before they're married, but at
this rate they'll soon start eating the turkey before plucking
it.'

Bigou listened a little longer to Baco and Chanu and the
stranger paring the shavings off the stump of another day.
Then he finished his drink and went out, but without saying
good-night so that Baco and Chanu might see that he still
dared to be annoyed. He went across to the flat, but Odette
was already in bed and asleep. When he had grown tired

of watching her, he came downstairs again, intending to walk off his distemper. As he turned up the Boulevard Exelmans, he was overtaken by the abbé Pécher skirting along in his cassock.

'Good-evening, monsieur l'abbé,' he greeted, and asked lest the priest should inquire why Odette was no longer going to Mass: 'Another death-bed?'

The priest nodded.

'We are God's bottle-neck,' he said. 'People filter in and filter out through us; the trouble is that we see so little of them in between. But perhaps it is not altogether their fault. Perhaps it is too much to expect them to be Christians when our civilization has made it so difficult to believe in God in railway termini and streets. And then there is the way we dress. Our Holy Mother the Church was wise in the Middle Ages when she instituted her guilds of craftsmen and tradesmen and their different badges and dresses. Men ought to be allowed to wear gay clothes for peace as well as for war, for the servitude of the bowler hat breeds boredom and boredom breeds disbelief in God, and disbelief in God breeds war. But perhaps it is no use philosophizing; perhaps the only thing we Frenchmen can do about France these days is to go on living in it.' The light from the street lamp fell briefly on him and let Bigou see what beautiful things forty years of ugly streets had done to the priest's face. 'But I also saw a young man today. One of our own parishioners. The Cardinal's going to ordain him a priest on the Feast of Saint Thomas 1939. You must come to the ordination. It will be very beautiful. There is nothing, I think, more lovely than the spectacle of a quite young man dedicating himself to the service of our Lord.'

Bigou said nothing. There had been so many young men who had been going to save France and who ought to have saved her if only God had been good. That was the worst of people like Chanu, Baco and Latérade: you could give them good example after good example, you could pump them full of Host and Holy Ghost, but they'd still go on being Chanu, Baco, and Latérade, lazy, irritable, lecherous, and ironic, waiting for the other fellow to sacrifice himself for them. He was thinking about this as he left the priest and was still thinking about it as he walked aimlessly along the Avenue Kléber towards the Arc de Triomphe. In the rue Boissière the last whores were leaving the *maison de rendezvous;* their silk legs shone as they came down the steps on the pavements and the high collars of their coats stood up in rectangles at the back of their necks. Down the Avenue des Champs Elysées the great white lights shone, like a serene necklace dropped from heaven, and beneath the Arc the pink sail of flame fluttered in and out on the cold slab of forgotten grave.

XIV

THE POLITICIANS went on getting down to things. It was decided to open the 1937 Exhibition on time. It was decided not to devalue the franc any more, although of course it might slip away to 130 to the pound. It was decided not to intervene in Spain. It was decided to take stern steps to suppress tax evasion and to do away with wooden railway carriages. It was decided to make the rich pay. It was decided not to abolish five-centime pieces because the owners of Rolls-Royces and Minervas found that they still came in very handy for putting in the plate on Sundays.

Georges Bernanos wrote *Les Grands Cimetières sous la Lune* in which he proved that Papal nuncios were wrong in imagining that Franco was defending the gospel of Christ and that the kingdom of God on earth could not be blasted in by force, and that if men were to be true Christians they must also be free not to be Christians. He said also that it was wrong to force Majorcans to go to Holy Communion at the point of an Italian bayonet. He said also that he believed just as much as did the Papal nuncios that Jesus Christ was really and truly present in the Blessed Sacrament and he said so in strong, unscented language of Céline, whose *Voyage au Bout de la Nuit* had scandalized propriety in 1931 by winning the Prix Théophraste Renaudot. Messieurs les curés of the padded parishes were shocked, but luckily for them the people still preferred Fernandel, for after all in these hard days one had to laugh, and if Christians started acting as though their religion were true, well, one wouldn't be able to say for certain if the stock exchange would open again on Monday.

Perhaps that was part of the trouble. Perhaps if stockbrokers had worn silk stockings the clergy might have smelt their sin. Or perhaps it was because it was becoming increasingly difficult to talk to people about things that really mattered. When it was hot one said: 'Good-morning, monsieur, it's not cold today,' and when it was cold one said: 'Good-morning, monsieur, it's not hot today.' One could not say: 'Good-morning, monsieur, don't you think Almighty God would have made a better job of creation if He had made men without bellies, for in that way they would not have had to be cruel to animals in order to live? For it must hurt like hell, monsieur, having your throat cut in a slaughter-house or being pulled through water by a hook in your tongue. And even bacilli, monsieur, it seems to me that God might have made them feast on contemplation rather than on men's lungs and glands. It seems to me, monsieur, that we require to revise our conventional notions of pity and to realize that small or ugly creatures can feel pain just as acutely as big or beautiful ones, and that even snails are alone behind their window.' One could not say it because then one would have been trying to make the world mean something, whereas most people were content that it should remain as it was: a hotch-potch of Holy Ghost, Adolf Hitler, and Danielle Darrieux.

It was decided that even although the 1937 Exhibition had not been ready on time, it had nevertheless been opened on time because Monsieur Albert Lebrun had been there to make a speech. It was the month of May again, the month of Mary.

XV

'*Au prochain de ces messieurs.*' Seated third down in the row of yobs waiting to have their hair cut, Bigou moved up one. *Paris-Soir* was full of the miracles that Georges Bonnet was going to work now that he had been called back from Washington to save the franc. The paper also forecast new measures to prevent tax evasion and appealed to Frenchmen to sink their political differences and join in the defence of the fatherland. '*Maintenant plus que jamais l'union de tous les français s'impose,*' the writer said and warned the enemies of France to beware, because in moments of common danger Frenchmen had always put their country first. On the back page there was a picture of the millionth visitor, looking like a sheep, clicking his way into the Exhibition, which, it was hoped, would be completely completed before it was closed. There were photographs, too, of Camille Chautemps and Georges Bonnet, also looking like sheep. Monsieur Albert Lebrun, too, had been photographed on his annual visit to Mercy-le-Haut, as had Herr Adolf Hitler explaining to Monsieur François Poncet that he thought war a terrible scourge. '*Au prochain de ces messieurs,*' the barber said again as he raked a streaky comb through the hair of the yob he had just sheared. The yob rose, paid, and carried his new head out into the sun. Chanu took his place.

'No lewd literature today?' he asked the barber as he wound the shroud round him.

'But certainly, Monsieur Chanu,' the barber answered, pulling a pile of *Sourires* and *Paris-Magazines* from under a bottle of O'Cap. 'After all, that's the only thing that makes people laugh.'

But Bigou saw that Chanu wasn't laughing as he flicked over the Euclid of streamlined thighs, pert breasts, and languorous flanks. Chanu was suffering as Saint Teresa of Avila had suffered when she thought about God. He was suffering because he was afraid that there was a joy in raping virgins which he had missed. Watching the misery in the butcher's unshielded pool of eye, Bigou remembered that Hitler and Mussolini had suppressed pornographic literature in their countries. He also remembered that in 1926 the abbé Bethléem had gone about tearing up the filthy magazines he found on bookstalls and had been laughed at for his pains. But why should priests be afraid to read about the geometry of the female body and brave to read about armaments factories and Jewish surgeons having their fingers burned with acid? Unable to solve his fraction of world, Bigou returned to *Paris-Soir*.

'That's the stuff to blow away the cobwebs, what?' the barber asked as he ploughed a runway up the side of Chanu's head.

But Chanu was too busy contemplating the beatific fornication to answer. He did not speak again until the barber was beginning to shampoo him.

'Going to the kindling of the flame?' he asked Bigou.

'Then this flame business still goes on?' the barber asked before Bigou could answer.

'Yes, worse luck,' Chanu said. 'It's the turn of the Point du Jour ex-soldiers' association tonight, so I suppose I've got to go.'

'The war seems far away now,' the barber said. 'Fancy still rekindling the flame every night.'

'Why they can't do it by pressing an electric button beats me,' Chanu said.

'Poor France,' the barber said. He dried the butcher's head with a brisk tussle of towel and scamped a parting. '*Alors on est beau, quoi?*' he asked as he held a small mirror to reflect the recurring decimals of Chanu's pate down the big mirror.

'*Je m'en fous de la beauté comme de l'an quarante,*' Chanu said as he see-sawed towards the door. 'I'm going to have a drink before the ceremony.'

'Well, what do you think of the political situation?' the barber asked when he came back from the till to find Bigou in the chair.

'I'm sorry for Blum,' Bigou said. 'After all he did his best.'

'So you think the Popular Front's finished?' the barber asked.

'I didn't say that,' Bigou said. 'Blum's been thrown out by the Senate, but the Popular Front still goes on under Chautemps.'

'They say that the franc will be at a hundred and thirty to the pound sterling before October,' the barber said.

'Paul Reynaud was right,' a waiting yob said. 'We ought to have devaluated long ago.'

'What beats me is that they've never punished the zebras who've bought foreign currencies,' the barber said. 'They said they were going to, and now that they haven't everybody who's bought pounds or dollars is laughing and those who've been patriotic are also rans.'

'Hitler would never have allowed the same thing to happen in Germany,' the waiting yob said. 'In Germany the law's the law and must be obeyed.'

'They say that there are lots of Hitlers who are all as alike one another as drops of water and that when one of them gets shot or murdered there's always another to take his place,' the barber said.

'What I like about Hitler is that he always tells us exactly what he is going to do and does it,' the waiting yob said.

Bigou let the conversation ramble on. He was wondering if he dared to save five francs by not having a dry shampoo; but when the barber asked what kind of dry shampoo he wanted, he hadn't the courage to say that he didn't want one at all. 'Eau de Cologne, medium,' he said because he was afraid that the barber would despise him if he asked for Eau de Cologne, ordinary. As hard fingers scrubbed the cool liquid into his scalp Bigou supposed that every other man in France was like himself and submitted to dry shampoos they didn't want in case their barbers would think them mean.

Outside Baco's café the ex-soldiers of the district were already assembling with their flags and their medals and their fripperies. Baco himself, his forehead washed to a high glaze, stood in their midst shooting out handshakes simultaneously with his right and left hands. Chanu, Lacordaire, Latérade, and Bacqueroët were all there and a lot of other square men whom Bigou knew by sight. The abbé Pécher was there, too, standing slightly apart with a strained smile on his lean apostolic face. Sewn out from a buttonhole of his cassock he wore the thin yellow and green ribbons of the *médaille militaire* and the *croix de guerre*. There was an air of forced joviality about the men as they stood horsily waiting for somebody to give the order to move off. Nobody else paid much attention to them, however, and young men and girls strode by without as much as a turn of their heads, although the tart's mother was looking down from her window.

'Everybody ready?' Baco asked.

'No drums or music?' somebody asked.

'No, but a senator waiting for us at the Etoile,' Baco said. 'He's going to make a speech, but we needn't listen if we don't want to.'

They all trolloped up to the bus-stop at the corner of the

rue Chardon-Lagache. Bigou and the abbé Pécher walked with Bacqueroët who kept tapping with his stick on the pavement before each step that he took.

'Please let me know if I can be of any assistance to you, Monsieur Bacqueroët,' the priest said.

'Thanks, monsieur l'abbé,' Bacqueroët said.

'I have often wanted to tell you how much I admire your courage in your great affliction, Monsieur Bacqueroët,' the priest said.

'Thanks, monsieur l'abbé,' Bacqueroët said.

Bigou knew that the priest was trying to tell Bacqueroët how much he wished the other would seek spiritual balm for his blindness by coming to Mass on Sundays and he also knew that Bacqueroët resented the priest's kindness because Bacqueroët didn't like priests even when, like the abbé Pécher, they had been brave and won the *médaille militaire* and the *croix de guerre*. With their premises flapping against each other, they walked in stiff silence to the bus-stop.

'I remember when the strafing was on at Verdun,' the confectioner was saying.

'Wherever I went there was strafing,' Chanu said. 'I remember only that.'

'There was strafing on the Somme too,' Latérade said. 'I remember once when a big pig of a Boche came up to me and pointed his revolver at me and said he was going to make my brains jump out, but I was too quick for him and slit up his tripes with my bayonet, *et la merde sortait par devant.* He was seeping his eyes out and said something about having a mädchen at home, so I had mercy on him and took his revolver from him and made his own brain jump out *et puis ça avait l'air de la merde aussi.*' As he spoke,

Latérade caught the priest's lonely eye and pulled off his hat. 'If you'll pardon the word, monsieur l'abbé,' he said.

'Please,' the priest said, raising his shovel hat back at Latérade.

But Baco felt that Latérade had been rude to talk about *'merde'* in the hearing of a priest, so, when the bus came at last, he crammed into a seat beside the abbé, determined to atone for his friend's lack of manners. Bigou sat down opposite them next to a pretty woman with a silver chain round her ankle which looked like a vein through the sheen of her stocking.

'There's a thing that's been troubling me, monsieur l'abbé,' Baco said. 'Ought one to call the transatlantic liner *le* Normandie or *la* Normandie?'

'I maintain that one ought to call it *le* Normandie because one is really talking about *le* paquebot *la* Normandie,' the priest said.

They did not seem to have much to say to each other after that and sat with uncertain smiles on their faces conjuring up from their bellies the familiarity that wasn't in their minds. The other people sticking to the seats all seemed to have been born in the bus. Nailed above their heads was a graph of the bus route from terminus to terminus. There was also an advertisement about how to keep your trousers up without braces or belt.

The senator was already waiting for them when they reached the Etoile. Impatient to get back to his new mistress who kissed like a vacuum cleaner, he strode up to the men as they came tumbling out of the bus.

'Come on, boys,' he said. 'Everything's ready.'

They all fell in under the trees at the top of the Avenue

de Wagram. There was some argument as to who should actually light the flame. Chanu had lighted it in the previous year and Baco in 1936, and Verneuil in 1935, so in the end it was decided that the flame should be lit by Bacqueroët, who had not lighted it since 1927. Then there was further argument as to who should carry the standard. Both Baco and Chanu wanted to carry it, but finally Baco gave in to Chanu. When these matters had been decided, they moved forward to cross the Place to the Arc, but couldn't immediately do so because of the buses and taxis that came swirling up and round from the Avenues Friedland, des Champs Elysées, Marceau, Kléber, and Victor Hugo, and those that turned to go charging down the Avenues de Wagram, MacMahon, and La Grande Armée. An inspector with gold braid round his cap and a natty new blue waterproof stood checking into a notebook the numbers of the buses as they passed, but neither he nor the policeman standing next him offered to stop the traffic for the ex-soldiers. Twice the inspector moved out into the roadway, but that was only to reprimand the driver of an AB bus from the Bourse for being late and to remonstrate with the conductor of a 16 bus from the Madeleine for having the red signboard up for the short run to the Porte d'Auteuil instead of the white one for the long run to the Rond Point de Boulogne. At length, however, the senator himself, losing patience, led the way off the pavement and the others followed. Even then the drivers of buses and taxis did not stop, but only swerved to avoid the ex-soldiers when these did not dodge out of the way in time. It was the rush hour and every day there was some delegation or other rekindling the flame and the war was a long way off anyway. The abbé

Pécher took one of Bacqueroët's arms and Bigou took the other. Chanu, who had been carrying the flag stuck out from the middle of his belly, brought it to the trail and ran.

Underneath the Arc itself two bored policemen stood and watched the group of ex-soldiers re-form within the garland of chains and advance with the red, white, and blue flag held high above their coming. . The monument under which they stood was inscribed with the names IÉNA, INKERMAN, SÉBASTOPOL, TOLÈDE printed on top of one another in capital letters, but they might have been JESUS NAZARENUS REX IUDAIORUM or CHAQUE FEMME ÉLEGANTE EST CLIENTE DU PRINTEMPS for all that the policeman cared. History, for them, was a rolled-up carpet and they were in a hurry to get back home and yawn at their wives and listen to the wireless and pick their teeth. Even when Chanu lowered the flag over the grave and Bacqueroët, his arm guided by the abbé Pécher, stuck the torch into the well to light the flame, their eyes were like marbles. Both Bacqueroët and the priest looked very grim and religious, and even Baco, Latérade, and Chanu were shadowed by passing awe. Re-reading the inscription on the bronze tablet, Bigou wondered what sort of man the unknown soldier had been, whether he had been a dirty dog behind his waistcoat like Chanu and Baco or an apostle like the abbé Pécher or a poet like Mallarmé, and what he thought of the stupid lying official faces which came to moon for a moment over his grave when decency demanded they simulate the gratitude they failed to feel. The senator took a piece of paper out of his pocket, unfolded it, opened the hinges of his teeth and read at a rate:

'My comrades, on this solemn anniversary I ask you to

salute the sacred memory of those who have given their all
that we might live. The sacred soil of France has been
hallowed by their blood. Never shall we forget their sacrifice nor the bond which binds them to us their brothers.
The tempest of war has departed from our land, but still our
thoughts go out in gratitude to those who have made the
supreme sacrifice.' Thinking of how his mistress giggled
when he tickled her, the senator read more and more rapidly. It was the seventh year running he had made more or
less the same speech, only last year he had said: 'My comrades, on this sacred anniversary I ask you to salute the
solemn memory' instead of 'My comrades, on this solemn
anniversary I ask you to salute the sacred memory.' Listening to him Bigou thought how very much more eloquent the
senator would have been if he had said: 'Soldiers, don't let's
forget the pals who went west when we didn't.' The language of the people had a tang which was not rusted by
repetition.

As soon as his speech was over, the senator waved a gloved
hand at them all, smiled his number three smile, and hurried
away back across the Place to where his big shiny car was
waiting for him with the chauffeur standing holding open
the door and showing the pale grey inside.

They stood in silence as they waited for an AS bus to take
them back because none of them knew quite what to say
with the priest standing there listening. The priest stood
with his eyes fixed back at the flame and with his lips moving as though he were praying. Bacqueroët stood with the
strands of his red matted wig blowing in the wind and his
eyes screwed in sightless and the war going on for him forever. Behind them a little girl standing with her mother

caught sight of Baco's flag and the tawdry jangle of their medals.

'Tell me, mother. What's it all about?' she asked.

'Ex-soldiers, I suppose,' her mother said out of her pale porcelain face.

'And what are ex-soldiers?' the little girl asked.

'They are old solidiers who've fought in the war a long time ago,' her mother said.

'And what are they doing here?' the little girl asked.

'They've been rekindling the flame at the Arc de Triomphe on the tomb of the Unknown Soldier or something,' her mother answered.

'And what's the Unknown Soldier?' the little girl asked.

'Look here, Ginette, if you don't stop asking silly questions I'll put you straight to bed when we get home,' her mother said. 'It's as old as the hills, all that.'

They managed at length to find room in an AS bus which had been specially turned back at the Etoile because of the number of passengers travelling direct to the Porte de Saint-Cloud from the Bourse. Baco and Chanu and Bigou and the priest found themselves sitting in a compartment together. The priest took out his breviary and began to read it. Chanu winked at Baco and Baco winked back, but Bigou thought the black and red Latin words looked beautiful. They travelled back in silence to the Boulevard Exelmans.

'So it's *la* Normandie, monsieur l'abbé?' Baco said as he shook hands with the priest.

'*Le* Normandie,' the priest corrected smilingly. '*Le* paquebot *la* Normandie.'

'*Le* paquebot *la* Normandie,' Baco repeated. 'Thanks, monsieur l'abbé, I must remember that.'

'Then till one of these days, Monsieur Baco.'

'Then till one of these days, monsieur l'abbé.'

They separated with an elevation of hats. The priest went back to his garret to finish his office and Baco, Chanu, and Latérade slouched along to the café for a drink. Bigou went with them because he was afraid the others would think him a prig if he didn't. Inside the café the painters, plasterers, and carpenters whom Baco had at length got in to do his renovation were scraping, thumping, banging, and sawing, but the counter itself had not been touched. In a corner, too, the lady with the black veil was holding hands beneath *Paris-Soir* with her elderly lover and the young couple were making love in the telephone box. Madame Turbigo was there too, swabbing down export cassis.

'Things go off all right?' she asked.

'Yes, it's all over and done with till next year,' Baco said.

XVI

THE POLITICIANS really began to get down to things. It was decided that foreigners should be hatless when they had their photographs taken for their identity cards. It was decided that in order to prevent fraud the printed formula on cheques should read: '*Veuillez payer contre ce chèque*' instead of '*Veuillez payer.*' It was decided to increase the stamp duty on cheques to seventy-five centimes. It was decided that it was wrong for policemen in the municipality of Marseilles to serve their sentences for theft during the period of their annual leave. It was decided to manufacture

more aeroplanes. It was decided that it was high time the
Cour des Comptes got a move on with auditing the govern-
mental accounts for 1924. It was decided not to reopen the
Exhibition in 1938. It was decided to suppress tax evasion
and to do away with wooden railway carriages.

His Eminence Cardinal Eugenio Pacelli came to Paris,
was met at the Gare du Nord by Monsieur Yvon Delbos'
nose, preached in Notre Dame and sang pontifical High
Mass at Lisieux. Maurice Chevalier brought out a new song.
Michelle Morgan proved that a film star could be an artist.
The project of a fiscal identity card was again mooted, but
it was decided that there were too many deputies in the
racket for the measure to be a success. It was decided, however, that very stern steps indeed must be taken to suppress tax evasion. It was also decided that Paris was open
to air attack and that taxi-drivers ought not to blow their
horns after nine o'clock at night, but that it would be undemocratic not to let everybody play their wireless sets as
loudly as they liked. It was also decided that Mistinguette
had youthful legs, that Cécile Sorel could come down a staircase divinely, that the Pope might die any day, that Hitler
didn't always tell the truth, that public security would be
increased if foreigners had their right ears photographed
on their identity cards and if Frenchmen were more united.

It was hoped that a wealthy American could be persuaded
to donate electric bellows for the metropolitan cathedral of
Our Lady of Paris so that the chapter would no longer have
to hire the services of toughs who didn't believe in God. For
was God flattered by music from an organ pumped full of
atheistic air? But why, since He was Perfect, did He require
to be praised at all? Zola had shot holes through a God Who

thirsted for praise. But had he been right? Had he seen far enough? Did not God desire men to praise Him because it was good for them rather than good for Him? Would not war and unkindness vanish forever if all men could take pleasure in praising God? Praising God was more than praising God just as the reflection of a leaf in water was more than the reflection of a leaf in water. It was not only in God that Zola had shot holes, but in the people of France as well.

It was decided not to make too much fuss over the members of the American Legion when they made their second decennial visit to Paris, because, after all, one had smiled at them quite a lot in 1927.

It was decided to decrease the stamp duty on cheques back to fifty centimes again.

XVII

BIGOU'S SERIES OF TRIPS to Geneva never came off. Monsieur Dupont always went himself and took Mireille with him, because he said there was so much typing to do. Bigou had, however, to put in a lot of overtime on Sundays. Odette, who now that she was fifteen had been engaged as an assistant bookkeeper by the company, generally went with him.

On Sunday, March 13, 1938, while her father was in conference with Monsieur Terrasse, she sat looking at the special edition of *Paris-Midi*, with photographs of the German tanks entering Vienna; but she soon grew tired of the boilers on wheels and the marching men and of Hitler as a baby of two months old, a boy of fourteen, and a corporal of twenty-nine. The letter-press did not interest her much either; she had scarcely been aware of the resignation of Camille Chautemps's Government and the announcement that Léon Blum as Premier and Paul Boncour as Foreign Minister would shortly tell Hitler where he got off left her cold.

Marie-Claire was much more interesting. Ought a girl to marry a man of the same age as herself or a man older than herself? Ought a girl of seventeen to make up like a woman of fifty? Ought a woman of fifty to wear the same sort of frocks as a girl of seventeen? Ought wives to walk about in front of their husbands with the tops of their stockings hanging down? *Marie-Claire* had photographic answers to all these questions. Entranced, Odette read on and forgot all about the boilers on wheels rolling into Vienna and about Monsieur Albert Lebrun receiving Messieurs Léon Blum, Edouard Herriot, François Piétri, Louis Marin, and Paul Reynaud. Politicians might come and go, but love and clothes went on forever.

She looked so pretty and grown-up in her new blue-and-white striped silk frock that even Monsieur Terrasse smiled at her when he came in with Bigou and saw her sitting there. Bigou almost loved Monsieur Terrasse for noticing her and was filled with pride. Then both men's faces grew grave as they stooped to look at the illustrations in *Paris-Soir*.

'Well, Hitler has now got a population of eighty million behind him against France's forty million,' Bigou said.

'That doesn't mean anything,' Monsieur Terrasse said. 'The Austrians won't fight for Hitler.'

'Cardinal Innitzger has said that he'll say Mass daily for the success of the new régime,' Bigou said.

'That doesn't mean anything either,' Monsieur Terrasse said. 'What worries me is whether the new Blum Ministry will last or not. Personally I hope it won't. We don't want any socialist utopias in France. And that's one good thing about Hitler: he's put down communism in his own country. And if ever we had a communist government in France, I for one would side with him if he marched across the frontier to overthrow it. Well, I think we've all worked enough for a Sunday morning.' He smiled again at Odette as he spoke and Bigou was so pleased that he forgot to resent or even to notice very much what Monsieur Terrasse had just said about Hitler.

Monsieur Terrasse had his car waiting for him in the sunshine with the leaves of the trees reflected in miniature on the shining mudguards. Bigou and Odette walked to the bus stop. Odette swung the pleated skirt of her new frock as she walked and tried to look haughty and disdainful when she realized that men were turning to look at her. Her breasts were full and firm in her bodice now and she walked with her mouth half-open, sipping away at the golden day. She looked so lovely that Bigou scarcely knew what to say to her.

'You're almost a young woman now,' he said.

'I *am* a young woman now,' she said.

'You seem very sure of yourself,' he said.

'I'm sure of myself because I know what I want from life,' she said, but she did not say the words as unkindly as she would have said them a year ago and opened the bow of her made-up lips in a full smile and took Bigou's hand in hers and gave it a gentle squeeze.

Inside, the bus was filled with the same sort of faces as

Bigou remembered having seen before Poincaré saved the
franc in 1926. Most of the faces were moving their lips as
they read their papers, bubbling the words up into their
brains. Watching their eyes run forward and backward
along the lines of print, Bigou wondered how many kilometres of journalese they must have read in the last ten
years. Stretched end on end, the silly words would probably stretch as far as Gibraltar: kilometres about Joséphine
Baker's loins; President Doumer lying in state; Violette
Nozières's motives for murdering her father; a metre or two
about the Pope saying to Cardinal Verdier, 'In our age nobody has the right to be mediocre,' more kilometres about
Marlene Dietrich saying with a girlish smile to reporters,
'Yes, I've come to Paris to buy clothes'; kilometres about the
conseiller Prince, the Secrets of the Kremlin, and the death
of Primo de Rivera. Opposite them a squirty little man sat
staring at Odette with huge unhappiness, but he turned
away and looked out of the window as soon as he saw Bigou
glaring at him. A few seats away another man said in a loud
voice: 'In two years from now I'll have made enough money
to retire and not do another stroke as long as I live.'

In the café, Chanu, Latérade, and Choiseul were all lined
along the counter discussing the yellow tart and her new
lover. The new lover did not actually live with the tart, but
he drove up to see her every day in a big white Voisin. The
tart had also changed her name from Mademoiselle Turbigo
to Madame Saint Georges, which was apparently her new
lover's name. The tart had also dyed her hair again to a
very pale blonde. Bigou was glad when Odette left him
and went over to sit with a young man in the corner. Bacqueroët was also at the counter, but he was not discussing

the tart. He was looking grim and angry as he brooded over a lonely glass.

'There's only one way to stop Hitler and that's to break his mug,' he said.

'The Austrians are Germans all the same,' Baco said. 'After all, they speak German.'

'I think Monsieur Baco is right, Monsieur Bacqueroët,' Latérade said. 'The Austrians are Germans.'

'*Tout ça c'est con comme la lune,*' Bacqueroët said. 'You're trying to deceive yourselves, that's all. You don't want to think that one day you will have to put on your uniforms and fight Germany all over again. Well, you will for the simple reason that Hitler has given his people a faith to believe in and a discipline to obey, which is precisely what we lack in France.'

'To a certain extent it seems to me that Monsieur Bacqueroët is right,' Bigou said. '*Sapristi,* you give them receptacles to put their used tickets in when they get out of the underground and they still scatter them about the platform like confetti.'

'France will muddle through all the same,' Latérade said.

'And then as Baco says they all speak German,' Chanu said.

'Hitler has no grudge against France,' Choiseul said, glinting his authoritative mean little eyes. 'I was talking to monsieur le commissaire only this morning and he says someone quite high up at the Préfecture told him that he was sure it was Russia that Hitler was after.'

'And between you and me and the door-post a nice little war between Germany and Russia would suit us nicely,' Baco said.

'I tell you that nobody is going to be able to save France except France herself,' Bacqueroët said. 'Oh, I know what you're all thinking. When one is blind one always knows what other people are thinking. You are thinking: "Poor fellow, he's been so badly wounded that he cannot forget that he's been in the war." Well, I do not care what you think because I know what I know. The politicians are rotten. The people are rotten. France is rotten. We are in the cart and we deserve to be there.'

'Those tanks are impressive, all the same,' Bigou said.

'The Pope's impressive, but that doesn't cut any ice with Frenchmen,' Baco said. 'Talk of the devil.'

A long white car slid by with the yellow tart and her lover inside it. The lover was wearing a grey top hat with a black band round it and the tart had lovely new golden hair like a saint.

'Getting a bit high-minded, isn't she?' Chanu said.

'Women are all swine in their souls,' Latérade said.

'That zebra opposite's a swine in his soul too,' Baco said. 'Do you see that hoarding he's putting up in front of his waste land? They say that he's going to rent it out for advertisements for Ce Soir and La Vache Qui Rit and that he'll pay the costs of his renovation that way. I've got no waste land to help me out.' He glanced pridefully round at the new red leather settees, shiny topped tables, mirrors and globes. 'I've accepted bills for sixty thousand to pay for that little lot.'

'Then there's only one thing left for you to do and that's to make a little Anschlüss on your own account,' Choiseul said.

They all laughed and began to drift away for lunch. Soon

only Bacqueroët and Bigou and the lady with the black veil
and her cavalier and Odette and her young man were left.
Out of the corner of his eye Bigou thought he saw the young
man reach out for Odette's hand, but he was feeling too sorry
for Bacqueroët standing there with his raw sightless face
and his wig all awry to pay much attention.

'If only Clemenceau were still here,' he said.

XVIII

'ALL THE SAME, I bet you all this is going to make Hitler sit
up and take notice,' Baco said.

'And then they say they've got a red carpet stretched
all the way along the platform at the Porte Dauphine,'
Latérade said.

'You can say what you like, a king's more impressing than
a president,' Chanu said.

'Perhaps it's a question of habit,' Bigou said. 'People
haven't time to get used to a president before he dies, re-
tires, or is assassinated. Take Millerand. He's been President of the Republic and given away cups at football
matches and reprieved murderers and today he travels in
the underground just like anybody else. But a king's different. People have known his father and his grandfather. All
their lives they've seen photographs of him. They've seen
him as a child and a young man. They've seen him standing
against the background of their national disasters and tri-
umphs. They've often dreamt about him. And then there's
the pageantry.'

'The fellow's the same age as I am,' Chanu said. 'We were both born in ninety-seven.'

'They say that even during royal dinners he changes uniforms,' Madame Turbigo said. 'They say that he's always dressed as an admiral when he eats fish.'

It was an evening in July, 1938. Bigou, Baco, Chanu, Latérade, Madame Turbigo, Odette and her young man were all standing waiting to see the King and Queen of England drive past in the company of the President of the Republic and Madame Albert Lebrun. Bunting was strung in red, white, and blue festoons from gold pillars. For days past the buses, normally carrying two tricolours in their route signs for the fourteenth of July, had been stuck with a tricolour and a Union Jack. Above the summer sky stretched away and away into banks of quilted clouds. It was so hot that when Bigou half-closed his eyes he could see the air vibrating.

On a grandstand opposite, the yellow tart sat with her lover. She was wearing a white frock and a little red jacket and a rhomboid pink-and-white hat tilted like a dish of strawberries and cream. Her lover, dressed in morning coat and top hat, had clever, cold, unfeeling eyes and lips like razor strops, and looked as though he understood all about Marcel Proust and nothing at all about the Curé d'Ars.

'Quand même, a daughter who won't recognize her mother,' Chanu said.

'Let me do the worrying,' Madame Turbigo said. 'I can look after myself.'

'And they say that everybody in England goes either to Eton or Harrow or Oxford or Cambridge,' Baco said.

'They say that the Queen has her hair done specially for her by a hairdresser every morning,' Odette said.

'England and France, that means something,' Latérade said.

'The misfortune is that England hasn't got conscription,' Bacqueroët said.

'*Tout ça c'est con comme la lune,*' Baco said. 'England's got her navy and we've got our army. And then we've got all our old generals, while Hitler has only got new ones.'

'Are the English Catholics or Protestants?' Chanu asked.

'I expect they're Catholics like everybody else, although I suppose it doesn't matter to them any more than it does to us,' Latérade said.

'When she was little, my daughter was the dead spit of Princess Margaret Rose,' Madame Turbigo said.

'The Queen was wearing black when she left London, but they say she's to be wearing white when she arrives in Paris,' Odette said.

'It must be wonderful to be a king,' Baco said.

'If I were king I'd drink and drink all day,' Latérade said.

'And I'd imprison all tax collectors,' Chanu said.

'And if I were queen I'd do good to everybody and never charge a halfpenny for letting anyone make love to me,' Madame Turbigo said.

Bigou gave up listening to their prattle. He thought he knew what Bacqueroët was thinking. Bacqueroët was thinking that France could be saved by nobody's effort except her own. Baco, Chanu, and Latérade were hoping that the might and panoply of Britain might strike terror into the heart of France's enemies but Bacqueroët knew that sacrifice alone could make France strong again. Bacqueroët knew that if France were to be saved, Frenchmen would have to pay their taxes and work and obey and love their common good and believe in the mission of their country as Germans and Italians paid and worked and obeyed and loved and believed. Bacqueroët knew that in the fatty hearts of the Bacos, the Chanus, the Latérades, the Duponts, the Terrasses, and in the hearts of all the politicians from Louis Marin to Maurice Thorez, God would have to work a miracle so that they might become saints and selfless and strong. Yet, even as Bigou watched Bacqueroët's stern, unhappy, angry sightless eyes staring along the rows of banners and flags asplash beneath the sky, such a hope was born in him. Perhaps even now it was not too late. Perhaps the King of England could do what the President of France could not: unite all Frenchmen in a love of their heritage and an understanding of their danger. Perhaps this glimpse of an ordered tradition might awaken the desire to emulate. In the sun and the sky and the trees and the banners Bigou's soul took new courage.

'Does the King say "good-day" to the President first or does the President say "good-day" to the King first?' Chanu asked.

'They all say "good-day" to one another all at once,' Odette said. 'Then they get into their cars and the King talks to the President about the kind of weather it is and the Queen talks to Madame Lebrun about the kind of weather it is. Then the President goes to call on the King at the Quai d'Orsay and the King goes to call on the President at the Elysée, and they all stuff themselves full and talk about the kind of weather it is. When one comes to think of it, it's not very difficult to be a king.'

There was shouting in the distance. On either side of the avenue the hedge of spectators broke out into a waving blossom. Along the rubber avenue on rubber wheels the tins of royalty rolled. In front of them rode the garde républicaine with their helmets set out in golden lines. As the car with the King and the President in it passed, Bigou thought that it looked easy to be famous. Everybody waved and cried 'Long live the King' and 'Long live England' and 'Long live France,' but almost nobody cried 'Long live the President.' The Queen passed smiling, with the squat figure of Madame Albert Lebrun stuck like a Buddha beside her. In a shimmer and a spurt the squirt of pageantry shone, passed, and was gone down the drain to Balaclava and Thermopylae. Bigou felt Bacqueroët pluck his sleeve.

'Tell me, does he look the sort of man who could say *"merde"* to Hitler?' Bacqueroët asked.

'In England it is the prerogative of the Prime Minister to say *"merde"* to foreigners,' Bigou said.

'I should have liked all the same to have had an invitation to the garden party at Bagatelle,' Odette said.

'The Queen was beautiful,' Madame Turbigo said. 'Did you see the way she smiled? And when she was little, my daughter was the dead spit of the Princess Margaret Rose.'

As he walked away with the others, Bigou noticed that there was a gaiety and an enthusiasm among the crowd which he had not seen in Paris for many years. Workingmen, priests, clerks, officers, young men of fashion, midinettes, mothers, and harlots, all were walking with happy smiles on their faces. Was France so empty of great men that she had to throw her love at a foreign king and queen? Could their dignity and elegance succeed where the eloquent baggy-trousered French politicians had failed? At the bus stop, people were barging and shoving each other as they tried to scramble onto the overladen vehicles, but it pleased Bigou to think that they were doing so with less acrimony than usual.

'A king's visit, that means free drinks all round,' Latérade said with a wink at everybody except Baco.

'*Quand même*, I bet you all this is going to make Hitler sit up and take notice,' Baco said.

XIX

THE YELLOW TART was in the cart again, and in the café she was telling them about it:

'Then Armand's son sees his father's car drawn up outside the house and off he runs to tell his mother. And along comes the real Madame Saint Georges to call on me. "Madame, have I the honour to be speaking to Madame Saint Georges?" she asks when my maid has let her in. "Yes, madame," I say, "I am Madame Saint Georges." "You lie, madame," she says, "*I* am Madame Saint Georges," and that's how the row started, but I certainly pulled her hair harder than she pulled mine. But Armand's never been to see me since, so now I'm back home again to live with mother. *Ce n'est pas gai, la vie d'artiste.*'

But nobody felt very sorry for Mademoiselle Turbigo, because she had been so snooty to them all when she had been in the money. Besides, there was much more important news to discuss.

'They say that this time he won't beat about the bush, but will tell us straight out what he wants,' Baco said.

'I saw Daladier arrive at Le Bourget when he came back from London,' Latérade said. 'There was a platoon of aircraftsmen drawn up for him to inspect. Bonnet got out of the aeroplane first with his great big nose and Daladier got out afterwards. Daladier was in such a dither that he almost forgot to inspect the guard of honour, and even when he was reminded, he only inspected half the front rank.'

'All the same, I don't wish to have my mug broken for a lot of Sudeten Germans,' Chanu said. He was dressed in a slouch of khaki uniform with horizon-blue puttees.

'*Faut pas s'en faire,*' Baco said. 'We're all in the same boat.'

'That's not true,' Chanu said. 'You're not going and Latérade's not going and Choiseul's not going. I'm forty-one years old and I nearly went west in the last war, and I've no desire to go west for a lot of Sudeten Germans, and all for fifty centimes a day. And why the devil aren't *you* going?' he asked, switching an angry red boiled eye on Bigou.

'I report tomorrow,' Bigou said.

'That's good,' Chanu said. 'We'll go west for the Sudeten Germans together. And why aren't *you* going?' he asked Baco. 'You're only three years older than I am.'

'I've got a blue card, thank God,' Baco said.

'It's a good thing that Clemenceau and Foch and Joffre aren't alive today,' Bacqueroët said. His wig was so askew that the scars on his scalp showed and his sightless eyes floated in their sockets like faded leaves. 'They'd die again of shame if they heard of what has been happening at Berchtesgaden and Godesberg.'

'That's the English,' Latérade said. 'As soon as you mention war to an Englishman, he trembles.'

' "Yes, madame," I say, "I am Madame Saint Georges." "You lie, madame," she says. "*I* am Madame Saint Georges," ' the yellow tart said.

'What's he going to say next?' Chanu asked, swilling at his pernod. 'That he's going to war against the whole world?'

'The Pope was all the same very moving,' Madame Turbigo said.

'He ought to be speaking soon now,' Bigou said.

'Pour me out another pernod, boss,' Latérade said.

'What I want to know is whether it was we or the Germans who won the war,' Baco said.

'And in any case who was it said that we had to fight for Czechoslovakia?' Chanu asked.

'Those swine of politicians gave a guarantee without ever consulting us,' Latérade said.

'They did consult you, but you were too busy with the "virgin, vivacious and beautiful today" to care,' Bacqueroët said.

'The English have a fleet,' Baco said. 'And we've got the Maginot Line. We're as safe as houses behind that.'

'All I know is that I've no desire to go west for a lot of Sudeten Germans,' Chanu said.

'We gave our guarantee to Czechoslovakia and it's our duty to implement it,' Bacqueroët said.

'It's about time now,' Bigou said.

There was silence while Baco reached up and turned on the wireless. He got several wrong stations before he got the right one. The voice of God spoke briefly out of burning bushes in Paris, Rome, London, and Madrid: '*A la Bourse les valeurs sont plutôt en baisse.*' '*Gl'italiani e i tedeschi desiderano la pace ma la pace con onore.*' 'The Socialist Party in

Great Britain still sets its face against any form of compulsory military service.' *'El enemigo fascista no llegará jamás hasta la puerta de nuestra ciudad.'*

Then a rasping voice spoke across a cavern walled with ice:

'*Wir wollen nichts von Frankreich.*'

'That's the boy himself,' Latérade said.

'What's he saying?' Chanu asked.

'*Il nous chante la messe, pardi,*' Baco said.

Nobody laughed, however. All along the counter men stopped drinking and talking and were silent. Their faces turned grave and lonely as the secret fear ran through their juices. Poured down within himself, each stood, poured down within himself and unable to get out. Sculptured in new holiness, stamped alone forever like heads on coins, Baco, Chanu, Latérade, Bacqueroët, Bigou, the yellow tart, and her mother listened to the world being threatened from a polished wooden box. '*England. . . Benes. . . Frankreich.*' The words kept recurring like invocations. Sometimes the voice snarled, sometimes it spoke evenly, sometimes it shrieked in angry twists; and sometimes from the cold belly of Berlin came the maniac roar of '*Sieg Heil.*'

'It says in the papers that means "Hail, victory,"' Madame Turbigo said.

'If only one could understand what he's saying,' Latérade said.

'I understand what he's saying all right,' Chanu said. 'He's telling us we're finished and that he's going to break our heads open. All the same, I've no desire to burst for a lot of Sudeten Germans.'

'We gave our guarantee,' Bacqueroët said. 'A great country like France cannot break her word.'

'I tell you I've no desire to go west for a lot of Sudeten Germans,' Chanu said.

'*Mein Freund, mein lieber Freund Benito Mussolini,*' the wireless said.

'He's talking about the macaronis,' Madame Turbigo said.

'*Tout ce que je demande c'est qu'on me foute la paix,*' Chanu said. 'Germans, English, Italians, Sudeten Germans, all that I ask them to do is to leave me in peace.'

'Sometimes I think that if there is anything worse than war, it is peace,' Bacqueroët said. 'At least the kind of peace we've been having for the last twenty years. An ignoble commercial brawl. A dishonourable war without blood. Now at last France has the chance to be true to herself. If she fights, she will show the world that she believes in an ideal greater than her own prosperity. If she fights, perhaps Frenchmen will again understand and respect one another.'

'*Herr Chamberlain hat mir in Godesberg gesagt,*' the wireless said.

'*Je t'emmerde, vieux salaud,*' Chanu said.

'*Faut pas s'en faire,*' Baco said. 'It's not the soldiers who are going to get it in the neck this time; it's the civilians. Paris will be bombed to ruins in no time. You hadn't thought of that, had you, Bacqueroët? There's nothing very noble in women and children having their arms and legs blown off.'

'If it's really war, mother and I are going to hide in the trenches,' Mademoiselle Turbigo said.

'In any case there'll be no war,' Baco said. 'It'll all blow over. You'll see.'

'*England,*' the wireless said.

'The only way for France to save herself is for her to

choose of her own free will to do the difficult thing instead of the easy thing,' Bacqueroët said.

'If I don't run, I shall lose my train,' Chanu said.

'*Frankreich*,' the wireless said.

Chanu shook hands all round. There was in the anonymity of his uniform a nobility which threw a priestly, monkish shadow up onto his unreflective face. Chanu tried to smile, but his mouth was a gape across, his teeth, like a slit in a letter-box. Baco said '*merde*,' and Chanu said that would bring him luck. The yellow tart and her mother kissed Chanu on both cheeks and said '*merde*' too, and the wireless went on saying '*England*' and '*Frankreich*.'

Even when Chanu had gone, the ghost of his lumpy uniform was still there. The cold fishy voice went on gargling away in Berlin's tin belly. Bacqueroët went up to the wireless and shook his fist at it and then stumped and clumped out of the café in an austere rage. Everybody felt relieved when he had gone, because they were ashamed to be afraid and unpatriotic when Bacqueroët was about. '*Frankreich*,' the wireless said.

'Let's turn on something gayer,' Latérade said.

'*Ça oui, alors*,' Baco said. 'We'll have the translation at nine-thirty.'

'*Tout est permis quand on aim-e*,' the wireless said.

' "Yes, madame," I say, "I am Madame Saint Georges," "You lie, madame," she says, "*I* am Madame Saint Georges," ' the yellow tart said.

XX

THE SPARE BUSES were strung right away up the rue de l'Assomption past the entrance to the church because there was no longer any room for them in the dépôt when Bigou and Odette's young man went to report there next morning. AS's, AB's, 16's, 15's, and 12's lay stretching away in green arithmetic progression. The sun shining in their lamps made them look like huge short-sighted frogs. The AS's, the AB's, the 16's, and the 15's were new, with cushioned seats in the second-class compartments as well as in the first, but the 12's were old and rickety.

'All that's to transport us to the front,' Odette's young man said. His name was François Letourneau and he was twenty-one years of age. Generally Bigou didn't like him, because he was jealous of him and because he thought Odette too young to be courted by him and because he didn't like the way they were always going into Baco's telephone box together; but today he loved him because he was young and had an unlined face and might die a sore death for France. 'Everybody's got to go through with it, even the buses.'

'Perhaps they'll mobilize the trains on the underground as well,' the man standing in front of them said, but nobody laughed very much.

'I scarcely think they'd use new buses to transport us to the front,' Bigou said to François.

'In fourteen they took us to the front in taxis,' the man standing in front of them said. 'It was bad enough then, but from what I can see it's going to be worse now. And then it's not only at the front that it's going to be bad. Hitler's going to let some lovely chocolates fall on Paris.'

'And we're going to let some lovely chocolates fall on Berlin,' François said. 'And the English will be with us and they'll let some lovely chocolates fall too.'

Bigou loved François forever from that moment. He loved him for his young ears and for the pity of his youth, but chiefly he loved him for having said a clean brave thing when so many were saying dirty cowardly things.

'That's the way to talk,' he said, patting François on the back. 'We Frenchmen must show Hitler that we're not afraid.'

'It's all very well to talk, but have we got as many aeroplanes as the Germans?' the man standing in front of them said. He had a thin, mean face with hard, disappointed lines running from the corners of his nose. A stub of half-smoked cigarette, stuck on his lower lip, moved up and down when he spoke.

'Daladier has not been twiddling his thumbs at the Défense Nationale,' Bigou said.

'All that's nonsense,' the man standing in front of them said. 'Hitler's got five times as many aeroplanes as France and England put together and the day he wants he can blow Paris and London sky-high.'

'Even so, we mustn't give in,' François said. 'France and England can't go on being threatened by Germany forever.'

'That's right,' Bigou cried, feeling the spirit of Bacqueroët fill him now that François was speaking out so grandly. 'We've got to show Hitler that we've got guts in our bellies.'

'All that's words,' the man standing behind them said. He, too, had a mean face.

'And then the English haven't got conscription,' the man standing in front of them said. 'As in the last war it's the French chests that are going to stop the bullets.'

'And I'll tell you why they're going to stop them: so that the big men can go on making their profits,' the man standing behind them said.

'The big men are conscripted like anybody else, or at least their sons are,' Bigou said.

'Money talks,' the man standing behind them said.

Bigou gave it up. He saw that it was no use arguing. The big men didn't want to believe in the good faith of the little men and the little men didn't want to believe in the good faith of the big men. Nor was it any use trying to convince them of the justice of France's cause, because such subjects were, in their opinion, extravagances reserved for the platform, the pulpit, and the microphone. Apparently nobody believed any longer that anybody could be impartial. Perhaps that was part of the world's trouble: the inability to talk of true things in private as well as in public. The noise of the buses and the cars snorting up the avenue killed his meditation. Noise by day and noise by night, the imperative meaningless clatter of haste. Perhaps that, too, was part of the world's trouble.

'*En voilà de vos gros qui foutent le camp*,' the man standing behind them said.

Turning, Bigou saw that a large number of the taxis and cars climbing the avenue were laden with trunks and mattresses, but nobody except the man standing behind Bigou and François seemed to think it worth while to bother to be indignant. The files of shabby underpaid men queuing up to be paid still less for shedding their blood for their country seemed to take it for granted that those who could afford to be cowards should be so. They were so accustomed to spiritual wickedness in high places that they no longer noticed it. But behind the fleeing chariots of the rich moved the patient aprons of the poor, square about their accustomed tasks. One had seen it all before, so what was the use of worrying?

The men who had arrived before Bigou and François were coming away with wads of uniform under their arms. Some were smiling and some waved a cocksure hand, but most were grave and hurried. Among them Bigou recognized the abbé Pécher, but the priest did not see him and passed, his thin ill face sorrowing with Christ. Bigou wondered how the priest reconciled this new war with his Lord's command to turn the other cheek, but he did not have time to wonder for long. Soon he was standing in front of an officer and a sergeant. The officer wore a black képi with 86 embroidered on it in silver and a pale khaki tunic with medal ribbons stuck in with brooches. The sergeant wore his medal ribbons painted on a shiny strip of tin. Neither looked shocked by the tactics now paining, grieving, saddening, shocking, and revolting Messieurs Chamberlain and Daladier. War was their business and their moustaches did not care whether it was fought about prayer-books or black women in brothels. Bigou showed his fasicule. The sergeant read it. Then the officer read it. Then the sergeant read it again.

'Report at the Gare de l'Est at two o'clock,' the sergeant said. 'The quartermaster over there will give you your uniform.'

'What about my rifle?' Bigou asked.

'They'll give you one at your headquarters if they've got any,' the officer said.

Bigou's uniform did not match when he got it and it did not look as though it would fit either. He waited at the gate of the dépôt until François came to join him. He, too, had a bundle of assorted uniform under his arm.

'Appears they're sending me to Sedan,' François said.

'You'll be as safe as houses there,' Bigou said. 'Disasters can never happen twice in the same place.' He was glad to be able to believe that, because now he loved the young man so much.

XXI

BIGOU PREFERRED the new sit-down lavatory with the rose-pink seat to the stand-up affair in his own house which he shared with his neighbour on the same landing, so he popped into the café on the Saturday evening after he had been demobilized, hoping that Baco would not see him passing the counter, because Baco would expect him to pay for a drink if he did. The last time he had seen the rose-pink seat, it had been fresh and newly painted, but already it was scratched with the marks of hobnailed boots, because many customers had been accustomed for so long to stand up that they now found it awkward to sit down. The walls, too, had been disfigured by pencilled inscriptions: DOWN WITH THE JEWS; LONG LIVE MAURRAS; DOWN WITH THE COMMUNISTS; DEATH TO BLUM; DOWN WITH THE PRIESTS; LONG LIVE BLUM, and THE UNION OF ALL FRENCH PEOPLE IS NECESSARY. When Bigou came out, however, he saw Baco's eye fixed upon him challengingly, so he was obliged to line up at the counter with the others and order a drink which he didn't want. As Baco went treading up and down, he kept frowning at the big new blue advertisement for Savon Cadum which his competitor had just had plastered up on the hoardings opposite. The advertisement represented an enormous baby's face smiling out at the huge blister of Paris.

'Well, like everyone else you've won the war?' Baco asked as he took Bigou's order.

'I was at a small village near Nancy,' Bigou said. 'There were no rifles and no equipment. We were billeted in farms, but there was no straw. There was no food either, and we had to buy our own, and the peasants made us pay through the nose.'

Everyone except Bacqueroët nodded knowingly. They were not surprised. They had known it all along.

'I still maintain that France ought to have kept her word to Czechoslovakia,' Bacqueroët said. 'We should have been in the cart, of course, but at least we should have saved our honour.'

'It's no use talking like Henri de Kerillis,' Chanu said from a few pernods farther down the counter. Back in his bloody smock, he was again bluff, domineering, and courageous. 'When I got to Rheims I was put behind an anti-aircraft gun, and when I asked the sergeant where the shells were he said there weren't any just yet, but that the gun would make the Germans frightened if they saw it from the air. If we'd gone to war, we should have lost and that would have been the end of everything.'

'It said right across the front page of *Paris-Soir* last Friday night that it was peace,' Madame Turbigo said. 'In great big letters, too. And they've opened a subscription to buy Monsieur Chamberlain a country house in France where he can fish.'

'Hitler, Mussolini, Chamberlain, and Daladier, they've all met and made peace forever and everybody's pleased,' Baco said.

'Except the Czechoslovakians,' Bacqueroët said. 'I maintain and I shall always maintain that we have betrayed Czechoslovakia!'

'*Je m'en fous de la Tchécoslováquie comme de l'an quarante*,' Chanu said. 'Let them get out of their own mess. I'm getting too old to want to go to war.'

'Me, too,' Baco said.

'It's all a matter of having guts in your belly,' Bacqueroët said.

'I think Léon Blum put the matter in a nutshell when he said that it was with a sense of grateful shame he'd learned that there wasn't going to be a war,' Bigou said.

'It said right across the front page of *Paris-Soir* last Friday that it was peace,' Madame Turbigo said.

Bigou thought he saw Bacqueroët give it up as a bad job. Behind his stitched-up smear of face he looked as though he were realizing that Jean-Jacques Rousseau had been eternally right when he had stated that with most men conviction would always coincide with convenience. Against the glass of the telephone box Bigou could see the blur of Odette and François making love, but he didn't worry about that any longer because Odette was big and well-formed for her age and he himself loved the young man so much. Gudule Flotte came in with a wad of newspapers under her arm. She was carrying a few copies of *Mein Kampf* as well.

'Evening, gentlemen and ladies,' she greeted. '*Paris-Soir*, last edition. *Mein Kampf*. All that Hitler's going to do to France. Published five francs, selling two francs fifty. *Paris-Soir*, last edition.'

Most of the customers bought *Paris-Soir,* but nobody seemed to want *Mein Kampf.*

'All that's baloney,' Chanu told Gudule. 'Hitler and Daladier are pals now. The Trojan war will not come off.'

Bigou read his newspaper with the rest. Splurged across the front page was an article entitled '*If Paris Had Been Bombed.*' The whole city, the writer said, would have been blasted into disorder in less than twenty-four hours. There were no barrage balloons because the town council hadn't had the money to pay for them. There were not sufficient anti-aircraft guns and there was not a great enough number of trained crews to man those that there were. The French air force possessed scarcely any fighter aeroplanes, although plans were being made which should remedy the deficiency within the next five years. There were not enough ambulances to transport the wounded, and in any case the streets would have been blocked with craters and the rubble of crumbled buildings. Gas and electricity and water would have been cut off and burst drains would have started epidemics. There would have been no food. Baco, who had not bought a paper, but who had come round to run his eye over Bigou's, snorted as he went quickly back behind the counter in case anybody should get out without paying.

'It's as well it's peace,' he said. 'Otherwise we'd have been in the cart.'

Bacqueroët banged down his empty glass. His sightless eyes did not see Odette and François leave the telephone box and come and stand near him, hand in hand.

'There was a time when Frenchmen cared more for their country than for their comfort,' he said. 'France and England have ratted and one of these fine days they'll pay for it dearly.'

Odette stood near him with the wind from the avenue blowing in through the door and skiffing the whisk of her frock in and out about her knees. Then she raised the pale moon of her face to the sore sewn-up gristle of his.

'I'm glad they ratted,' she said. 'I'm glad they ratted because now François won't be killed. Oh, I know he thinks the same as you do, but I don't want him killed all the same. And it's easy for you to talk because you've got all your pain and suffering behind you, but François is young and he's got it all in front of him. Sometimes I hate all of you who've been to the war because I think you want the young men to suffer like you did.'

Bacqueroët did not answer, but raised his hat at the direction her voice came from and then put it on again all squint and knocked the coarse carpet of his wig squint too. Then he tapped his way out of the café back into his seventh-floor loneliness with no water laid on.

'Cabbage, you shouldn't have spoken to poor Bacqueroët like that,' Bigou said to Odette.

'I don't care,' Odette said. 'It's wrong of him to wish that there should have been war. I love François and I don't want him to be killed and I don't care who knows it.' She dried the tears from her eyes and went away back into the telephone box with François.

'It serves Bacqueroët right,' Chanu said. 'Even though he has been badly wounded in the war, he's got no right to talk like that.'

'It said right across the front page of *Paris-Soir* last Friday night that it was peace,' Madame Turbigo said. 'In great big letters too. And they've opened a subscription to buy Monsieur Chamberlain a country house in France where he can fish.'

Bigou realized that it was no use arguing with them because they were too afraid of being wrong not to be certain that they were right. He paid for his drink and went out to find a poor woman giving suck to her baby against the big blue advertisement for Savon Cadum. People pretended not to see her as they passed, hurrying away from a misery which they knew it was their duty to succour. They had defiant, accusing expressions on their faces, but Bigou knew that it was only because they were angry with the woman for making them see how unkind the world would be to them, too, if they hadn't any money. Bigou, too, would have liked to pass the woman or to persuade himself that she had hired the baby from a friend in order to defraud people, but he gave her five francs and ran away from her when she thanked him, because he knew that he ought to have given her food and shelter as well.

Monsieur Lacordaire was standing in the door of the house as Bigou entered. With his hands stuck in his pockets, he was stretching his trousers out sideways as far as the moorings of his buttons would allow. A crumpled copy of *Paris-Soir* lay wedged under his armpit, but his gobby eyes did not seem to have been impressed by what they had read.

'One day more, one day less,' he yawned as Bigou came in under his nose from the night.

XXII

THE 51 TRAMS had been replaced by buses running directly from the Place de la République to Drancy, so Bigou hadn't to change when, with Odette and François, he went to visit

Marie's grave on All Saints' Day. As it was a public holiday
under the Napoleonic Concordat, swarms of other mourners
were also flocking to the cemetery because it was the near-
est leisure they could get to All Souls' Day when the priests
wore black vestments and said three Masses, that the dead
might be loosed from their sins.

They bought some flowers in a shop at the cemetery
gates. They had to wait a long time because the shop was
full of shiny sweaty smelly people who were also wanting
to buy flowers. The girls' cheap shoes squeaked as they carried bouquets up and down avenues of writhing popular
model Christs with REGRETS on the scroll above the head
instead of I.N.R.I. The girl who at last served Bigou didn't
even pretend to be sorry that he was having to buy flowers
for his dead wife's grave.

Although it was now more than two years since he had
last been to the cemetery, Bigou found his way along the
paths without having to think of the turns. He walked in
front and Odette and François walked behind, holding
hands. Odette was wearing a new pale green frock, but on
top she was wearing an old lumpy black coat which she had
borrowed from Madame Turbigo because it would have
been indecent for her to visit her mother's grave looking too
gay.

When they came to the bare ranks of dusty mounds, they
had some difficulty in finding Marie's grave because of the
mould which had eaten away the names on the squee-gee
wooden crosses. When at last they had identified it, Bigou
and François took off their hats and Odette crossed herself
and said a prayer. Bigou knew that he should be praying,
too, but the only words which came to him were those which

the priest used on Ash Wednesdays when he made the sign of the cross on people's brows with the ashes and he hadn't heard them since he was a boy: '*Memento, homo, quia pulvis es et in pulverem reverteris.*' Then he thought of Marie and of the time he had kissed her behind a haystack with the stubble tangled in her hair. Where the wall of the cemetery dipped, he could see a bus charging up the rue Henri Barbusse with CHEZ DUPONT TOUT EST BON written on its roof.

'It must be two years since mother died,' Odette said at length.

'Nearly two and a half years,' Bigou said.

'And in another two and a half years they'll be burying somebody else on top of her,' Odette said. 'What a pity we're so poor.'

'I'll have to try to find the money to renew the lease,' Bigou said.

Odette slid her arm through her lover's.

'Darling, when I die you won't let them bury anyone on top of me, will you?' she asked.

'Of course not,' François said. 'But what if I die first?'

'Then I shan't let them bury anyone on top of you,' Odette said.

'I don't want you to die before me,' François said. 'I want to die first.'

'No, I want to die first,' Odette said.

'In that case we'd better both die together,' François said.

They laughed out loud with their young mouths because it seemed so impossible to them both that either of them should ever die. Then they remembered that they were standing in front of Marie's grave and became serious again.

Bigou stood thinking of Marie for a few minutes longer. Then they all walked back to the cemetery gates. Odette walked in front with François because she said they wanted to discuss private things.

The bus was filled with other poor mourners returning from visiting their dead. Screwed down on their hunkers they sat, eyeing one another with stolid, indifferent, hostile disinterest. They were all, Bigou thought, in the same boat, but none of them cared about anyone getting out of it except himself. As the conductor came lumbering along the corridor for the fares, a small girl of three insisted on taking the tickets for herself and her mother. For a second or two the scowling faces smiled and were lit with a brief beauty as though they could love and be loved; but almost immediately they clouded over again and became opaque with the hatred they were too disillusioned to feel ardently.

In their pens outside the slaughter-house at La Villette, the patient cattle stood, waiting to be hewn in pieces so that men and women might get up tomorrow as ugly and stupid as they were today. With lowered heads and sad eyes they stood, boxed in their uncomprehended Gethsemane. The yard of the slaughter-house was succeeded by a line of small cafés, their windows strung together and punched like photographs on a film. Behind each counter a Baco stood, pouring out drinks for his clot of Chanus, Latérades, and Choiseuls. Like the cattle they stood, only they weren't beautiful and going to be killed.

Because it was a holiday and none of them felt like travelling home by underground, they took the N bus from the Place de la République to the Louvre. In the rues Blondel and Sainte Appoline the early tarts were already on the tout.

Outside the windows of *L'Intransigeant* a bored holiday crowd stood gaping at enlargements of photographs of the last Tour de France. When the bus stopped outside Saint-Germain L'Auxerrois, the congregation was coming out from the last Mass. As they were crossing to climb into an I bus, they ran into Verneuil standing on the edge of the pavement with his hands thrust deep into his pockets and a moody expression on his face.

'*Merde alors*,' Bigou said, as he threw his arms round Verneuil's neck and kissed him on both cheeks. 'It's good to see you, all the same.'

Verneuil kissed Bigou back, and then he kissed Odette because she had grown such a big girl and so pretty, and then he kissed François because he was in love with Odette. Then they all stood on the pavement together laughing at one another with happy teeth.

'What about the war down there?' Bigou asked. 'How did it go?'

'I was wounded in the thigh,' Verneuil said. 'I've been invalided out.'

'The Spanish Government has given you a pension, all the same?' Bigou asked.

Verneuil shook his head.

'Old man, I'm beginning to believe that it is stupid to make war or revolutions,' he said. 'For both war and revolutions are only a means of robbing Peter to pay Paul and one is always oneself Peter, a little bit more robbed than one was before. But I can't complain. Things might have been worse. The company is giving me back my job on the buses as soon as my leg's completely strong again, but I'm not coming into the café till then because I don't want Baco and Chanu's dirty sympathy.'

Bigou did not know what to say. He felt sorry for Verneuil for having been wounded, but he knew that he did not feel sorry enough. On the other side of the river the Institut de France sat on and on. From an invisible voice came the sound of a ragwoman singing:

'*Ma-archand d'habits, chiffo-ons.*'

'*Ce n'est pas gai, la vie d'artiste,*' Bigou said.

'On the contrary, I'm beginning to be hopeful again,' Verneuil said. 'Let's go and have a quick one and I'll prove to you all that Hitler doesn't really want to make war, but only to paint pictures.'

But Bigou wasn't thinking about Hitler as he followed Verneuil and the others into a near-by café, but about Marie and how he could save up enough money to prevent somebody being buried on top of her in two and a half years' time.

XXIII

THE POLITICIANS went on getting down to things. It was decided that it was high time that the Cour des Comptes got a move on with auditing the public accounts for 1924.

'Corsica, Nice, Tunis,' shrieked members of the Fascist Party at a meeting in Rome. '*Pas une arpente de notre territoire,*' declared Monsieur Daladier, so it really looked as though there were going to be trouble; but Herr von Ribbentrop smiled quite pleasantly at Monsieur Georges Bonnet when he came to Paris to sign a declaration that Germany and France would never, never, never make war on each other again without first trying to settle their differences by negotiation. Of course, it was a pity that his visit had had to be put off a few days because of the threatened general strike on the thirtieth of November, but when he came he behaved like a perfect gentleman and went off to the Louvre to give the Vénus de Milo the once-over for Hitler and dined with Monsieur Bonnet at the Quai d'Orsay, and Frau von Ribbentrop looked very pretty and friendly talking to Madame Bonnet on the back page of *Paris-Soir*.

It was decided that there would be no European war in 1939 because the leading astrologists all said there wouldn't be, although Madame Geneviève Tabouis wasn't quite so sure and the headmistress of the whorehouse on the Boulevard Edgar Quinet said the gentlemen were very gloomy these days.

It was decided to take stern steps to suppress tax evasion.

XXIV

'IT'S A PITY, all the same, that the Pope's always got to be an Italian,' Verneuil said.

'There have been heaps of Popes who weren't Italians,' Bigou said.

'In that case I vote for Verdier,' Madame Turbigo said. 'He's got a nice face. He's the dead spit of monsieur, my late husband.'

'They'll elect an Italian,' Latérade said. 'They'll spin us a yarn about only an Italian being able to get on with a dirty dog like Mussolini and they'll disgust millions of honest fellows like myself. Whereas if they'd only do something daring like choosing an English or an American Pope, but they won't.' He glanced with brief soulfulness round the café and then stuck his gloomy nose back into his pernod.

'If they choose an Englishman, it'll have to be Hinsley, and if they choose an American, it'll have to be O'Donnel or Mundelein,' Baco said with heavy knowledge. For the past fortnight he had bought ten newspapers a day in order to study the forecasts of the Papal election, and in the lavatory with the rose-pink seat a little pad of photographs of the late Pontiff, at the age of two, immediately after his first Mass, blessing the city and the world after his coronation, lonely and shrunken on his death-bed, hung swinging on a string from the pipe of the cistern.

'They needn't necessarily elect a cardinal,' Bigou said. 'I believe they can even elect a layman if they want. They might even choose you, Monsieur Baco.'

Beneath his waistcoat Baco threw his chest out against his braces.

'*Sapristi*, I'd do the job as well as the next man,' he said.

'You'd be able to excommunicate the fellow on the other side of the street,' Chanu said.

'All the same, I don't think they'll choose a foreigner,' Baco said. 'I think they'll choose dalla Costa of Florence. He's a holy man and Mussolini and Hitler like holy men because they're too busy singing Mass and putting the wind up people who make love without being married to have any time for politics.'

'What about Schuster of Milan?' Latérade asked. 'He's got a fine face.'

'Or Goma of Toledo,' Verneuil said.

'Or Hlond of Warsaw,' Chanu said.

'Perhaps they'll choose Verdier,' Madame Turbigo said. 'He's got a nice smile. He looks just like monsieur, my late husband.'

'Perhaps your daughter will be able to tell you that better than anyone else,' Verneuil said. He pointed through the window to where the yellow tart and the abbé Pécher were pacing up and down on the other side of the street. 'That makes at least half an hour they've been together.'

'It's a little compromising for your daughter to be seen walking with a priest in public,' Chanu said.

'They'll choose Pacelli because they want to defy Hitler and Mussolini as much as possible without going so far as to choose a foreign Pope,' Bacqueroët said.

'They never choose a Secretary of State,' Baco said. 'When Benedict XV died, they didn't choose Gasparri.'

'Here's somebody who'll be able to tell us,' Verneuil said as the yellow tart came into the café. 'Tell us, mademoiselle, who goes for walks in broad daylight with priests: who's going to be Pope?'

It was some months since Mademoiselle Turbigo had her hair dyed. Her hair was now yellow at the edge and black at the roots, like an uncooked kipper. Her neck, too, was beginning to look scraggy and there were lines on her brow and down her cheeks. Watching her sad eyes, Bigou realized that she was beginning to grow old and would probably have some difficulty in finding a new lover.

'We weren't talking about that,' she said defiantly.

'All the same, darling, I do wish you'd be careful,' her mother said. 'We've got a reputation to live up to, you know.'

Surprisingly Latérade ordered drinks all round, perhaps

because he suddenly remembered that he was in receipt of two pensions and that nobody else except Bacqueroët had any at all. Then they started again discussing who was to be Pope, tossing names like Seguro, Liénart, Baudrillart, Gerlier, and Maglione in the air like lighted balls; but Bigou knew that for the most part it was the shine and the ceremony which held them and not the still small voice behind. In a few days' time they would be back with their noses in *La Veine*, trying to spot winners at Vincennes.

'They have three white cassocks laid out,' Baco said. 'A long one, a short one, and a medium one.'

'Perhaps they'll know something on the wireless,' Chanu said.

Baco turned to fiddle with the knobs. From a mighty depth came a Latin voice:

'*Habemus Papam: Reverendissimum Dominum Eugenium Pacelli.*'

'*Ça, par exemple,*' Baco said.

Then a trembling voice sang out over the bottles of Byrrh and Suze Menthe and the stains on the counter and their worldly ignorant faces and Bacqueroët's pouched-up face and the elderly couple holding hands under the table and Odette and François cramming against each other in the telephone box:

'*Sit nomen Domini benedictum.*'

'*Ex hoc semper et usque in saeculum.*'

'*Adjutorium nostrum in nomine Domini.*'

'*Qui fecit coelum et terram.*'

'*Benedicat vos Omnipotens Deus, Pater et Filius et Spiritus Sanctus.*'

For a second even the bottles looked holy, but the yellow

tart was the only one except Bigou who made the sign of
the cross and Bigou only made it because she did.

'The next round's on me,' Baco said. 'This doesn't happen
every day and it'll be another ten years at least before the
new zebra bursts.'

'All the same, this ought to make Hitler and Mussolini
think,' Chanu said.

'What a pity it wasn't Verdier,' Madame Turbigo said.
'He's the dead spit of monsieur, my late husband.'

XXV

THE POLITICIANS really began to get down to things. It was
decided to take stern steps to suppress tax evasion. It was
decided that it was even higher time that the Cour des
Comptes got a move on with auditing the public accounts
for 1924. Monsieur Deibler died in the underground station
at the Porte de Saint-Cloud, was buried from the new and
uncompleted church of Saint Jean de Chantal, and his chief
assistant was elected executioner in his stead. It was decided that something ought to be done about Germany having more soldiers than France, so it was decided to institute
a Family Charter to encourage an increase in the birth-rate,
so that in twenty years' time there might be sufficient soldiers to meet the German onslaught which, so the headmistress in the Boulevard Edgar Quinet told her clients, might
happen any one of these fine days; but of course it wasn't
possible to get the Charter going immediately, but it was
hoped, nevertheless, that the preliminary project would be

drafted in about a year's time. It was decided that it was immoral to photograph the public executions even of monsters like Weidmann, so it was decreed that henceforth all public executions should take place inside the prison gates. It was decided that the best way to frighten men with faces like Hitler and Mussolini was to elect a man with a face like Monsieur Albert Lebrun President of the French Republic for another seven years. It was decided that Hitler had broken his word when he marched his troops into Prague. It was decided that Paris was open to air attack and that bags of sand should be delivered to each householder, so that the sand might be spread under the rafters, but it was decided that it would be undemocratic to take any steps to prevent the sand being handed over to the children or the cat. It was decided to guarantee Great Britain's guarantee to Poland. It was decided not to prosecute those who had illegally concealed their holdings of foreign securities and bullion, as their punishment might deter other delinquents from declaring theirs. It was decided that Mussolini was a dirty camel when he invaded Albania on Good Friday and that he really ought to have waited till Low Sunday or until his opponents had had more revolvers and bicycles. It was decided that Paris was open to air attack. It was decided to speed up rearmament. It was decided that Pope Pius XII and President Roosevelt were very great men indeed, and that French politicians might impress the dictators more if they dressed like Mr. Eden. It was decided that it had been exceedingly wise to send Maréchal Pétain as ambassador to the victorious General Franco in Madrid. It was decided that the continued existence of two previous civilly married wives did not prevent a man marrying a girl of twenty-one in church because there had been no sacrament, and the headmistress at the Boulevard Edgar Quinet said that that was what the best theologians had always taught her to believe. It was decided to issue gas-masks to the civil population and to add their cost to the taxpayers' assessment. It was decided that aeroplane fuselages needed aeroplane motor engines to make them fly. It was decided that when Signor Gayda said that no Frenchman was worth an Italian's spit, he didn't mean that no Italian was worth a Frenchman's spit. It was decided that electric candles on altars were not in accordance with the rulings of the Sacred Congregation of Rites. It was decided that a famous man was a dirty dog, but not as dangerous as Hitler and Mussolini. It was decided that Hitler might really mean what he said when he said that he had always meant what he said. It was decided that Paris was open to air attack. It was decided to do something about doing something about speeding up rearmament. It was decided to take stern steps to suppress tax evasion, but the headmistress said that *cela ne lui faisait ni chaud ni froid*. It was decided to run the Tour de France anti-clockwise that year.

XXVI

ODETTE AND FRANÇOIS had grown tired of making love in the telephone box, so they had persuaded Bigou to ask the abbé Pécher to marry them in the new parish church of Saint Jean de Chantal to which the priest was now attached. Because Bigou was a friend of his, the abbé Pécher arranged to marry them at the high altar, although Bigou hadn't paid nearly enough money, and he wore one of the best white satin chasubles, which shone and gleamed and glinted in the light of the candles. A funeral was going on at a side altar at the same time, with another priest in faded black vestments muttering away in front of a cheap wooden coffin and a smudge of mourners. The man inside the coffin had once been a baby and had grown up and had learned Latin irregular verbs and had fought for France and known about President Roosevelt and Mistinguete and Henri de Monthérlant, but nobody cared. Dumped along the best seats in the nave, Bigou, Baco, Chanu, Latérade, Verneuil, and Madame Turbigo and the yellow tart, and François's parents and friends didn't care either because Odette was looking so young and so pretty in her wedding dress.

As soon as the ceremony was over, they all went to have a snifter at the café where Bacqueroët was waiting for them, because his principles wouldn't let him enter a church, although he had promised to come to the lunch. Baco went behind the counter and shuttlecocked up and down, pouring champagne as fast as he could. He poured each glass full to the brim, so that the champagne slopped over and down onto the counter because he knew that they would think that he was trying to cheat them if he didn't.

'Weddings are beautiful, all the same,' Madame Turbigo said. 'I remember when I was married. Monsieur, my late husband, told me that I looked the dead spit of Queen Alexandra of England.'

'Ladies and gentlemen, I give you the health of the bride and bridegroom,' Bigou said.

Everybody drank to the health of the bride and bridegroom, including Baco, who had noted down the cost of his drink with that of the others on the slate. Odette swayed on the stem of her new white silk dress. François grew beside her and creaked in his too-new shoes. The elderly couple mooned up and joined them and Bigou nodded to Baco to pour out drinks for them as well. When she drank, the woman did not remove her veil, but raised it only far enough to uncover her lips. The bridesmaids in their narrow-waisted blue and green and red frocks looked like crackers waiting to be pulled.

'It's lucky you haven't been called up,' Baco said to François.

'I only go if there's general mobilization, but in any case it'll probably blow over like last time,' François said, slipping his arm round Odette's waist.

'That's what I say,' Latérade said. 'Children, you can sleep soundly tonight,' he said, raising his glass and winking lubriciously along the counter.

'You're wrong,' Bacqueroët said. 'Hitler's asking for impossible conditions from the Poles. He won't give in either. The two tyrannies have joined hands and it's entirely the fault of France, England, and America for not having understood that democracy was a duty as well as a privilege.'

'It's bad luck to talk politics at a wedding, Monsieur Bacqueroët,' Madame Turbigo said.

'Ça oui, alors,' François's father said. 'One must be gay, what?'

'What else can one talk of and how can one be gay when the world may go up again any minute in flames,' Bacqueroët said. 'And there's another thing: France has no longer got any discipline and you can't make good soldiers without discipline.'

Everybody glared at Bacqueroët because they knew that he was telling the truth. The yellow tart was the only one who did not glare. Instead she glanced at him with wide, tired, appraising eyes. She had found a job now: packing new tennis balls in boxes three afternoons a week. She was also going to Mass on Sundays and to Holy Communion on the first Friday of each month, because Our Lord had told Mother Margaret Mary Alacocque that He would never let anybody go to hell who went to Holy Communion nine first Fridays running, so the abbé Pécher had said. At first Bigou glared with the others, because he was angry with Bacqueroët for spoiling Odette's wedding; but he glared no longer when he saw the prophetic misery on Bacqueroët's puckered face and the squat figure of a soldier in his bumphled uniform drinking by himself at the end of the counter.

'Yes, I suppose we do need discipline,' he said, but not with too much conviction so as not to annoy the others.

'Sacré Bigou, va,' Baco said. 'You're a fine one to talk about discipline. *Tu t'en fous pas mal de la discipline, toi.* Like Chanu and me you've got a blue card and things'll have to be pretty serious before we're called up.'

'We were through the other war,' Chanu said. 'It's for the young to get us out of the mess this time, what?'

'The young are ready,' the squat soldier said, turning a sad face over them all. 'And we're not afraid.'

'I'll have to go, too,' Verneuil said. 'I was wounded in the last war and I was wounded in the Spanish war, but I'll have to go again, all the same.'

'We have generals,' Latérade said. 'We have Gamelin and Georges and Weygand and Pétain.'

'We've got an Italian chimney-sweep and he told me only

yesterday that there won't be war because Mussolini can't stand the sight of Hitler,' Madame Turbigo said. 'How pretty weddings are, all the same. I remember mine so well. Monsieur, my late husband, told me that I looked the dead spit of Queen Alexandra of England.'

'I'm off to Belfort tonight,' the soldier said.

'Swear to me, François darling, swear to me that there won't be war,' Odette said.

'Of course there won't be war,' François said.

'Of course there won't be war,' his mother said.

'Of course there won't be war,' the woman with the black veil said.

'It's quite easy really,' Baco said. 'Everybody talks about war, but everybody's afraid to make it. "The Trojan War Will Not Take Place." I don't like Mauriac, but for once he's right.'

'You mean Giraudoux,' Bigou said.

'The name doesn't matter,' Baco said. '*Vingt-deux, voici les flics.*'

Choiseul marched into the café with his silly moustache scratched on his hard face. He did not greet anybody, but ordered a pernod and stood pouring it in behind his teeth.

'*Ça y est,*' he said.

There was silence all over the café. Everybody looked at Choiseul and then at one another. Odette swung ever so slightly on her pinnacle of white dress and then slipped her hand into her husband's. Bigou stared at the bottles lined along the shelf and at the reflection of Baco's shiny waistcoat in the mirror. They looked just as they had looked the day before yesterday.

'Germany invaded Poland at five-forty-five this morning,'

Choiseul said. 'It's Hitler himself who says so. "We've been shooting since five-forty-five this morning," he says.'

There was another silence. Poured down within himself, each stood, poured down within himself and unable to get out. Behind Baco's eyes Bigou could see his own fears darting: 'Will I come through all right? Will it hurt to be bombed? Will it be sore being buried alive? Can I stand the splintered iron, the stench, the knowledge that I may never drink wine again or dine with a girl by a river?' Through them all the same terrors tore, through the barrel of their tubes and tripes the jagged edge of God was pulled and each knew himself alone forever. Tears filled Odette's starry eyes. François crammed his glass against her mouth and made her drink. The yellow tart made the sign of the cross. Madame Turbigo tottered on her high heels, but Latérade put his arms round her and steadied her. 'All the same, we're French, aren't we?' he said.

'I'm sorry for being silly,' Madame Turbigo said. 'I was thinking of monsieur, my late husband. He was killed at Verdun. And to think that there are other wives and mothers . . .' She stopped as she caught sight of Odette, all white and thin and stricken. 'No, darling, God couldn't do that to you,' she said. 'You're much too young and pretty.'

'And then it's in the trenches that one will be the best off,' Latérade said. 'It's the civilians who are going to get it in the neck.'

Everybody laughed, but everybody felt a shiver run down his spine, so everybody laughed again. Bacqueroët was the only one who did not laugh. With his wig askew and his knobbly hand clutched round his stick, he stood like a priest before an altar, although Bacqueroët didn't believe in altars, but only in courage, decency, and honour. Baco's hand shook as he wobbled more champagne into everybody's glass, but he didn't mark the cost down on the slate, and everybody laughed no end when he splashed some in on top of Choiseul's pernod.

'To France,' Bacqueroët said as he raised his glass.

Everybody felt a little theatrical, but they drank in a spurt of solemnity. Choiseul looked more solemn than anybody else, but perhaps that was because he was a policeman and only that morning had arrested a woman for burning her baby with lighted cigarettes.

'And to England,' Chanu said, but nobody took this toast very seriously because nobody knew much about England now that the King and Queen had gone back to London.

'And to Poland,' Bigou said.

Everybody looked grave as they drank this toast and everybody tried to think of farmhouses burning and of men having their arms and legs blown off and being killed and of babies being thrown out of windows onto naked swords; but the drink was having its way with them and they soon found that they were unable to feel miserable for long.

'Perhaps it'll all blow over,' Latérade said. 'After all, we haven't declared war yet.'

'France and England have given their word and this time they'll keep it,' Bacqueroët said.

'Probably the British navy's already sailing into Warsaw,' Madame Turbigo said.

'In any case it's general mobilization,' Choiseul said.

'There's no getting out of it,' the soldier said. 'We've got to go through with it. We've got to make Hitler understand that he can't go on making a fool of France forever.'

'*Et puis merde!*' Verneuil said. '*A un de ces jours alors.*
I've got to report at Saint Ouen.' He began shaking hands
all round, but when he shook hands with Odette he kissed
her on both cheeks as well. '*Faut pas s'en faire,*' he said.
'It's not because one goes to war that one gets a bullet in
the head.'

'Of course not,' Baco said. 'I remember in fourteen. We
were going up the line in a truck — ' But nobody paid any
attention to him because François was telling them that he
would have to be off, too, but that he hoped that he wouldn't
be long because the authorities would be almost certain to
give him a few hours' grace when they learned that he had
just been married. Most of the other young men started
saying good-bye, too, but François took Odette into the
telephone box so that he could say good-bye to her in private.
Through the glass door Bigou could see Odette's dress flow
out in a milky skim, so he looked the other way.

On the hoarding next the café on the other side of the
avenue a small man was posting up the orders for general
mobilization. There were two little red, white, and blue
flags crossed above the text. Plastered against their windows
the patient wives of the poor went on with their sacramental
stirring and scrubbing, but down on the pavement men and
women were gathering and talking in little clots. When
Odette came out of the telephone box, her eyes were wet,
but her lips were thin and brave. François and the other
men walked quickly through the open door without turning
round. Baco poured out some more drinks for everybody,
but his hand didn't shake so much this time because the
champagne already inside him had tied his terrors in broad
golden strands.

'*Faut pas s'en faire*,' he said. 'War's all a question of luck. One either cops a packet or one doesn't. I remember in fourteen. We were going up the line in a truck and the fellow next me was weeping his eyes out. "All the same," I say to him, "it's no use worrying; we're all in the same boat." "I can't help it," he says. "I've got a wife and two children at home." "We've all of us got wives and children at home," I say to him. But he wouldn't listen to reason and he said that he knew he was going to be killed and, *bon sang*, the first time we went into the line a bullet went clean through his nut and killed him on the spot.'

'It was often like that,' Latérade said.

'A soldier must do his duty all the same,' Bacqueroët said.

'*Dame, oui*,' Choiseul said.

'All the same, I don't understand how it's happened,' Madame Turbigo said. 'We've got an Italian chimney-sweep and he told me only yesterday that there wouldn't be war because Mussolini can't stand the sight of Hitler.'

Nobody said anything. Everybody went on drinking, poured down into themselves, alone with themselves, with God in a bottle. On the other side of the avenue the little man went on posting his notices over the advertisement for Savon Cadum, slapping paste first underneath and then on top.

François came rushing back into the café.

'They've given me till five o'clock this afternoon,' he said. 'We've time for a good lunch. And I'm likely to be stationed in Paris for a month at least. And then in the barracks they say it'll be as easy as falling off a log. We'll sacrifice three hundred thousand men. We'll take the Siegfried Line.'

'And this time we'll make a proper peace,' Baco said.

'Ça oui, alors,' Chanu said. 'And we'll occupy Berlin.'

'And we'll insist on the destruction of all their armaments,' Latérade said.

'And after that, if Germany as much as makes a single gun, we'll declare war on them at once,' Baco said.

'A revolver, you mean,' Chanu said.

'And then, after all, we've got the Maginot Line,' Latérade said.

'Hitler can bellow as much as he likes,' Baco said. 'We're as safe as houses.'

They were all feeling quite cheerful again when they trooped through behind the partition where a luncheon was to be served on six of the glossy-topped tables joined together.

XXVII

IN SPITE OF THE FACT that he knew that the chances were a million to one against his being killed or wounded, Bigou's belly felt as though it were made of tissue paper when the sirens shrieked at two o'clock one morning in November. As in his lonely square of darkened room he lay listening to the thumping of his heart, he was sure that this time it was the real thing and that within the next few minutes Paris would be laid waste. Odette scrambling into her clothes on the other side of the room sounded as though she thought so, too. He rose and offered her some brandy, but she refused and he took a swig himself. The fiery liquid burned the walls of his stomach back solid again. When he had

finished dressing, the sirens were still too-hooing away.
Down on the street the fire alarms were jangling as well. The
windows were shaking in their frames as though heavy traffic
were passing.

Their official shelter was in the cellar under Baco's café,
as their own house was not solidly enough built. The sirens
and the fire alarms were still going full blast when Bigou
and Odette clattered down to the bottom of the staircase.
Baco stood on the pavement outside the café with his fingers
jammed in his ears and shouting *'merde'* up at the placid
pattern of the sky. Mesdames Baco and Turbigo, tousled in
their dressing-gowns, were directing with flashlamps to the
cellar tenants from other houses.

To pretend that he wasn't afraid, Bigou let Odette go
down alone into the cellar and himself remained outside on
the pavement with Baco. As they stopped, the sirens made
a noise like air being let out of a tyre. In the middle of the
roadway Choiseul was shrilling on his whistle and shouting
'lum-ière' whenever a chink of light appeared at a window.
When he finished whistling and shouting, the night became
so silent that Bigou could hear the stars. The policeman
lumbered across the cobbles to Baco and Bigou.

'I can hear nothing,' he said.

'It must begin one day,' Baco said.

'I remember during the last war,' said Madame Turbigo
who had joined them. 'I was near Saint-Germain-des-Près
when the shell fell. The dead choir boys looked very pretty
when they were carried out.'

'If the Germans won't bomb Paris, then we ought to bomb
Berlin, otherwise the war's going on till doomsday,' Baco
said. *'Nom de Dieu,* this isn't war. In the last war we were

fighting all the time. When we weren't killing with the rifle, we were killing with the bayonet. I remember on the Somme I once killed nine Germans one after the other. They all had their hands above their heads, but I skewered my bayonet into their bellies just the same. Their tripes came gushing out like quicksilver and it was funny to see the way they tried to stuff them back.' He looked Choiseul full in his shifty eyes as he spoke. 'And in 1914 everybody had to go to war,' he said. 'Even policemen.'

'Somebody's got to stay at home and keep order,' Choiseul said. 'In 1914 there weren't communists and fascists.'

'There were Jaurès and *Le Bonnet Rouge*,' Baco said. 'And why should people like Chanu and Bigou and I have to pay the new fifteen per cent tax and you get off scot-free when you've never fought in a war at all?'

Choiseul shrugged his shoulders. He knew the answer to Baco's question, but he also knew that he couldn't give it to Baco: the Government might risk offending ex-soldiers, but it must at all costs keep the police sweet.

'They say that Paul Reynaud's going to exempt those who hold the old soldiers' card,' Bigou said.

'Even then he shouldn't exempt policemen,' Baco said.

'All the same, on the day of victory we'll all dance in the street and there'll be champagne for everybody,' Madame Turbigo said.

'That won't be tomorrow,' Baco said.

'I was talking to a woman yesterday and she said that the men would all be back in their homes for Christmas,' Madame Turbigo said.

'That's stupid,' Baco said. 'How can it finish when it hasn't even begun?'

'It's the macaronis who are going to mess up everything,' Madame Turbigo said. 'The macaronis are going to come in with us and then Hitler will do it in his trousers and we'll have peace.'

'One of these fine days the strafing's going to begin good and strong,' Baco said. He cupped his hand to his ear and listened. 'I rather think I hear something,' he said.

Madame Turbigo and Choiseul and Bigou put their hands to their ears and listened too. There was no sound except that of silence. A piece of old newspaper went skittering against a dustbin. The night and the stars went on.

'I hear nothing, but I see something,' the policeman said. He made a trumpet with his hands round his mouth and shouted to a patch of light shining from a window high up on the other side of the street: '*Lum-ière*. Put out that light at once or you'll get two hundred francs in the arse.' When he had blown his whistle several times, the light went out.

'The burgesses don't know what war is,' Baco said. 'It might do them good to get a few bombs on the nut, but unfortunately most of them have cleared out into the provinces already. Sometimes I think I'd rather kill burgesses than Germans.' He went on hating up at the sky in silence. Then he turned and shuffled back into the café. Madame Turbigo and Bigou followed, leaving Choiseul planted alone in the cold empty world.

Down in the cellar the lights were burning brightly. Chanu, Latérade, Verneuil, who was home on leave, the yellow tart, and Odette all sat in a corner together. Near to them a little girl of six was teaching her doll to say the rosary: '*Je vous salue, Marie, pleine de grâce; le Seigneur est avec vous . . .*' The child's voice rose in a cool spiral, and some of those around her smiled tenderly. Bigou took out *Paris-Soir* and tried to read. A columnist who signed himself 'XXX' was sneering at Hitler whom he called 'the corporal-strategist.' Soon the bad taste of the article and the noise of the others talking made Bigou give it up.

'You can't expect a fellow to fight on fourteen francs a fortnight,' Verneuil said.

'They say that they're going to increase soldiers' pay to seventy-five centimes a day,' Chanu said. 'And ten francs a day under fire, five francs of which is to be kept back till they come home on leave.'

'Fifty centimes a day,' Verneuil went on. 'If you're careful, you can buy yourself a packet of issue cigarettes every three days. The English soldiers are paid seventeen francs a day and the proprietors of the cafés and the estaminets know it. After ten o'clock at night, they throw out the French and only serve the English. And the women know it too. No, but sometimes. We are in France, what?'

'*Et Jésus le fruit de vos entrailles est béni,*' the child said.

'I never liked the English,' Baco said. 'It was the same in the last war. When we were alongside the English at Saint-Quentin they had plenty of food and chocolate and we had nothing and they guzzled it all themselves and never offered us any. Now if the boot had been on the other foot . . .'

'You're swallowing German propaganda,' Bigou said. 'You're doing the work of Ferdonnet. "*Les anglais fournissent les machines mais les français fournissent les poitrines.*" The English are our allies, and it's only the enemy we're aiding by speaking ill of them. And then this war is not like the last war; it's a crusade of right against wrong.' He felt awkward and self-conscious when he had said this, because it sounded like preaching.

'They always say that to soldiers during a war, but when the war is over and the soldiers come back home *couverts de gloire et de merde,* then it's another story,' Verneuil said. 'When I went to the last war the curé said to me: "Be brave, my son. You are fighting for Jesus Christ in the Blessed Sacrament of the altar and for the Blessed Virgin and for all the saints." But when I came back, the old swine pretended not to recognize me in the street because he knew I was out of a job and was afraid I might try to borrow money. And when I fought in the Spanish war, it was the same thing. And in this war it will be the same thing again. They tell us all sorts of fairy stores on the wireless about how grateful those behind the lines are to the brave boys at the front; but when we come home on leave, we see all the fat Jews, who are back again in Paris now that it hasn't been bombed, smoking cigars on the terraces of the cafés and pawing the expensive tarts.'

Everybody looked for Bacqueroët to reply, but Bacqueroët wasn't there. Bacqueroët was lying alone in bed beneath his lonely slates because, although he was lame and blind and couldn't run quickly if a bomb hit his house, he was not going to get out of bed, all the same, in the middle of the night and dress for any German.

'At least we have alerts in Paris and that's more than you can say for the front,' Latérade said.

'That's what's killing us,' Verneuil said. 'We've been twiddling our thumbs for nearly two months now. If it goes on like this much longer, I shouldn't be surprised if most of us packed up and cleared off home.'

Once again everybody looked round for Bacqueroët, but as Bacqueroët wasn't there Bigou felt that it was up to him to say something instead.

'Perhaps that's what Hitler means when he says that he will take the Maginot Line without losing the life of a single German soldier,' he said.

'It's all very well for you to talk,' Verneuil said. 'You're a civilian. You sleep in your own bed every night. You earn decent money and you even grumble because the Government's going to make you pay fifteen per cent of your salary to provide for the wives and children of the soldiers.'

'I've never grumbled,' Bigou said. 'And it's not my fault I'm a civilian. My firm's been authorized to open a new armaments factory and I'm to be chief accountant. In other words, I'm in a reserved occupation, but I'd go to the front tomorrow if I were called up.'

'We are all soldiers, what?' Baco said.

'We all have the same duties, what?' Latérade said.

'Only some of us don't have to perform them and hope that we never shall,' Verneuil said. 'They told us that this war wasn't going to be like the last and that nobody was to be allowed to make money out of it. Well, I've heard of quite a few who are making fortunes.'

'There's a chap at Levallois,' Latérade said. 'He's a colonel at the arsenal and earns five or six thousand francs a month for doing sweet Fanny Adams, because he's never there. All day long he's at his private factory working as a director and earning another salary of ten thousand francs a month and a commission of at least two hundred thousand francs a year into the bargain.'

'It's a disgrace,' Madame Turbigo said.

'. . . *maintenant et à l'heure de notre mort, ainsi soit-il,*'
the child said.

'All I know is that I wish François were home again,'
Odette said.

Bigou smiled gently at her and tried to make her smile
back, but her lips ran away from her teeth and her eyes were
grave pools, so it wasn't at all a smile which she gave him.
Ever since François had gone away from Paris a month ago,
she had been like that, brooding, brooding, brooding. The
rumble of gunfire sounded grandly in the distance.

'Guns,' Baco said. 'I always said that the war must begin
some day.'

'Perhaps it's bombs,' Madame Turbigo said.

'If they bomb Paris we'll bomb Berlin,' Chanu said.
'Daladier has said so quite plainly.'

'That poor Daladier, all the same,' Madame Turbigo said.

'*Effectivement ça doit être un type immensément em-
merdé,*' Verneuil said.

The noise sounded again and rolled away in rippling
reverberations.

'Perhaps they're going to gas us and I left my gas-mask in
the underground,' Madame Turbigo said.

'In that case, madame, you'll have to make water in your
stocking and dab it against your nose,' Latérade said.

The guns sounded out once again and then were silent.
The pink cellar lay and lay with all their faces stuck around
it. Bigou read *Paris-Soir* again. '*Le caporal stratège,*' 'XXX'
jeered, 'the corporal strategist.'

'Evidently it's not happening yet,' Latérade said.

'All the same, it must begin one of these fine days,' Verneuil said.

'Either one is at war or one is not at war,' Baco said.

'Everybody seems to be frightened to be the first to start,' Madame Turbigo said.

The yellow tart sat in silence with her knees drawn up under her chin. Her hair looked more like an uncooked kipper than ever. Her eyes were lonely and solemn, but from time to time they shone as they lighted on the small girl teaching her doll the rosary. Bigou wondered if it were really true that she had been converted by the abbé Pécher.

'And then the English aren't sending us enough soldiers,' Verneuil said. 'Two hundred thousand's not enough when France has mobilized five million.'

'England is slow to start, but once she has begun she won't stop,' Bigou preached again. 'And then we are both fighting for a just cause.'

'It's exactly the same as it was in the last war,' Verneuil said. 'We are fighting for the rich and their moneybags, for the two hundred families, what?'

'And the rich think they're fighting for the communists,' Bigou said for the ghost of Bacqueroët beneath his slates. 'When will people understand that we are fighting for France and Christian civilization?'

'I think *I* understand that,' the yellow tart said.

Nobody else seemed to want to argue about why they were fighting. France and Christian civilization were words they had to listen to on the wireless, that was all. Verneuil began to whistle through his teeth, stretching his mouth into a slit. When the sirens sounded the all clear, Baco was the first to bound upstairs into the street where he stood shouting *'merde'* until the noise stopped and the windows ceased shaking. Bigou came and stood beside him, bathing his face

against the night. Choiseul ambled across the avenue, twirling his bâton and humming, *'Tout est permis quand on
aim-e.'* Madame Turbigo loomed up beside them, scratching
herself.

'All the same, on the day of victory we'll all dance in the
street,' she said.

XXVIII

THERE WERE NOT ENOUGH red dalmatics and tunicles for the
new deacons and sub-deacons, so, although it was the feast
of Saint Thomas, Apostle and Martyr, the sacristan of Saint
Sulpice had had to dole out to the ordinands green, violet,
and white ones as well, although the future priests all carried red chasubles folded over their arms, to wear when they
should offer the one true perfect oblation and sacrifice with
the Cardinal Archbishop. Almost the whole nave had been
cleared of its chairs and *prie-Dieu* to make room for the
ordinands to lie flat on their faces and pray that God might
send them His Paraclete to make them worthy ministers of
His mysteries. Bigou, who still had not been called up to his
armaments factory, knelt among the sparse congregation at
the back of the church, wedged in between an English officer
young and clean in prayer and a man who kept turning
round to stare up at the organ loft when he wasn't trying to
lick away the milky rain stains from the black ribbon round
the rim of his bowler hat. Bigou couldn't recognize the abbé
Pécher's friend amongst the ordinands, but he knew that he
must be there, because the abbé Pécher had written to him

from the front to tell him that he was coming home on leave to be ordained. Heavy in his scarlet vestments the Cardinal knelt in front of the altar and the young men who were to be made priests and deacons and sub-deacons lay humble and proud in their albs stretched out in a sweet white carpet beneath God. The Cardinal intoned in his strong old voice:

> 'Veni, Creator Spiritus,
> Mentes tuorum visita,
> Imple superna gratia,
> Quae tu creasti pectora.'

At the side altars, however, the daily drudgery of the Church was going on with its usual Latin apathy. At one altar a funeral was taking place, with an inattentive priest gabbling through a requiem. Lonely in his box the dead man lay, with his rubble of mourners behind him, come from God, gone to God, and nobody caring. At another altar a young corporal and a girl with big ears were getting married, with another tired priest yobbling away at them as fast as his great tongue could clack: 'Le mariage est en effet une alliance sacrée, instituée par Dieu même, et le symbole de l'union de Jésus Christ avec son Eglise.' Behind at the font another priest was baptizing a baby, hoicking at a grand rate a child of sin into a potential saint and an inheritor of the kingdom of heaven. Beginnings, middlings, endings, how busy God must always be. Bigou wondered how long it would take the new priests to become like the old priests, with hairs growing out of their ears and dolloping out sacraments with indifference.

> 'Deo Patri sit gloria
> Et Filio, qui a mortuis
> Surrexit, ac Paraclito,
> In saeculorum saecula.'

When the Cardinal stood up to pray, the tired priest was still yobbling away at the marriage altar: '*Recevez donc ce Sacrement si grand et si saint avec respect et dévotion*'; but it wasn't the same couple he was yobbling away at, because this time the soldier had bigger ears than the girl.

Bigou turned back to watch the ceremony unwinding away at the high altar. One by one the ordinands approached the Cardinal, knelt before him and received the Holy Ghost and became priests or deacons or sub-deacons. From beneath most of their cassocks as they knelt Bigou could see the heavy boots and puttees sticking out. Young, erect, given to God, they came back in their vestments. 'Dear God,' Bigou prayed, 'make more Frenchmen like these. Make more, make more.' His eyes were so wet with tears that the tongues of flame on the candles spread into one huge sea of gold and he could not see the new red priests stand round the Cardinal and bend and kneel as Christ came again in a swift serene wind beneath the Host. When it was all over, the coffin was gone and the baby was gone, but the tired priest was still yobbling away at the marriage altar: '*Vous allez donc contracter une union indissoluble, que la mort seule peut rompre*'; but it wasn't the same couple he was yobbling away at, because this time both the soldier and the girl had big ears.

Outside, the grey and black Paris was going on as usual, held like an etching while men and women moved through it. A small girl with a circle of dirt making her mouth look like a target was bouncing a ball against the wall of the church and swinging completely round on her feet before she hit it again. '*Sainte catholiqu-e, vous allez trop vit-e,*' she murmured as she swung. A trollop of soldiery oozed desultorily across the square, out-of-step, blurred and miserable in their hodge-podge of bumphled uniforms. The abbé Pécher and the new priest looked blurred in their uniforms, too, when they came down the steps of the church, but their eyes were shining.

'How's tricks?' asked the abbé Pécher, who had learned a lot of slang again since he had been back in the army.

'Not so dusty, thanks,' Bigou said.

'That's good,' the abbé Pécher said.

For a little while nobody knew quite what to say, but as they walked towards the underground together the older priest began to talk.

'I am beginning to be confident,' he said. 'It seems to me that France is beginning to be reborn again. All these young men giving up all to follow Him, and most of them soldiers, too. It was very moving. The Cardinal was almost weeping when he knelt in the sacristy to receive the blessing of his own new priests.'

Bigou did not answer immediately because in the cold old world his doubts were again about him. The harvest indeed was plentiful, but the labourers were few. Each year a few hundred new keen priests were ordained, but their zeal was quickly blunted by the yawn of habit around them and by the timidity, cowardice, and sloth of their superiors.

'Yes, it was moving,' he said.

'And now when I go back to the front I can say Mass every day,' the new priest said. 'I have a portable altar and vestments which are gold on one side and black on the other.'

'You see, life is not always a bed of roses up there,' the abbé Pécher said.

'But when you take out your rosary, you feel very near to God,' the young priest said.

'A lot of men are beginning to turn to God,' the abbé Pécher said. 'During the long peace they have "fled Him down the years," as the English Catholic poet Francis Thompson has it, but they are afraid to do so any longer now that they know they may die at any moment. Every Sunday the churches behind the lines are full to overflowing, and not only for the last Masses, but for the early Masses and Holy Communion as well. I'm always being asked to hear their confessions by men who haven't been to the sacraments for years. Prayers are worth more than tanks and aeroplanes. Perhaps God and His holy Mother will send France a great victory to reward her sons for their reawakening faith.'

Bigou did not answer this time, because he was unable to accept this concept of a haggling God. Down in the underground the rulers of France did not seem to accept it either, because the walls were plastered with gaudy bills: WITH YOUR SCRAP WE SHALL FORGE THE VICTORIOUS STEEL; and, WE SHALL CONQUER BECAUSE WE ARE THE STRONGER.

There was no train in the station. The male ticket-puncher on one side was shouting to the female ticket-puncher opposite:

'And then I am not going to give up Corsica to Mussolini.'

'*Mussolini me fait chier,*' the woman shouted back.

'And then all this talk about parachutists.'

'*Les parachutistes me font chier,*' the woman shouted back.

When the train came in, it was so full they had to get into the first-class compartment. Soldiers on leave from the front with their steel helmets on and packs on their backs were blocking the corridors and the pretty women seated scowled when their dirty overcoats brushed against their frocks. The soldiers' faces looked monkish and apostolic above their uniforms, but none of the bland clergymen of banking and finance stood up to offer them their seats.

'Yes, there's no mistake about it; France is beginning to be her old self again,' the abbé Pécher said.

XXIX

THE POLITICIANS really began to get down to things. It was decided to take stern steps to suppress tax evasion. It was decided that French blood must be economized. It was decided that the bulk of Notre Dame floated more beautifully in complete darkness than when it was floodlit. It was decided that the Cardinal Archbishop of Paris was a great Frenchman. It was decided to increase the price of Gauloises bleues cigarettes from four francs to four francs fifty. It was decided to take impressions of all foreigners' fingerprints as well as to photograph their right ears. It was decided that the five hundred priests from the archdiocese of Paris serving with the forces were very brave men indeed, but that the communists serving were even braver men, because they were more numerous and more dangerous. It was decided that *Le Monstre Sacrè* by Jean Cocteau and *Elvira* by Henri Bernstein and *L'Ecole de Médisance* by Sheridan were good plays. It was decided that the Italians were only playing for time before they made common cause with France and Great Britain. It was decided that a man who had never risen higher than a corporal in the last war could not possibly hope to equal the strategy of men who had been generals for the last twenty-five years. It was decided that it had been a pity to board up the high altar of the Madeleine, but that the bunches of tricolours and union jacks stuck up behind looked quite aesthetic. It was decided to get a move on with the Family Charter and the manufacture of armaments. It was decided that Edouard Daladier no longer represented the resolve of the country when the number of deputies abstaining from voting was greater than his majority, but that Paul Reynaud fully represented the same resolve, even although he had a majority of only one. It was decided that both André Maurois and Georges Duhamel wrote good patriotic articles in the *Figaro*. It was decided by the scribes of Jean Prouvost of *Paris-Soir* that a corporal could never win a war and that the Franco-British Alliance was stronger than ever. It was decided that Notre Dame looked very beautiful in the blackout, or at least so the headmistress in the Boulevard Edgar Quinet said. It was decided that Cardinal Verdier had lost a lot of publicity by dying on the day that Germany invaded Denmark. It was decided that the war might not be fought in France at all, but in Norway and Sweden instead. 'Faux pas Sans Fer,' jeered *Paris-Soir*, meaning, of course, 'Faut Pas S'en Faire,' meaning, of course, that there was no need to get het up because Hitler hadn't got any iron anyway.

The dead Cardinal lay in front of the high altar of Notre Dame, with his scarlet hat and his *cappa magna* on top of his coffin. The bells of the metropolitan cathedral rang out over the darkened city for the office of the dead, but the sirens were sounding at the same time; in the chancel, however, the tiers of bishops and canons and Dominicans looked just like ice on a wedding cake and the words '*Circumde-derunt me dolores mortis*' rumbled finely to the gunfire. The next day the whole cabinet was there, staring down at their boots in shamed uncertainty, as though wondering whether God might matter after all. The Cardinal Bishop of Lille sang the Mass with lithe devotion. Monsieur Albert Lebrun was there, too, taking good care to look as though he were neither praying nor scoffing, but he brightened up when he went to the Opéra the same evening to hear Maurice Chevalier and Gracie Fields.

It was decided that stern steps must be taken to suppress tax evasion. It was decided that Monsieur Paul Reynaud was a strong little man and that the soldiers at the front wouldn't stand for another change anyway. It was decided to send men between forty and forty-five to work in the powder factories. It was decided to get a move on with the manufacture of tanks and aeroplanes. It was decided that it was perhaps imprudent to say '*Je m'en fous comme de l'an quarante.*' It was decided that Paris looked really quite beautiful in the blackout, or at least so the best prostitutes said.

It was decided to take stern steps to suppress tax evasion and to do away with wooden railway carriages.

It was the month of May, the month of Mary.

XXX

BIGOU WAS NOT FRIGHTENED when he heard the sirens screech early in the morning of the tenth of May. They had screeched so often and nothing had ever happened. He got up and dressed at leisure and insisted on Odette getting up and dressing too, because she was now eight months gone and big with child and couldn't be expected to move quickly if bombing suddenly started. Even when they had finished dressing, however, they did not go downstairs immediately, because nobody went down to Baco's cellar any longer, but they assembled instead in the café where they drank and argued the toss.

He went to the window and looked out at the new blue sky, stretching all the way to Spain. High up in one of the expensive houses on the other side of the street a pretty servant girl was hanging her red hair out of the window. Bigou smiled and she smiled back. 'It doesn't look as though anything were going to happen this time either,' he shouted across to her, but apparently she could not hear him, for she laughed and shook her fuzzy head. Down on the pavement a dirty tyke trotted tranquilly among the dustbins. 'He doesn't seem to be worrying about the war,' Bigou tried to shout to his new friend, but once again his voice was lost in the stretch between them, so that they could only go on laughing at each other.

The yellow tart came out of the front door and walked rapidly away in the direction of the church of Saint Jean de Chantal. Bigou supposed she must be going to early Mass and pulled his head back in case she might look up and see him smiling at the girl opposite. When he stuck his head out again, the girl was gone, but there was an aeroplane in the sky, far away, tiny and benevolent, like a safety razor flying. He knew that it must be a German aeroplane because of the puffs of smoke which kept bursting around it. Filled with a swirl of importance, he told Odette and then went down with her to the café to tell everybody else.

In the café there was a whole cram of people jammed along the counter and jabbering away at a hundred kilomètres an hour. Latérade, Bacqueroët, Chanu, and Madame Turbigo were all there, swigging red wine for all they were worth.

'Talk of the devil,' Baco said as Bigou and Odette entered. 'Chanu's just been called up to work in a powder factory at Saint-Etienne and he's wondering why they haven't called you up as well.'

'It's a disgrace,' Chanu said. 'I'm a family man with a business to run and I fought in the last war. Why pick on me?'

'I expect they'll find a site for the new armaments factory any day now,' said Bigou, who was tired of explaining that, by nature of his firm's business, he was now in a reserved occupation. 'I saw a German aeroplane in the sky just now,' he added.

'The war must begin some day, all the same,' Baco said.

'Perhaps it's come to drop some more tracts,' Madame Turbigo said.

' "Parisians, prepare your coffins for the fifteenth of June," ' Latérade mocked. 'They've already warned us for the twenty-ninth of February and the fifteenth of March, but I've never seen the tracts and I've never met anyone who has.'

'It says in *Paris-Soir* that Hitler says he'll be in Paris by the fifteenth of June,' Madame Turbigo said.

'That's stupid,' Bacqueroët said. 'We are all soldiers. Frenchmen may have tried to keep their country from getting their money, but they've always been willing to give their blood.'

An explosion sounded in the distance. Everybody rushed to the door, but when they got out onto the pavement there was nothing to be seen, except the blue empty oyster of the sky and the new advertisements on the hoarding opposite: WE SHALL CONQUER BECAUSE WE ARE THE STRONGER; WITH YOUR SCRAP WE SHALL FORGE THE VICTORIOUS STEEL; and, AFTER MEIN KAMPF MY CRIMES BY ADOLF HITLER. They all trooped back into the café again.

'I sometimes wonder what they're going to do with the unknown soldier underneath the Arc de Triomphe after the next victory,' Madame Turbigo said.

'Probably they'll put a new one there,' Baco said.

'But will they leave them both there together or will they take away the old one?' Madame Turbigo asked.

Bacqueroët did not say anything, but Bigou could see that behind his smashed face he was thinking a lot. The sirens screeched the 'all clear' and Baco shouted '*merde*' until they stopped. Choiseul came into the café, but for once he wasn't twirling his bâton or humming, although he leered knowingly at Odette's swollen belly.

'*Ça y est*,' he said. 'Hitler invaded Holland and Belgium at four o'clock this morning. The shoemaker next door heard it on the wireless.'

Poured down within themselves, clapped down, prisoners, bottled in their tripes, once again they all stood, Baco, Bacqueroët, Chanu, Latérade, Madame Turbigo, Bigou, and Odette. Poured down, clapped down, shut in forever and ever, each knowing that the great sore thing could happen to him and that nobody else would care. Outside, the new day went on, a blue and gold ribbon invisibly pulled by.

'It's fourteen beginning all over again,' Bacqueroët said.

'François,' Odette said.

'The wireless,' Latérade said.

Baco's thumbs were so frightened that he could not immediately get the right station. At Paris P.T.T. they were shrieking the old advertisement for furniture:

'*Bien le bonjour, Monsieur Lévitan,*
Vous avez des meubl-es,
Vous avez des meubl-es,
Vous avez des meubles qui durent longtemps.'

At Radio Paris they were putting over a play: '*Je vous répète, monsieur, que je n'ai pas couché avec votre femme.*' At the Poste Parisien, however, the cool voice of the announcer was impersonally relating tragedy: '*. . . ont envahi ce matin la Hollande, la Belgique, et le Luxembourg. Les armées francaises et britanniques se sont immèdiatement portées aux secours des pays envahis.*' Bigou did not stay to listen to any more, because he thought that Odette looked as though she were going to faint. As he was helping her across the avenue, he was met by Lacordaire who handed him a letter to the effect that he was to report for duty with the seven hundred and fourth regiment of infantry next morning at Noeux-les-Mines.

XXXI

Bigou left for the Gare du Nord an hour earlier than he need have because he was afraid that there would be a crush at the station. Madame Turbigo said that she would come and see him off instead of Odette, but Odette said that even if she was in the family way she was still well enough to see her father off to the front. Madame Turbigo said that she quite understood and said good-bye to Bigou in the café with Baco, Latérade, Chanu and Bacqueroët. Chanu, who was to leave for Saint-Etienne the next day and had been drinking like a fish all afternoon, kissed Bigou several times and told him to be sure to put his steel helmet over his testicles when he went over the top. The woman with the black veil and her lover were there as well and they both said 'merde' to Bigou because that would bring him luck.

Although he felt self-conscious in his unaccustomed lumpy uniform, nobody took much notice of him in the underground. There were a number of other soldiers in uniform as well, with sad, sore, lonely, determined looks in their eyes, but nobody took much notice of them either. Bigou and Odette changed at Chaussée d'Antin and Gare de l'Est, trudging along the long dreary passages with the scuttling crowds. The workers returning to Villette and Belleville from Boulogne and Billancourt looked as miserable and angry as they had in 1926 and 1933, but they all made way politely enough for Odette with a new little Frenchman in her belly held out in front of her like a big drum. The train which they boarded at the Gare de l'Est came from the Halles and smelt of vegetables. They sat down in front of two pretty girls in yellow silk dresses.

When they reached the Gare du Nord, the ticket-collector told Bigou that his train wouldn't be in at the platform for another half-hour. They went and sat on the terrace of a small dirty café outside the station. The only other customers were four fat middle-aged civilians gathered round a pale blue corporal who was telling them how to win the war. 'Now if I were in Gamelin's shoes,' the corporal said and began to draw maps on the table with his wet coffee spoon. The night fell like ink tipped out from an invisible bottle, drenching the streets dark blue and blurring warehouses till they looked like churches. The corporal went on talking about what he would do if he were in Gamelin's shoes and the civilians nodded their heads and said that, *bon sang*, that was precisely what they would do too.

'If he's a boy I'll call him François,' Odette said.

'And if it's a girl?'

'It won't be a girl. Madame Turbigo says it's always boys who are born in wars.'

They did not know what to say to each other after that. Bigou thought how grown up Odette looked to be only seventeen and how like her mother she was and of how glad he was that they had been so much more friendly lately, but he knew that Odette did not love him as much as she loved François and that she would rather he were killed than François.

'Can soldiers still write letters home during battles?' Odette asked.

'When they're out on rest they can. At least they could in the last war.'

'Perhaps this war won't be like the last war, though.'

When they went into the station again, they couldn't see at all. People were making round holes in the night with their flashlamps. In a sago of lovely silver blobs the invisible soldiery surged back to the front. Bigou held his torch well in front of them so that nobody should bang into Odette. At the entrance to the platform the ticket-collector was snatching the soldiers' passes from them as well, reading them with his whole blotched face and handing them back rudely. He swore at Bigou when Bigou showed him his calling-up notice instead of papers and said that people like Bigou made him sweat and ought to have been called up long before.

Two soldiers were singing an obscene song in the compartment which Bigou entered, but they stopped when they caught sight of Odette and rammed bottle-necks down their throats instead. When he had taken off his pack, Bigou went out of the train to say good-bye to Odette on the platform, but still they didn't seem to have much to say to each other. Beside them a group of young soldiers was saying good-bye to a cluster of girls. 'You mustn't weep,' one of them was saying. 'You must smile. You must be pretty. You must be pretty because we're going away to see the Germans who are not nearly as pretty as you are.' Bigou laughed with the girls. It pleased him to think that not all France was foul-mouthed and hating the great golden thing. A little farther along the dull outline of a British officer was handing out cigarettes to other French soldiers. 'Merci, mon pote,' one of the soldiers said. 'Oui, nous sommes tous des potes,' the British officer said back in an uncertain accent.

'They seem to be nice, the English,' Odette said.

'Yes, they're nice,' Bigou said.

'En voiture,' the guard said.

'If it's a boy I'll call him François,' Odette said. She kissed Bigou on both cheeks. 'Look after yourself. You're not a bad old stick,' she said.

When he was back in his compartment with his head stuck out of the window, Bigou suddenly knew exactly what he had wanted to say to Odette all these years, but already she was being pulled away with the platform. He waved at her frantically and the young soldiers crowded out over him and waved frantically at their girls. When the young soldiers sat down, they all had cheerful young grins. Bigou was glad of their presence because he didn't want to be alone with the two slovens who were still drinking.

'When the war's over I'm going to be an architect and marry Jeannette,' one of the young soldiers said.

The two slovens scowled, but Bigou smiled, and after a little the young soldiers smiled back. Bigou felt how much older his face was than theirs. He sat in the blue light and watched them till they fell asleep, loving their youth and their strong dark hair.

XXXII

ON THE AFTERNOON of Wednesday fifteenth May, Bigou was working in the orderly room, to which he had been attached because he was an accountant. The sergeant was staring moodily out of the window.

'Say what you like, the Dutch were right in throwing up the sponge,' the sergeant said.

Bigou wanted to shout at him to shut his mouth, but he couldn't because the sergeant was his superior officer and could put him on a charge. Instead he tried to think of all the brave soldiers he had seen marching away to the front, with a smile to hide the fear that lay deep down inside them. Perhaps the sergeant would look like that when the time came for them to enter the battle.

'There's a return to be made for mares in foal,' he said.

212

'It seems a little ridiculous since the unit has never had any mares.'

'*Ça, mon vieux, je m'en fous comme de l'an quarante,*' the sergeant said. 'Regulations say the return's got to be made in sextuplicate.'

'But we're at war and the Germans are on French soil and who's going to read the six copies anyway?' Bigou said.

'Regulations say the return's got to be made in sextuplicate. *Un point; c'est tout,*' the sergeant said.

'But I haven't any carbon paper,' Bigou said.

'Then you'll have to indent for some,' the sergeant said. 'And regulations say that all indents for stationery have to be made in sextuplicate.'

As he had no carbon paper with which to indent in sextuplicate for carbon paper, Bigou set about typing out the indent six times. After that he would have to type out six times that the unit possessed no mares in foal. Outside, the sky was nailed so blue against the window that it did not seem that war could be going on anywhere. The sergeant sat on with his hands in his pockets and smoked up at the roof.

'It's England's fault we're in the cart,' he said. 'The Germans are right when they say they're fighting the war with French chests.'

'They've sent us four hundred thousand men all the same,' he said.

'That's no good against Hitler's millions,' the sergeant said. 'And then the English aren't soldiers. Just look at Narvik. And then I don't like their faces. *Et puis ils me font chier. Et puis merde!*' He seemed to wait for Bigou to say something, but as Bigou didn't he went on: 'Say what you like, this time we're properly in the cart. They admit the Germans have broken through at Sedan and Montmédy, but they don't say how far they've got. Then the Government's already left Paris for Bordeaux. And what are we going to do if the Boches suddenly turn up here? The latest lot of ammunition they've sent us doesn't even fit our rifles. Of course, the officers say we'll muddle through. And what are we fighting for anyway? The Jews and the two hundred families. And are they up here with us risking their lives? Of course not. They're down in Biarritz and Saint-Jean-de-Luz.'

Bigou thought of Bacqueroët and his sore smashed face. He wanted to tell the sergeant that when he talked like that he quenched the tiny flicker of a flame that had once burned so high that it lit not only France but the whole world as well; but the only words he could think of were curses. The major stood in the doorway, with his black képi and the silver number on it. Bigou stood to attention, but the sergeant sat on smoking.

'Go and fetch the colonel,' the major said to Bigou.

Bigou put on his cap, saluted, and went out. The streets were full of troops slouching about with their hands in their pockets, but there were some civilians as well. Two men in straw hats were walking in front of Bigou.

'All the same, we're all soldiers,' one of them said.

'Yes, we are all soldiers,' the other said.

'And those armoured cars that have penetrated are bound to be destroyed,' the first said.

'Certainly they are bound to be destroyed,' the other said.

As he expected, Bigou found the colonel in his billet. The colonel wore an old-fashioned khaki tunic buttoned right up to the neck with a rim of white collar sticking out on top. His war medals were stuck on his breast on brooches with big silver knobs at the ends. A fierce little iron-grey moustache brisked on his upper lip. As they marched back together, most of the soldiers they met tried to avoid saluting the colonel and did so only when they saw his angry blue eye screwing itself right out at them. Thinking about the colonel's eye, Bigou concluded that the majority of honest men in France were to be found among the professional soldiers and the clergy, most of whom put the cause they served before their comfort.

'We are paying now for the sins of the past, Bigou,' the colonel said. 'People in Paris used to laugh at me when I told them that the used underground tickets strewn about the platforms were a sign of our decadence. You never saw used tickets lying about platforms in Germany. And those novels by Raymonde Machard, Victor Marguéritte, Maurice Dekobra, we're going to pay for them through our noses now. And all because we wouldn't listen to Bernanos, Mauriac, Péguy, and Maritain. If France had been a pious Catholic country, today she need have feared no battle; but even as things are we'll still throw the Germans out.'

In the courtyard of the house in which battalion headquarters was located a woman was teaching her grandson to say his prayers. The colonel stopped to beam at the baby, crossed himself and passed on. The major was waiting for them in the orderly room. His uniform looked very new beside the colonel's.

'Mon colonel, things are serious,' the major said.

'War is always serious,' the colonel said.

'But this time it is more serious than usual,' the major said.

'I've just had a message from brigade. The break-through is bigger than we feared. Motorized detachments have been reported at La Bassée. We've got to go up at once and stop them. It seems the whole of the Ninth Army's been smashed. Bridges that were mined have not been blown up. I've taken it on myself to give the necessary orders, mon colonel. The battalion will be ready to march off in ten minutes' time.'

The colonel was silent for a little before he answered.

'Don't worry, major,' he said. 'We got them before and we'll get them again, eh, Bigou?'

'Frenchmen have always known how to defend their soil, mon colonel,' Bigou said.

'Do you know, I think I rather like this chap,' the colonel said to the major. 'What about making him my runner?'

'I'm afraid you can't do that, mon colonel,' the major said. 'It seems that his posting here was a mistake. He's an accountant and is to return to Paris at once to take up a job at a new armaments factory run by his firm. You'd better go and pack your kit at once,' he said to Bigou. 'If you're lucky you'll be able to catch a train at Saint-Pol. At the double, old man. Those chaps in Paris seem to be in a hurry to see you.'

Bigou stood waiting for the colonel to say something else, but the colonel took no more notice of him and went on talking to the major. Crossing the courtyard to the barn in which he and another twenty men were billeted, Bigou did not know whether to be glad or sorry that he wasn't going with the battalion to the front. The barn was full of men stuffing socks and shirts into kit bags. Some were laughing and boasting, but most were as solemn as saints. Bending to pack, Bigou told his neighbour that he had been called back to Paris. He had to repeat the remark several times before the other was willing to believe him.

'Your wife must have been unfaithful to you,' the man said. 'Here's a lucky devil,' he called out. 'He's going back to Paris to sleep in a bed.'

But the others were too busy with their own private fears and darings to pay much attention. Bigou hadn't been with them long enough for them to care what happened to him; and the bloodiness of death had not yet made them love one another. Wrapped and trapped in their accoutrements most of them went away to fall in without saying good-bye. Bigou was the last to leave the barn. When he went back to the orderly room, the battalion had already fallen in along the road. Through the window Bigou saw them, austere, anonymous, their faces all the same, with the cook-house at the tail, like a miniature shunting engine. The major was no longer in the orderly room, but the sergeant was there, handing a sheaf of papers to the colonel.

'Nil return of mares in foal in sextuplicate and indent for carbon paper in sextuplicate, mon colonel,' he was saying. 'And I typed them all myself, mon colonel,' he added with a scowl at Bigou.

The colonel signed the papers without grumbling. The guns could be heard in the distance as he shook hands with Bigou, but they did not sound as though they were killing anybody.

'Good luck, little man,' the colonel said.

'Good luck, mon colonel,' Bigou said.

The sergeant did not look at Bigou as he stumped out after the colonel. Bigou waited in the orderly room until he heard the battalion march off, because he did not want to stand outside and be watched watching them go away to the front without him. When the sound of their feet had died into gunfire, he realized that he had forgotten to ask the major for a pass.

XXXIII

LIKE SPOKES ON A CARTWHEEL, like veins on the back of a hand, the roads ran across the tilted tray of countryside, with here a village and there a church steeple, pointing, pointing, pointing. As Bigou first stepped out into the afternoon there didn't seem to be anybody in the world except himself. In the distance the bells were ringing for Benediction, with God glad in the centre of the monstrance. Soon, however, cars began to pass him at a speed, with a powder of dust on their mudguards. Some had white and red number plates, with a big 'B' on top. Gradually the torrent of them increased, then slowed until it became a clutter moving no faster than Bigou, trudging his boots along the road. Quickly, too, there were other pedestrians, humping through the afternoon with suitcases and birdcages, pushing perambulators filled with tins of sardines and gramophone records, a great juice squirted out from nowhere, hurrying, panting, scattering, tumbling, tripping. Old men, old women, young men, young women, children carrying babies, nobody took any notice of anybody else, but with eyes set and mouths grim stamped and stumbled along the pale grey road toward Saint-Pol. On Bigou's right a yellow Rolls-Royce rode empty but for a big fat man with a cigar in his mouth at the steering-wheel. On his left toddled a little girl of five with her mother. The big fat man didn't offer a lift to the mother and the little girl, but the mother looked as though she had been alone and unhappy for so long in the world that she didn't expect him to do so. Once a soldier appeared in the middle of the road and waved them all to one side. They all stood still while the fluff and fur of the sky moved on and on and a great lurch of painted-over Paris buses came up the road with sticks of soldiers inside them and their old sign plates with the numbers and letters gouged out. Then, when the soldier jumped onto the platform of the last bus, they all scuffed on again, in starts and strains, in squirts of consternation and fear. In the distance the gunfire rumbled more often, but it still didn't sound as though it could be killing people. Bigou found that he was no longer walking beside the yellow Rolls-Royce and the little girl and her mother, but beside an old woman with tousled dirty grey hair who stumped along carrying a package wrapped in old newspaper under her arm. Bigou smiled at her and she smiled back, her whole face breaking out into kind thoughtful wrinkles and their tributaries.

'What a business!' she said to Bigou.

'Where are the Germans now?' Bigou asked.

'I don't know where they are,' the old woman said. 'All I know is that they are coming. I was saying my prayers in church when the grocer's wife rushed in to say that the Germans were coming. I was out of that church in no time, but first I had to ask the curé to come in and take the *Bon Dieu* out of the tabernacle and eat Him in case the Germans would get at Him. This is the third time they've come in my lifetime. I was ten years old when they came in seventy, monsieur.'

'But where are they?' Bigou asked. 'Are you sure somebody hasn't made a mistake?'

'They're everywhere,' a middle-aged man walking on the other side of the old woman said. 'It's the tanks that have done it. They come on and nobody can stop them. And then the aeroplanes. They bomb you and they machine-gun you and they bomb you again. A Belgian woman came into our house yesterday. Her baby was dead with a hole in its head, but she said she must go on carrying it because she still loved it.'

'It seems it was all the fault of the Ninth Army,' another man said. 'It seems that our tanks were all drawn up, but there was nobody to give any orders because the officers were all drunk or with their mistresses.'

'And there are motor-cyclists too,' the first man said. 'They say there are sixty thousand of them and they all go in front of the tanks or behind them.'

'And then there are parachutists,' the second man said. 'They let German soldiers drop from aeroplanes and they blow up telephone exchanges and power stations. And sometimes they're not dressed as German soldiers, but as civilians or even as priests. And some are even dressed as French soldiers.'

'All that's nonsense,' the old woman said. 'It's not because of tanks or motor-cyclists or parachutists that France is in the cart today; it's because France has said "*merde*" to God and now God is saying "*merde*" back to France.'

Both men looked at each other meaningly, with sardonic smiles hating round their lips. They knew, they knew that

God hadn't made the world because the world had made itself. They knew that it had been foolish of Christ to have hung upon the tree. They knew that flowers and sunsets weren't really beautiful, because they were only gradations of light impinging upon the retina.

'I still maintain it's the parachutists that are the bottom of all the trouble,' the second man said.

'And the tanks,' the first man said. 'The soldiers can't stand up to the tanks. They are so heavy and they come at such a rate.'

'I expect it's all three really: tanks, motor-cyclists, and parachutists,' Bigou said. 'It's all right,' he added when he saw them eyeing his uniform at first with surprise and then with suspicion. 'I'm an accountant. I'm going back to Paris to take up a job in an armaments factory.'

'You're lucky,' the first man said. 'In the last war they didn't let soldiers leave the front in moments of danger to take up jobs as accountants in armaments factories. In the last war when one was in the trenches one was in the trenches.'

'I'm more certain than ever that it's the parachutists who are at the bottom of the trouble,' the second man said. 'Just think, German soldiers whom everyone takes for French soldiers mixing themselves with the population and blowing up telephone exchanges and power stations.'

'They wouldn't be able to speak French,' the first man said. 'They would speak German all the same.'

'Don't make any mistake about it,' the second man said. 'They speak French as well as you and I. That's how they're able to mix with the population and pretend they're French.' He looked meaningly at Bigou. 'That's why the Grand Quartier Général has ordered that all parachutists not dressed in German uniforms are to be shot at once.'

'*Ça oui, alors,*' the first man said. 'Where's your pass?' he asked Bigou.

'I haven't got one,' Bigou began foolishly. 'The major forgot to give me one.' He saw at once that the two men didn't believe him and that even the old woman was looking at him with distrust. Instead of waiting to argue, he thrust forward through the crowd, pushing people out of his way. Behind him he could hear the two men shouting, but he scrambled through a fence and onto a field and ran across it, making for where the road bent back to join it again. A few kilometres away the town of Saint-Pol lay dumped against the lid of the sky with its spires and its steeples and the smoke from its chimneys blowing out like a girl's hair and disappearing. Bigou could hear his heart pounding and tasted blood and salt in his mouth as he ran across the field, but he ran on steadily. He looked over his shoulder, but nobody was following him. In front of him the dark procession of refugees swerved away like a river and swerved back again to the far corner of the field. Bigou's feet made no noise as he ran on and on, but his empty water-bottle kept banging against the hilt of his bayonet. When he scrambled through the fence again, some people looked at him curiously and then looked away again, back down into their own sorrows, hurries, and hopes. There was no sign of the two men and the old woman he had just left and Bigou judged that they must be at least half a mile behind him on the road, curving round to circumvent the field which he had run across. Conscious, however, that he was the only one of the whole turgid tatter in uniform, he thrust forward as quickly

as he could. There was a traffic block ahead and the pedestrians moved on while the cars stood still. Even when the
cars began to ooze on again, they moved more slowly than
the pedestrians and Bigou passed the big fat man in the
yellow Rolls-Royce driving on behind his cigar.

As they drew near to the outskirts of the town, Bigou
jostled against a man who looked at him angrily and said:
'Then it's true that the army's ratting?'

'Of course not,' Bigou said. 'The army's staying to fight.
I've been released for a special job.'

'When I was a soldier, nobody was released for special
jobs,' the man said. 'Everybody stayed to fight and deserters
were shot.'

Several other people looked at Bigou with suspicion, but
Bigou took no notice and hurried on. Although the ground
moved away under his feet, the sky above him seemed to be
standing still, but the town was already much bigger on the
horizon, and as they drew nearer it spread out and melted
across the fields to meet them. Bigou tried to walk away
from the eyes which were looking at him, but he walked
only into more eyes which were also looking at him. At the
entrance to the town an officer sat growing up into the sky
from his horse with a group of soldiers beside him. From
time to time one of the soldiers stopped a car and made the
driver show his papers, but for the most part they stood
mooning out at the world from unreflective faces. For a
second or two Bigou thought he was going to get past without being stopped, but the officer himself leant down from
his horse and caught him by the shoulder strap.

'Where the devil are you going?' he asked.

Bigou saluted and stood to attention. The officer had a
hard foxy little face and numb spiritless eyes.

'I've been called back to Paris to take up a job in a new armaments factory as an accountant, mon capitaine,' he said.

'Where are your papers?'

Bigou fumbled in his pockets, found his papers, and handed them up to the officer. The officer's eyes ran along them as though they were trying to score the words out.

'They seem to be in order,' he said. 'Now let me see your pass.'

'Mon capitaine, I regret that I haven't got one,' Bigou said. 'Orders had just come through for the battalion to move up the line when the major told me that I had been ordered back to Paris. Everything was done in such a hurry that they must have forgotten that I'd need a pass. It's not as unreasonable as you think, mon capitaine. I'm as ready as the next man to fight for my country, but I'm overage and an accountant by profession.'

'It's the first time in my life I've heard of an accountant making armaments,' the officer said.

'Armaments factories need accountants just as much as any other industry, mon capitaine.'

'*Ça alors c'est con comme la lune,*' the officer said. 'You don't need to calculate the cost of armaments, as it's the State that pays.'

'We are the State, mon capitaine.' Fearing that he had angered the officer, Bigou explained. 'My firm's the Entreprises Françaises d'Installation de Chauffage Central, Boulevard de la Madeleine, Paris. Since the beginning of the war, we've been requisitioned by the Government. Now we're to open a new armaments factory and I'm to be chief accountant.'

'What did you say was the name of your firm?'

'The Entreprises Françaises d'Installation de Chauffage Central, mon capitaine. Can I go now, mon capitaine? You see, I'd like to get back to Paris tonight if possible.'

'So would we all, my friend. You too, Ricaille, you'd like to get back to Paris tonight, wouldn't you?' The officer laughed mirthlessly through his mean teeth. 'Let's have another look at your papers.' He took the papers which Bigou handed to him and scanned them deliberately. 'They seem to be in order,' he said as he gave them back.

'Then I can go now, mon capitaine?' Bigou asked.

'Seeming to be in order and being in order are not the same thing,' the officer said.

Bigou did not answer. He knew that the officer was trying to be awkward and he did not wish to make matters worse by losing his temper. The motley of refugees stared as they passed with their packages and then tramped dully on to their next misery. Disdainful, the officer sat hesitating on his horse. Bigou was going to ask him again if he might move on when he saw the two men from whom he had run away farther back on the road advancing towards them. The old woman was no longer with them. Bigou supposed that they must have walked so fast that they had left her behind.

'Yes, it's him all right,' the first man said.

'Mon capitaine, you did well to arrest him,' the second man said. 'He's a parachutist. He's been dropped by a German aeroplane to blow up telephone exchanges and power stations.'

'When I asked him if he had a pass, he took to his heels and ran hell for leather across a field,' the first man said.

'I only did that because I knew they wouldn't understand,' Bigou said.

The men stood hating him on the dusty road and the captain sat hating him on his horse. The captain had a triumphant little smile slitting his lips as though he were glad to discover that there were dirtier swine in the world than himself.

'You know the orders,' he said. 'Parachutists caught otherwise than in German uniform are to be summarily tried and shot.'

'That's what they deserve,' the first man said.

'They deserve worse than that,' the second man said, and told Bigou all the obscene things which he would like to do to him. Then he tried to hit Bigou, but the officer made his soldiers push him off. Some of the crowd which had gathered round tried to hit Bigou too. The officer made the soldiers push them off as well and gave orders that Bigou should be fallen in in the middle of them and marched into the town.

The two men marched along beside the soldiers shouting insults at Bigou and telling him how glad they were that he was going to die. 'Dirty Boche,' they said, 'now you are going to die like you've made our women and children die.' For a while Bigou was able to grin at them, because he knew that he was innocent of the charge which they had brought against him. He thought that they must really know that he was innocent and could only be pretending that they didn't, but after a little he understood that neither they nor the officer could see right down inside him and read how innocent he was.

To grin became such an effort that he brought his lips together. He wondered what it was going to feel like to die. Would he feel something before he felt nothing or would he pass straight from the pain of the bullets to the pain of God judging him and telling him what a low-down ignoble dirty lying selfish prayerless fornicating swine he had been, or would he just one moment be and the next moment not be? If death was just a dreamless sleep, then he would be happier than most times when he had been alive. He was dead in Paris at this moment and he was happy in Paris at this moment as he had been happy in China a thousand years ago and as he was happy there now. If death was just extinction, then all that it meant was being happy over all the world instead of in just every place except one.

He laughed aloud at his own definition, but he stopped as he saw the two men still marching along scowling at him. He looked away to the horse's high hunkers steaming haughtily in front. They entered the town. The horse's hooves pounded a pentameter on the cobbles, but nobody seemed to stare at them very much, perhaps because they were getting used to the sight of the surge of distress or perhaps because they were too distressed themselves or perhaps because they didn't realize that Bigou was a prisoner marching along in a patty of other soldiers.

The officer halted the squad in front of the commissariat with its red, white, and blue flag drooping dirtily. He told the two men who had accompanied them that they would be required as witnesses. The two men said that they were in a hurry to be on their way, but the officer said that they must wait, and that in any case Bigou's trial would take place almost immediately. Two policemen came out of the commissariat, and when the officer had told them what was the matter, they marched Bigou away into the prison and locked him up. There were three other men in the cell. They were dressed in shabby civilian clothes and sat moodily on the edge of bare bedsteads. They looked up dully as Bigou was pushed into the cell, but none of them was interested enough to speak. There were only three bedsteads, so Bigou sat down beside the least dirty of them. A week-old copy of *Paris-Soir* was spread out as a mat on the floor; its headlines said: FRANCE AND GREAT BRITAIN ARE MORE UNITED THAN EVER. There were also smaller headlines which said: WHILE CARRYING OUT STRATEGIC RETREATS AT VARIOUS POINTS, OUR TROOPS HAVE HELD ON TO THEIR POSITIONS IN THE MAIN.

Bigou looked up from the paper to see a soldier with rifle and bayonet standing over him.

'You're to come with me,' the soldier said.

Bigou followed him out of the cell and along a corridor stamped with gates of other cells. The soldier marched with his rifle at the slope, pointing his feet like a duck. At the entrance he stopped and faced Bigou.

'You're free,' he said. 'The captain wanted to have you shot at once, but the colonel insisted on telephoning your firm in Paris. Luckily for you, they got through, because already they can't telephone to anywhere any longer. You've had a close shave, my friend. They've been ordering people to be shot all day long: deserters and so-called parachutists. Some of them can't speak a word of German, but they shoot them all the same.'

Bigou tried to thank the man, but the words wouldn't come.

'It's all right,' the soldier said. 'I understand how you feel, but if I were you I'd clear out at once in case that swine of a captain persuades the colonel to change his mind. Sometimes I wonder what we are fighting for, but one fights just the same, although, when I think of some of the swine in Paris, I want to fight them instead of the Germans. Take my firm, for example. The directors make millions a year, but although I'm in the army they don't give me any balance of civil pay. I'm expected to die like a hero for seventy-five centimes a day while they and their wives sit on their fannies and keep the home fire burning. *Ce n'est pas gai, la vie d'artiste.'*

Although he had never seen the soldier before, Bigou shook hands with him because it pleased him to think that the other was glad that he was not going to be shot. Outside in the street the crowds paid no attention to him. From the café came the rasp of wireless: 'A council of war was held this morning at the Elysée with Monsieur Albert Lebrun presiding,' but the crowd paid no attention to that either.

XXXIV

THE GARE DU NORD was crammed with troops and refugees when Bigou arrived on a crowded train late the next evening. There were no buses running, so he had to take the underground. On the number nine line the train jogged along at a speed, running grandly through the stations which had been closed since the beginning of the war: Saint-Augustin, Iéna, rue de la Pompe, Jasmin, Exelmans. The people in the carriage looked much the same as they had looked a month previously, except that Bigou was the only soldier among them. He had to stand for most of the way, but at Trocadéro he got a seat, opposite a girl with spectacles who was reading a volume of Racine. Bigou tried to see the time on the clock at the end of the station, but he was sitting too near the window. The clock had been a friend of his for a long time, but not as great a friend as the little black clock with orange-coloured hands which used to stand in the station-master's office at Porte Saint-Martin. Bigou wanted to tell the girl who was reading Racine about the war, but when he tried to smile at her she looked away from him and went on reciting her poetry by heart, closing her eyes and bobbing rounded silent words up at the lights. On the other side of the carriage two middle-aged women sat with a pale-faced scruffy boy of about eight. 'And then, when he's finished his studies, I'll put him in the post-office, because like that he'll always be certain of earning his living, and when he's sixty-five he'll have a pension,' one of the women said.

Bigou found them all in the café when he reached it: Odette, Baco, Bacqueroët, Latérade, the elderly couple, the yellow tart and her mother, but of course the yellow tart wasn't a tart any longer because she had repented and went to Mass on Sundays, but everyone still thought of her as the yellow tart because she had been such a long time in business. They all wept and kissed him when he came in, but Bigou was pleased that Odette wept and kissed him more than the others.

'Talk of the wolf and you see his tail,' Baco said when they had recovered from their astonishment. 'We were just wondering how you were getting on. You've got leave quickly all the same.'

Bigou told them that he hadn't got leave, but had been called back to take up the job of chief accountant at the new armaments factory. He told them also that he had been mistaken for a parachutist. Odette slipped her arm through his while he was talking. The genuineness of her concern made Bigou realize that at last he and she were really friends.

'Tell us, though,' Bacqueroët said when Bigou had finished, 'how are things going up there?' He pushed his scarred sightless face right out from the stem of his neck, as though trying to read deep down inside Bigou. 'Are we going to be able to stick it?'

'We'll stick it all right,' Bigou said. 'And what's more, we'll win through in the end. I passed bus-loads of troops going up the line.'

'They say they're at Beauvais already,' Madame Turbigo said.

'Hitler can't keep it up,' Baco said, pouring Bigou out a drink. 'He's throwing in all his mechanized forces, but if only we hold out he's bound to crack up soon.'

'It seems to me that we haven't paid enough attention to the Polish campaign,' Bacqueroët said.

'It seems to me more correct to say that we haven't paid enough attention to religion,' the yellow tart said. Her hair was growing out black all over her head now, but there was a keen new light in her eyes.

'As a good family man I've never had anything against religion,' Baco said.

'Nor I,' Latérade said. 'I've always said: "Let the priests leave me in peace and I'll leave them in peace."'

'Prayers don't seem to do much good,' Odette said. 'I've prayed for more than a week now and it hasn't brought me a letter from François.'

'Chanu's a lucky devil to be in Saint-Etienne,' Latérade said.

'He won't be so lucky if Italy comes into the war,' Bacqueroët said.

'I was in the Italian grocer's only this morning and he said that if Mussolini went to war, he would be on our side,' Madame Turbigo said.

Poured down, clamped down, sealed in their tubes and tripes, screwed into God forever, they stood raising their glasses to their lips, Bigou, Baco, Bacqueroët, Latérade, Odette, the elderly couple, Madame Turbigo, and her daughter. In the long mirror behind the bottles their reflections raised glasses back.

'It's eight o'clock,' Latérade said.

The shiny silk back of Baco's waistcoat fiddled with the knobs on the wireless set. From the polished wooden box came the husky warm little voice which they had got to know so well during the last two years, telling them that rich people paid more taxes than poor people, that Daladier was a pal of his, that they would have to rearm, that Hitler wasn't a Christian: 'These rumours are false. The Government is in Paris and remains in Paris . . . A bulge has been produced between Sedan and Montmédy. We are trying to straighten it out. We have straightened out a good many others before now. France will once more astonish the world.' Poured down, clamped down, sealed in their tubes and tripes, screwed into God forever, Bigou, Baco, Bacqueroët, Latérade, Odette, the elderly couple, Madame Turbigo and her daughter stood and listened. '*Vous venez d'entendre Monsieur Paul Reynaud, Président du Conseil,*' the wireless said. Baco stopped drying his glasses and saucers while the *Marseillaise* was played.

'The little man has, all the same, got guts in his belly,' Bacqueroët said.

'I still maintain that Hitler's bound to crack up sooner or later,' Baco said.

'It said in *Paris-Soir* that if only Hitler had once lain in the arms of a pure young girl there wouldn't have been any war,' Madame Turbigo said.

'And if the swine does try to take Paris, we'll all go out and fight on the barricades,' Latérade said.

Bigou could stand it no longer. He paid for his drink and went out with Odette. She still kept her arm in his.

'I rather think that I like you more for having been mistaken for a parachutist,' she said.

'You remind me of when you were five,' he said. 'Your mother was staying with friends in the country and I took you to dine in a restaurant. You were very sleepy, but when we were coming home you slipped your hand into mine. "Papa, I love you and I like you," you said.'

They both laughed into each other's eyes at the memory. Then they became shy again, because both of them were grown-ups and could no longer communicate their affection with ease.

On the other side of the street the Lacordaires were sunning their evening faces on a bench and Gudule Flotte was selling *Paris-Soir*. Bigou bought a copy: France and Great Britain were still more united than ever, the enemy was still retreating forward, and the allies were still advancing backward.

XXXV

A PEPPER OF POMPOUS PERSONS came scattering across the hall of the Ministère des Finances. They had bald shiny heads and wore the red rosette in their buttonholes. A commissionaire hastened to open the door. As they passed Bigou, they looked as though they were thinking about Socrates.

'Yes, Vichy is very pleasant,' Bigou heard one of them say.

'I go there every August,' another said.

'I go in September; it's cheaper then,' another said.

The rulers of France flowed through the door and spilled out onto the pavement. Bigou waited for the commissionaire to come back, but one of the bald-headed important men came back first. Bigou surmised that he must be an official seeing a deputation off the premises. With uneasy daring he planted himself in the way of the approaching trousers.

'Please, monsieur, I must ask the favour of an interview,' he began. 'My business is of national importance.'

'I am forever interviewing people whose business is of national importance,' the official grumbled; but he led Bigou into a high and thickly carpeted room and sat down at a mahogany desk bare except for a blotting-pad. He folded his hands across his stomach and rolled his marble eyes up at the chandelier. 'Please state your business of national importance as briefly as possible,' he said. Across the bowl of evening outside came the voice of the ragwoman skirling up at the chimneys:

'*Marchand d'habits, chiffo-ons.*'

'It's like this,' Bigou said. 'Two days ago I was called back from the army to take up a job as chief accountant in the new armaments factory run by the Entreprises Françaises d'Installation de Chauffage Central in Belleville. I reported there yesterday and found that a full staff of managers, technicians, workmen, and clerks had been engaged, but there was no work for them to do because there wasn't a cog of machinery in the place.'

'Monsieur, you are wasting my time and your own,' the official said. 'The matter of which you speak comes solely within the competence of the Ministère de la Défense Nationale.'

'Unfortunately that is not so,' Bigou said. 'The machinery and the machine tools necessary are not there because they have been ordered from England and applications for the permits to purchase sterling are necessary in order to pay for them. In view of the urgency of the matter, we were wondering if the necessity for these permits might be waived.'

The official looked thoughtful.

'What you say is very interesting,' he said. 'I am afraid, however, that what you ask is impossible, as the exigencies of the emergency in which we are living demand that the franc be assured of adequate protection.'

'And is not the protection of France of even more importance than the protection of the franc?' Bigou asked. 'The enemy has invaded our soil. Surely this is not the moment to impose unnecessary restrictions? France needs armaments and munitions. Armaments and munitions cannot be made without machine tools. These machine tools have got to be ordered and paid for in Great Britain, who is an ally and has placed her resources in the pool with ours. Surely in this case at least discretionary powers might be granted for the purchase of the necessary sterling?'

'Monsieur, I appreciate and I applaud your impatience which does you credit as a loyal son of the fatherland, but I am afraid that you do not understand . . .'

'On the contrary, monsieur, I understand only too well,' Bigou said. 'I understand that you and your like are ruining and risking France in her hour of danger because you are too bound by custom and sloth to realize that good-will must be backed by energy. Machine tools have to be purchased from England now because those ordered by our buying commission in America arrived in a useless and rusty condition owing to having been bought by fools and sold perhaps by knaves. This time there must be no mistake and, more important still, there must be no delay. Therefore, monsieur, I entreat you to ask your minister if there is no concession that can be made in this matter.'

'Monsieur, I repeat, the exigencies of the emergency in which we are living demand that the franc be assured of adequate protection,' the official said.

Bigou nearly lost his temper and kept it only because he knew that rage could not convince where argument had failed.

'But, monsieur, it is the life or death of France which is at stake,' he said.

The official shrugged his shoulders.

'What will you?' he said. 'The law is the law. And then things are perhaps not so serious as you think. The Germans are putting all their resources of men and materials into this battle. I have it on the highest authority that their offensive may break at any time. And then has not Gamelin himself told his soldiers that they must conquer or die? And perhaps, after all, conquering the Germans is not as difficult as we are sometimes apt to imagine. Remember 1914. We can prove now as we proved then that if Frenchmen can retreat before Germans, Germans can also retreat before Frenchmen. In order to set your mind at rest, however, I shall go and consult my superior, although I warn you that I think his ruling will be the same as my own. It is not always easy for the layman, monsieur, to appreciate the subtlety and foresight of the experienced official mind.'

While he was gone, Bigou read and re-read the scroll on the ash-tray: '*Tout femme élégante est cliente du Printemps.*' If the Germans took Paris, would there be any elegant women left to be customers of the *Printemps?* He walked to the window and looked down on the rue de Rivoli unwinding itself from the hurried lethargy of the dead years. The official came back into the room waving excited hands.

'Good news,' he said. 'Paul Reynaud's just spoken on the wireless. He's taken Pétain in as Vice-Premier. For the duration of the war. "*Il y demeurera jusqu'à la victoire,*" he said, "he'll stay there till victory." That'll give old Hitler a fright, won't it? So you see there's no need for you to worry about permits to purchase sterling. As I had expected, my colleague is of the same opinion as myself. You'll have to fill in the necessary forms and forward them in the usual manner, but as soon as we receive them every effort will be made to expedite the matter. Besides, things are going to improve; with Pétain in the cabinet we can all sleep soundly tonight.'

Bigou thought so, too, as he went away down the broad stairway and back out into the street. Pétain, conqueror of Verdun, practising Catholic and patriot, a man who had never dirtied his hands with political intrigue! High in their niches Boileau, Mazarin, and Mirabeau seemed to be smiling beneath their birds' droppings. Bigou walked happily until he came to the tailor's shop with the mechanical dwarf still tapping on the window. 'France has conquered before; France will conquer again,' his cane said. The windows of the Tour Saint-Jacques burned and glowed with sun, as though candles had been lighted behind them.

XXXVI

ON THE AFTERNOON of Tuesday twenty-first May, the staff of the new armaments factory sat about doing nothing because the permits to purchase sterling had not yet been received from the Ministère des Finances. Bigou, however, had plenty to do, cooking out the profit and loss account of the Entreprises Françaises d'Installation de Chauffage Central for the year ended thirty-first December, 1939. Normally the accounts should have been completed and deposited with the fiscal authorities before the end of March; but the directors had obtained an extension, because the profits had to be subdivided into those earned before and after the outbreak of war.

Through the open window could be seen the gold lettering running across the façade of a wholesale shoeshop, with the two 'S's' in the middle of 'CHAUSSURES' missing. A scrabble of dirty children played noisily in the hot street, swinging on rusty gates and kicking old tin cans. A coffin was carried out from a mean house next door and dumped on a hearse and the children gathered round with popping eyes to ask who it was who had kicked the bucket. A woman in a ragged black costume was the only mourner. The woman next door again was cooking tomatoes stuffed with garlic, but she scarcely turned round from her stench as the procession passed: it was not her turn yet, and deep down within her was the feeling that she would never kick the bucket in quite the same manner as the man next door and Anatole France and Pope Pius XI and all those other silly fish. Watching the ruck of Napoleon's backwash, Bigou was almost inclined to believe that the object of any intelligent man ought to be the achievement of non-existence. A typist came to tell him that Monsieur Terrasse, who was managing the new factory, wished to see him in his private office.

'Still no news?' Monsieur Terrasse asked as Bigou entered. Bigou shook his head.

'Well, perhaps it's an ill wind that blows nobody any good,' Monsieur Terrasse said. 'This delay gives you and me all the more time to finish the accounts of the parent company. Monsieur Dupont has just been speaking to me on the telephone. He says that in his opinion there is no reason why we shouldn't add another five million on to the stock figure as at thirty-first August, 1939. And sales delivered after that date but for which the orders were actually passed before, there's no reason why they shouldn't be shoved forward. He says the great principle to bear in mind is that the more profits we can show ourselves to have made in the three years immediately preceding the outbreak of war, the higher will be the percentage basis on which we shall be allowed to make profits during the war. In other words, my dear Bigou, for once we want to inflate our profits instead of deflating them. Up to the thirty-first of August, that is.' He giggled thickly. 'And another thing. Monsieur Dupont said that he did not think it just that either he or I should pay the fifteen per cent war tax on our full salaries and commissions. He said that he knew perfectly well that the object of the tax was to benefit the wives and children of our soldiers, but that he still thought that fifteen per cent on the *full* amount was excessive. He has, therefore, decided that a portion of our salaries and commissions should be shown in the profit and loss account as travelling and entertainment expenses, and he wants your opinion as to what increased amount can be safely charged under this heading without exciting suspicion. In any case, I told him that there was no need to worry, as the Government had their hands too full these days to be able to probe deeply into anybody's accounts, but he said he wanted your opinion all the same. And about the Swiss subsidiary . . . Well, what is it?' he asked as the typist whom he had sent to fetch Bigou entered with tears in her eyes. 'Can't you see I'm busy?'

'I beg your pardon, monsieur, but it's Monsieur Paul Reynaud speaking before the Senate. He says that we have been betrayed. He says that the bridges across the Meuse weren't blown up. He says that the Germans are in Arras and Amiens.' She stood dabbing at her streaming eyes with a ridiculous flip of a handkerchief. 'I know it's stupid of me, monsieur, but I have two brothers in the army and I'm sure neither of them would betray France.'

Monsieur Terrasse said nothing, but strode out into the main office. Bigou followed him. The employees were all listening to a wireless set blaring down the stairs from the canteen: '*Si l'on me disait que seul un miracle pouvait sauver la France, je dirais: "Je crois au miracle, car je crois à la*

France.' ' 'If one were to say to me that only a miracle could save France, I should say: "I believe in miracles, because I believe in France."' When the speech was finished, there were tears in almost everybody's eyes.

'They say that the station-master at Compiègne was caught with a secret transmitter in his cellar and that he's been shot,' somebody said at length.

'They say that Gamelin's in a fortress,' somebody else said.

Monsieur Terrasse ordered them all to be silent and marched away back into his office. When he came back ten minutes later, he was smiling.

'I've good news,' he said. 'I've just been telephoning the Ministère de la Défense Nationale and they say there's been a mistake. We were never supposed to come here at all. There's a big new factory waiting for us in the rue des Goncourts. It's all fitted up with machinery, so we can get started at once. You can all go home now. We meet to-morrow morning at nine o'clock in the rue des Goncourts.'

Out in the street people were standing gesticulating in doorways. The lady opposite had left off cooking her garlic and was out with her big stomach on the pavement swearing her head off, but the street itself looked just the same, running in a humphle across the rue de Belleville into the squalor of the rue Piat.

It was beginning to rain by the time Bigou reached the métro and the sirens were sounding. Nobody, however, was taking shelter in the underground, except a Jew boy plastering his girl against an advertisement for La Vache Qui Rît, halfway down the dreary steps.

XXXVII

THE NEW FURNITURE in the café had now become so familiar
to Baco that he always talked to it in the mornings as he
walked around cleaning it. On the morning of Tuesday
twenty-eighth May, he was feeling cheerful. There had been
no bad news for the last forty-eight hours. Weygand had
come back from the Middle East and had taken over command on the Western Front. Pétain was a member of the
cabinet. 'And I rub you and I polish you and I wipe and
rub you again,' he said to the shiny-topped tables as he
rubbed them with his duster. 'Why that long face?' he asked
as Bigou came in from the morning.

'That's easy to explain,' Bigou said. 'I told you that the
Défense Nationale were moving us to another factory in
Belleville already fitted up with machinery. Well, between
you and me and the door-post when we got there we found
there wasn't any machinery there either. When we rang up
the Défense Nationale, they said there had been a mistake
and that they would shift us to another factory in a day or
two. Now they say that it was a mistake about there being
a mistake and that we'll have to begin buying machine tools
in England again and fill in forms to purchase sterling. And
how are we going to get machine tools across with the Chan-
nel ports either in or about to fall into the hands of the
Germans? And with the machinery still to be bought, trans-
ported, and set up, when is one going to be able to start
manufacturing? In the meantime I'm back in my old office,
swindling out the accounts for last year so that my employers may still further weaken France in her hour of need

by not paying their proper income tax. Sometimes I think that if I'd any guts I'd go and blow the gaff to the fiscal authorities, but I don't suppose they'd pay any attention if I did.'

'*Sacré*, Bigou,' Baco said. 'Things are not as bad as all that. Hitler's tanks can't keep it up forever. And they say he's lost more than a million killed already. *Tant va la cruche à l'eau qu'à la fin elle se casse.* Remember 'eighteen. In March we believed the game was up, but it wasn't up until November, and then it was the Germans who had lost it. And then we are French, what? We got them once and we'll get them again.'

'We mustn't count our chickens before they're hatched, all the same,' Bacqueroët said as he entered with Latérade and Madame Turbigo. Like all other ex-service men these days, Bacqueroët and Latérade were wearing a thatch of miniature war medals in their buttonholes, but Bigou thought there wasn't much need for Bacqueroët to wear his, as he couldn't possibly have got so smashed up in an ordinary accident.

'Sometimes I wonder if the big men really want to win the war,' Bigou said. He wanted to tell Bacqueroët and Latérade and Madame Turbigo about the new factory not having any machinery in it either, but he decided he'd better not in case he would make them feel too depressed.

'And Odette?' Madame Turbigo asked. 'How are things?'

'It ought to be here in a fortnight now,' Bigou said. 'She's given up working, of course.'

Madame Turbigo nodded sympathetically.

'It's an uncomfortable business,' she said. 'I remember when I was carrying Nicolle, monsieur, my late husband, used to say that I looked just the dead spit of the Tower of Babel.'

Baco turned on the wireless. The interval signal was now a bar of the *Marseillaise*: '*Aux armes, aux armes, citoyens.*' Bigou, Baco, Bacqueroët, and Madame Turbigo all felt very patriotic while it was being played over and over. With a national anthem like that, Bigou thought, France could never be properly in the cart. Baco was right: France had muddled through before; she could muddle through again. '*Aux armes, aux armes, citoyens.*' He would have stood to attention if he hadn't been afraid that the others would think him theatrical. '*Monsieur Paul Reynaud, Président du Conseil, va parler à la nation,*' the wooden box said.

'*Nom de Dieu,* what's the next bad news?' Bacqueroët said.

The furry little voice began its furry little tones. Poured down, clamped down, sealed in their tubes and tripes, screwed into God forever, Bigou, Baco, Bacqueroët, Latérade, and Madame Turbigo stood and listened. The king of the Belgians had capitulated. ' . . . *une trahison sans précédent dans l'histoire,*' the furry little voice said, but France and her ally, Great Britain, would fight on. '*Vive la France!*' When the speech was finished, Bigou, Baco, Bacqueroët, and Madame Turbigo all stood to clumsy Gaulish attention, and none of them thought the others theatrical because they were all weeping their eyes out. Even when the music stopped playing, it was some time before any of them could speak.

'All the same, the dirty swine,' Bacqueroët said.

But Baco was too upset to make any comment. To relieve his feelings he began polishing the bottles on the shelves.

'And I rub you and I polish you and I wipe you and I say *"merde"* to you,' he said.

XXXVIII

THE PRIESTS PRAYED, the people prayed, the politicians prayed, but still the German tanks came rolling on. On the Sunday within the octave of the feast of the Sacred Heart, the usual canopied altars were set up outside all the churches of Paris, but within the railings, so that Benediction of the Blessed Sacrament might be given in the open air without contravening the state regulations about out-of-doors religious processions. On the porches of the churches of the Madeleine, Saint Roch, Saint Etienne du Mont, Saint Eustache, Saint François Xavier, Notre Dame des Champs, Saint Pierre de Chaillot, Saint Pierre de Montrouge, Notre Dame des Victoires, Notre Dame de Lorette, Saint Germain des Près, Saint Germain l'Auxerrois, Saint Honoré d'Eylau, Saint Philippe de Roule, Notre Dame d'Auteuil, Notre Dame de l'Assomption, Notre Dame de Grace de Passy, the blistered wooden tables were trundled, so that the Most High Lord Jesus might be adored in the Holy Sacrament of His Love.

The same ceremonies had taken place on the preceding Sunday, which had been the Sunday within the octave of Corpus Christi, but they hadn't seemed to help very much, because the German tanks still kept on advancing. Today, however, was to be a very special day, because in the afternoon in the metropolitan cathedral of Notre Dame de Paris,

Monseigneur Beaussart, vicar capitular, was to pray to Saint Clothilde and Saint Geneviève and Saint Denis and Saint Rémy to pray to God to stop the tanks. Of course, it was a pity that the new Cardinal Archbishop was still away on his pilgrimage to Spain, but Monsieur Reynaud was to be there and the baggy trousers of his cabinet and a whole horde of important political hooks who hadn't been to Mass since the Lord knew when, but who had been persuaded at the last moment that there might be something in this God business after all.

In the partially completed Church of Saint Jean de Chantal it was also to be a special day, because the abbé Pécher and the newly ordained young priest were back home from the front on leave. The abbé Pécher was to preach a special sermon and the young priest was to sing High Mass for the first time and carry the Host in the procession. Although they never went to church as a rule, Baco, Latérade, and Madame Turbigo had promised to be there, because they liked the abbé Pécher and wanted to show their respect and because they wondered if, after all, a little wisp of prayer might not induce God and His Blesséd Mother to do something about stopping the German tanks; but Bacqueroët had refused to go because, although he liked the abbé Pécher a lot, he liked free-thinking more.

The young priest had never given the *Asperges* before and he got a bit mixed up when he had to sprinkle the congregation with holy water, because he tried to sprinkle both sides of the centre aisle at once; but the abbé Pécher, who was his deacon, put him right. 'To the left, to the left all the time,' Bigou heard him whisper to the young priest as they passed in their stiff white vestments, and after that the young priest got on all right, sprinkling one side of the aisle as he walked down and the other side of the aisle as he walked up. Baco, who was standing beside Bigou, got a great swish of the water behind his ear and he nearly said '*merde*' out loud, but he remembered in time that he was in church and whispered it only under his breath.

The yellow tart was the only one of their group who appeared to be at ease, for as soon as the Mass began she knelt quite openly on her knees and raised her face with eyes shut towards the altar, so that she looked still and holy; but her mother stuck only her chest against the prie-Dieu and balanced her bottom on the seat of her chair. Baco and Latérade stood in a non-committal attitude and Bigou stood, too, because he didn't want to appear more holy than his friends. Up at the altar the new young white shining priest prayed sweetly and cleanly to God, but his alb and his cassock were hitched up too high and his puttees and his heavy military boots stuck out underneath.

For the subject matter of his sermon the abbé Pécher took the mystery of pain and suffering. If we were as wise as God, the priest said, we should understand that sorrow could be a blessing as well as a curse. Men were ennobled by suffering. The man who had never known pain and disappointment was to be pitied rather than envied, because the man who always got things his own way was less than a man. God also used pain as a means of punishment. France had neglected God for years and spurned His commandments and therefore she must expiate her sins. But God was merciful and just. He would not permit the bodies of French boys to be torn and crushed by German tanks without some good coming out of it. France was the eldest daughter of the Church and it was God's Will that she return to the integral practice of the Faith. Pain and sorrow and suffering were God's inscrutable means of accomplishing this return. In God's good time the inexplicable would be made plain. To a savage who didn't know anything about photography it would seem the reverse of reasonable that negatives had to be developed in the dark. Pain and sorrow and suffering were God's dark-room through which poor human souls must pass before they could be made perfect. They were also God's discipline, with which He chastised men for their failings.

The priest started out with assurance, but as he proceeded his voice stumbled and broke, as though he were more sure of his grief than his logic. Looking at his lean tortured face, Bigou wondered if the priest, too, were wondering why God always seemed to allow the wrong people to get killed and maimed in wars. If He wanted to punish people for their sins, why didn't He punish the politicians and the money-grubbers instead of those who had only been their victims? Why didn't He crush a Bonnet or a Laval or two beneath the treads of German tanks? He looked along at Baco and Latérade to see what they made of the priest's sooth and was surprised to find that they were both crying their eyes out. The yellow tart and her mother were crying their eyes out, too. Everybody in the whole church was crying their eyes out. Up in the pulpit the priest was crying his eyes out. As the Mass continued in its blurred golden glory, Bigou began to weep his eyes out, too.

When the Mass was over, they all went and stood outside in the yard to wait for the procession.

'All the same, that was a sermon,' Baco said.

'*Ça oui, alors,*' Latérade said.

'To me Monsieur l'abbé Pécher looks the dead spit of His Holiness the Pope,' Madame Turbigo said.

The yellow tart said nothing, but she smiled away to herself and looked pleased. When the young priest came out carrying the Host, she dropped at once to her knees and Bigou could see that she was praying for their conversion. Baco and Latérade took off their hats, but at the bus terminus the conductors and drivers went on smoking, because they thought that only a fool could believe that God could strike Himself down beneath a white circle of bread. The young priest placed the Host on the open-air altar and the hot sun shone down on it and made the spikes of the monstrance shine. They began to sing the litany of the Blesséd Virgin, praying to Mary to ask her Son to stop the tanks:

> '*Turris eburnea,*
> *Domus aurea,*
> *Foederis arca*
> *Ora pro nobis.*'

Baco, Latérade, and Madame Turbigo hadn't been to Mass for donkeys' years and had eaten great juicy steaks on every Friday of the year except Good Friday, but they caught up the chorus and prayed to the Tower of Ivory and to the House of Gold and to the Ark of the Covenant to pray to her Son to save France.

> '*Janua coeli,*
> *Stella matutina,*
> *Salus infirmorum*
> *Ora pro nobis.*'

A battalion of motor-cyclists roared by on their way to the front, but still the crowd went on singing. When the litany

was over, the saints and martyrs of France were also called
in.

> 'Saint Rémy,
> Priez pour nous.
> Sainte Clothilde,
> Priez pour nous.
> Saint Louis,
> Priez pour nous.
> Saint Denis,
> Priez pour nous.'

With the humeral veil round his shoulders, the priest
made the sign of the cross over the people with the
monstrance.

'What's he doing now?' Latérade asked.

'Dame, il nous fout la bénédiction apostolique,' Baco answered, making a monster sign of the cross all over his new
waistcoat.

Bigou walked back alone to his flat, because he wanted to
see how Odette was getting on. Through the open windows
the wireless sets were sounding: 'Aux armes, aux armes,
citoyens.' Soon the news began to trickle through: Général
Huntziger had issued an order of the day to the troops,
urging them to look forward, never backward, and to clutch
on to sacred French soil. Gudule Flotte was dumping along
the pavement selling Paris-Midi. Bigou bought a copy from
her, but the news was the same there, except that a council
of the war cabinet had been held that morning with Monsieur Albert Lebrun presiding, that French troops had held
on to their positions in the main and that France and Great
Britain were more united than ever.

XXXIX

THE ELECTRIC ADVERTISEMENT for Balto cigarettes still looked the same as in 1934, only it was no longer lighted at night because of the blackout. Opposite its dry bones Bigou worked on as usual, surrounded by previous trial balances and balance sheets of the company stretching away back in still more faded ink to the happy days of 1923. The sky was darkened by a thick black mist as though a thunderstorm were blowing up. The windows of the bank on the other side of the street were squares of glowing amber. It was the evening of Monday tenth June.

Outside the mist thickened and the windows of the bank turned a deeper gold, but Bigou supposed the police couldn't say anything because it was not yet the official hour for screening lights. The familiarity of his task calmed his sense of impending gloom. Screwing out his row of figures, he found it easy to believe that he would screw them out forever. Down in the deep ravine of the street he could hear the rip of the rushing, panting, fleeing cars and taxis, but he forced himself not to think of them. All those directly and indirectly connected with munitions work had been ordered to remain at their posts. *Un point; c'était tout.* Besides, the complications of his cookery were interesting. The firm had the option of basing their maximum wartime profits computation either on their turnover or their profits for the three years ended thirty-first August, 1939 and he was trying to find out which would be the more advantageous. He looked up to see Monsieur Terrasse's white terrified face peering at him out of the gloom.

'About this percentage basis, monsieur —' Bigou began.

'To hell with the percentage basis!' Monsieur Terrasse said. 'I'm clearing out.'

'But I thought that the Government had given definite orders for all those connected with the munitions industry to remain in Paris,' Bigou said.

'The Government can give what orders it likes,' Monsieur Terrasse said. '*Tout ce que je sais c'est que je fous le camp.* Besides they've gone themselves. They're at Tours now. All the newspapers are at Tours too. The Germans may be here any moment. And they say they're terrible. They say they shot a one-legged civilian at Lille and a boy of seventeen. The boy of seventeen began to cry, so they blindfolded him and flung him to the ground and machine-gunned him till he was dead. And that mist looks mighty like gun-smoke to me.'

'All the same, orders are orders,' Bigou said.

'*Tout ce que je sais c'est que je fous le camp,*' Monsieur Terrasse said. 'Besides these orders apply to employees, not to directors. The directors have got to go first to prepare new offices and factories for the employees. Dupont cleared out to Saintes this morning and he's given me orders to follow him. He's going to rent new offices and a factory and he told me to come along at once with the books and accounts. You'd better help me to pack them up. I've got my chauffeur waiting with the car downstairs.'

Bigou said nothing. He tied up his books and accounts and carried them down to the waiting car. He was afraid and Monsieur Terrasse was afraid, but Monsieur Terrasse was not afraid to show that he was afraid; that was the only difference between them. As soon as all the parcels were in the car, Monsieur Terrasse jumped in after them and banged the door. He pulled down the window and stuck his whole face out at Bigou.

'Remember, as soon as you receive the order to leave Paris, you're to make for Saintes,' he said.

Bigou nodded. He was too angry and disappointed and frightened to speak. He watched the car drive away piled with its mattresses and trunks and suitcases. Then he went back into the office to get his hat, because now that the books and accounts had gone, it was no use trying to work any longer.

When he came down again the mist had grown thicker and it tasted acrid in his mouth. There were no buses running. All along the kerb people were piling furniture onto lorries. Taxis and private cars crammed with luggage came hurtling along on top speed. The pavements were almost empty. Two pretty young harlots came sailing in wide frocks like apéritif glasses held upside down. They smiled at Bigou and Bigou smiled back, pleased to believe that his face looked younger than it felt. They wanted Bigou to go with them, but Bigou said that he hadn't enough money, but he'd stand them a drink instead. As they stood along a counter, the girls kept crushing their bodies against him. The boss of the café splashed out their vermouths with an unsteady hand.

'Drink up,' he said. 'Drink up so that there won't be any left when the swine come. They're supposed to be at Pontoise already. That mist's either gun-smoke or a barrage they're using for crossing the Seine or oil-dumps burning or all three of them together. That's why I say "drink up" so that there won't be any left when the swine arrive.'

Bigou and the two girls clinked glasses.

'Were you frightened during last Monday's air raid, darling?' one of them said.

'It was pretty shattering, but I wasn't as afraid as I thought I'd be,' the other said.

The girls kept crushing their long legs against him. Bigou rather liked it, but he didn't know what to say to them, so he just smiled inanely through a slit in his mouth. Seeing that he wasn't reacting, they began to jig and hum, swaying on their heels and bouncing, and Bigou didn't like them pressing against him any longer.

'We'll be able to cross the streets tomorrow without looking round with all those funks running away,' one of them said.

'I'm thinking of running away myself, and if I were you I'd run away too,' the boss behind the counter said.

'The Germans are men, all the same,' one of them said.

'And a hundred-franc note is always a hundred-franc note,' the other said.

Neither Bigou nor the boss behind the counter felt like talking to them after that. The girls finished their drinks and twitched away out onto the boulevard in search of customers. The boss had a drink with Bigou and Bigou had a drink with the boss. When they had spoken about where the Germans were now, they didn't seem to be able to think of anything else to say, so they had a third drink, and the boss said that he'd pay for that, too, as he didn't want there to be any left when the dirty Germans came. A copy of that noon's *Paris-Midi* lying on the counter said that the French troops were holding on to their positions in the main and that France and England were more united than ever. It also quoted Clemenceau: 'We will fight in front of Paris, in Paris, and behind Paris,' and the boss said that that meant that the generals meant business. Then a man who had just been bombed out of Chantilly came in and said that he had tried to get a train out of Paris, but had found all the stations closed, and the boss started to stand him drinks too. Remembering Odette at home waiting for her baby to arrive, Bigou said good-bye and slipped out.

The mist was now so thick that the street was quite dark and the windows of the bank were glowing more brightly than ever. Bigou could hear gunfire in the distance, but he couldn't decide whether it came from anti-aircraft cannon or artillery. The rasp of wireless from the concierge's loge in the bank made him cross the street to see if he could hear the news, but the concierge had closed the window and he couldn't make out the words. He was about to move on dejectedly when the concierge came out and stood thrusting her brave tired face up at the darkening sky.

'That was Paul Reynaud speaking again,' she said. 'The macaronis have done it on us. They've declared war on France and England, but President Roosevelt says that America is going to declare war on Germany at midnight.'

'You're sure of that?' Bigou said.

'I tell you it was Paul Reynaud himself speaking,' the woman said.

There didn't seem to be anything more to say, so Bigou took off his hat at the woman and left her. The mist was so thick that the lighted windows looked as though they were shining through real night, but there didn't seem to be any customers on the terrace. Bigou walked on along the almost empty street, down the rue Royale filled with the ghosts

of those who had rioted there six years ago. The Place de la
Concorde was deserted save for the tear of a taxi charging
with luggage towards a closed station. At the corner of the
Avenue des Champs Elysées and the rue de Tilsit a pop-
eyed policeman creaked in his shoes and surveyed the deso-
lation, but beneath the Arc de Triomphe the flame on the
tomb of the unknown warrior waved up and out and fluttered like a lovely pink sail.

When he got home, Bigou found that Odette had gone
across the road to stay with Madame Turbigo, because she
was miserable about not having heard from François for so
long and was frightened her pains were going to begin any
moment.

XL

WHEN HE WENT DOWN to the café early next morning, Bigou
found that America hadn't declared war on Germany after
all, but only Italy on France and England, although Baco
said that he was pretty sure that Russia would come in one
of these fine days and that Stalin would wipe the floor with
Hitler. Baco also said that it had just come over the wireless
that all able-bodied men between the ages of sixteen and
sixty were to leave Paris immediately, on foot if necessary.
He also said that he was beating it himself right away, as
he was sure Paris was going to go up in flames like Warsaw
and he didn't want to stay and get burned to death. He also
said that he would give Bigou and Odette a lift in his car
if they wanted. He had to take his wife, of course, and he

had also promised to take Madame Turbigo and her daughter and Bacqueroët and Latérade, but he was certain that there would be room for Bigou and Odette as well if they all squeezed up a bit and didn't mind going to La Rochelle where his wife had relations. Bigou thanked him and said that it would suit him excellently, as Saintes wasn't far from La Rochelle. Bigou also said that he supposed that the order for all able-bodied men to leave Paris immediately included munition workers and Baco said that he was sure it did, because the Government couldn't want munition workers to fall into the hands of the Germans any more than potential soldiers. Bigou said that he would go up to Madame Turbigo's flat at once and see if Odette was well enough to travel.

Bigou found Madame Turbigo standing in the middle of her carpet as naked as a worm, with her wrinkled fat belly looking like a pile of Michelin tyres, but she said she didn't mind men seeing her naked any more, as she was no longer the dead spit of the late Gaby Deslys. Odette was still in bed and she smiled at her father and kissed him warmly when he bent over her. Bigou said that Baco had said that the only safe thing for them all to do was to clear out of Paris at once, but that of course he would stay behind with Odette if she didn't feel well enough to travel. Madame Turbigo said that in that case she would stay behind, too, as she couldn't have Odette having a baby and perhaps twins with the shells and the bombs and the bullets flying around, but Odette said she was sure now that her pains weren't going to start for another three days, at least, and that she had never been quite certain of the date, anyway. Bigou said that he would wait for them in the café while they were dressing, and Madame Turbigo said that her daughter was at Mass, looking the dead spit of Sainte Thérèse of Lisieux, but that they could pick her up on the way if she hadn't got back by then.

Latérade and Bacqueroët were already in the café when Bigou got back. Bacqueroët was saying that he had never run away from the Germans yet and didn't want to begin now, but Latérade said that it was his duty to go, as he could do no good if he stayed and would only get in the way of the fighting troops anyway.

'Vingt-deux, voici les flics,' Baco said as Choiseul came in, twirling his baton and humming, 'Tout est permis quand on aim-e.'

'The Germans are at Pontoise,' the policeman announced.

'We're clearing out,' Baco said.

'I'm staying,' Choiseul said. 'It's an order from the Préfecture. Besides, my wife's Alsatian. Perhaps we can be useful to them, since she speaks German.'

'I'd rather be shot than be useful to those swine,' Bacqueroët said.

'That's a matter of opinion,' Choiseul said.

'And another thing,' Bacqueroët said. 'Now I know that the Government lied when they said that they were going to fight in front of, in, and behind Paris.'

'What makes you say that?' Choiseul asked.

'Because if they were going to fight, there would be strafing, and if there was going to be strafing, a wretch and a coward like you wouldn't be staying here.'

'It's a good job for you you're blind and a cripple,' Choiseul said.

'Only a wretch and a coward would sing when France is

dying and you can hit me if you want,' Bacqueroët said, holding out his sore sightless face.

Choiseul said nothing, but glowered at them all and walked away out of the café again.

'Perhaps things aren't as bad as we think,' Baco said. 'Perhaps we'll be able to stop them on the Loire.'

'Even if the Government were obliged to clear out into North Africa, that wouldn't necessarily mean that we had lost the war,' Latérade said. 'There's always Pétain, remember.'

The name of Pétain sounded so sweet to Bacqueroët that he forgot his anger and smiled.

'Yes, there is Pétain, all the same,' he said. 'He at least has never cheated.'

They all looked happier when Bacqueroët had said that. Baco said that he would stand them as many free drinks as they wanted, as he couldn't take all the stuff away with him, but that he hoped a real customer or two would come in, because he had a bad ten-franc piece he wanted to get rid of before leaving Paris. When Madame Turbigo and Odette came in, they were all beginning to get as drunk as Poles, but Baco still had his bad ten-franc piece because there had been no real customers.

'Perhaps we'd better be moving,' Latérade said. 'They can't be far off now. And they say that those tanks can travel at a hundred kilometres an hour.'

'Perhaps it doesn't hurt so much getting crushed under them when they go so fast,' Baco said.

'It said in the papers that they were at Rouen on Saturday,' Madame Turbigo said.

'That means that they were at Rouen on Thursday,' Latérade said. 'I know a chap who works the lift in the *Matin* and he told me they always publish the news forty-eight hours late.'

Baco put on his coat and looked round the café with a sad globby eye.

'It hurts me to leave all that new furniture for those swine,' he said.

'Perhaps it'll still be there when you come back,' Latérade said. 'After all, the Germans are going to have to retreat some day.'

'And how we'll all dance in the street on the day of victory,' Madame Turbigo said.

'Fortunately it's not all paid for,' Baco said, laughing aloud and showing his gold teeth. The thought consoled him, and he began to bundle some of his best and fullest bottles into a bag. His ten horse-power Citroën was already drawn up alongside the pavement with Madame Baco sitting inside in case anyone should jump in and drive off with the car. None of Baco's friends knew his wife very well, because she gave herself a lot of airs, so they all stood around while Baco pulled down the shutters. The shutters made a clamp and a clash and a rattle as they came down, but everybody was able to laugh all the same, because someone had scrawled across them in white chalk, 'Vive la Rocque,' and they all knew that a fascist like him hadn't a dog's chance now that France had really and truly woken up.

What with the luggage and Baco's bag of bottles, it was difficult trying to fit them all into the car, but in the end they tied all the baggage on the roof with a mattress on top and Baco's bag of bottles behind. Madame Turbigo and

Odette and Latérade and Bigou crammed in beside Madame
Baco and Bacqueroët got in in front beside Baco. Before he
started up the engine, Baco took one last look at the outside
of the café and at the hoarding opposite with the slogans
plastered across it: WE SHALL CONQUER BECAUSE WE ARE THE
STRONGER; WITH YOUR SCRAP WE SHALL FORGE THE VICTORIOUS
STEEL. Just as he was about to let in the clutch, the elderly
couple came running round from the Boulevard Exelmans
and asked Baco to take them, too, because they had been to
all the stations and found them closed, with one crowd outside the gates shrieking to get in and another crowd inside
the gates shrieking to get a train. For the first time since
Bigou had known her, the woman was wearing her black
veil thrown back from her face. When Baco told them that
there was no room for them in the car, as he had still to pick
up the yellow tart at the Church of Sainte Jean de Chantal,
they both started to cry their eyes out and to say that they
would give him any money he wanted for a lift. Madame
Baco and Madame Turbigo and Odette and Latérade and
Bigou all looked out of the opposite window and pretended
not to see them, but Bacqueroët hadn't any pretending to
do. Then Gudule Flotte came along and said that she was
in the cart, too, because *Paris-Soir* had cleared off to Tours
without saying a word to her. Then she started to weep her
eyes out, too.

'*Bon sang nom de Dieu merde,* I'm not your wet nurse,
bon sang nom de Dieu merde,' Baco shouted and drove off
with a hard, hating face. Behind him Madame Baco,
Madame Turbigo, Odette, Latérade, and Bigou had hard,
hating faces, too, but it was really themselves they were
hating for not being able to do as Jesus Christ would have

had them do: get out of the car and give up their seats to
Gudule Flotte and the blubbering elderly couple.

Bigou was still hating himself when they drove up at the
church. He jumped down and ran up the steps into the
porch, where a notice hung to say that *La Femme du Bou-
langer* was not at all the sort of film a good Catholic should
see. Inside, the candles on the altar had just been put out
and there was still a smell of burnt grease in the air. The
yellow tart was kneeling alone in a corner. The curé came
tripping along on his toes towards the confessional and put
his arms round the shoulders and looked long into the eyes
of a boy of fourteen who was waiting there. Bigou knew
quite well what that loving gesture meant. It meant that the
priest didn't want the boy to grow up and lie and shirk and
fornicate like other men, but that he was afraid he would,
all the same. Bigou wanted to ask the curé if the abbé
Pécher and the young priest had gone back to the front, but
before he could make up his mind the curé and the boy vanished into the confessional and he was left alone in the
church with God's Body and the yellow tart's straight back.
For a flicker he knelt and told God that he was sorry for not
having been able to give up his seat in Baco's car to Gudule
Flotte or one of the elderly couple. He also told Him that
he was sorry for all the sins that he and other Frenchmen
had committed: lying, stealing, lusting, doing the easy
thing instead of the difficult thing, eating fish on Fridays,
keeping the feasts and not the fasts of religion, stuffing their
bellies with turkey on early Christmas mornings without
having been to midnight Mass first; not paying their taxes,
being dirty swine because everyone else was a dirty swine,
too. Then he went down the church and tapped the yellow

tart on the shoulder and told her that she must come at once.

The yellow tart sat in front of the car with Baco and Bacqueroët, because there was no room for her behind. Baco tried to make the car go on top speed, but it was so heavily laden it could go only in second. They intended to leave Paris by Saint-Cloud, but halfway along the Avenue de la Reine a policeman turned them back, saying that the road was blocked and that they would have to make for the Porte de Châtillon. So back along through Paris they chugged, along the silver sash of the gleaming Seine. At first there didn't seem to be many cars on the road and they passed through the rue de Rivoli at a fair trundle. Beneath the statue of Sainte Jeanne d'Arc an officer and his men were crowded round a map and Bigou hoped that, if Joan could no longer defend France, France would still defend Joan. In the tailor's window the mechanical dwarf was tapping away with his cane, but there was no golden glow behind the panes of the Tour Saint-Jacques because it was ten hours too early yet. In the Boulevard Raspail they tacked on to the tail of a traffic jam which stretched away into the sky and Baco had to go down to bottom gear.

'My petrol won't take us very far if things go on like this,' Baco said.

'Perhaps there won't be so many cars when we get out into the country,' Madame Turbigo said.

Some of the branches of the Société Générale had lights in their windows, but their doors were closed and there were queues of men and women on the pavement waiting to draw their money out. The mist still lay over the city and once again there was an acrid taste on Bigou's tongue. The church of Saint Pierre de Montrouge stood with its doors open waiting for the people to come and pray, but they were all clearing out on their bicycles. On the pavement a girl of ten was pushing a baby in a perambulator. Wrapped in a stockinette hood, its big blunt head looked out on the skelter with blank uninterested eyes, but the small girl had a brave tilt to her chin. There didn't seem to be any parent with them. Bigou lost sight of them once, saw them again, then lost sight of them altogether. At one of their many stops they stood behind a hearse-load of pretty girls showing their knees. As soon as they got out of one sludge, they fell into another: lorries, taxis, private cars, perambulators, bicycles, all panting away down the sewer of escape. It took them more than four hours to get out of Paris. Even then the traffic block still went on, stretching in front of them and curving away round the trees like a tail. Bigou thought for a moment that he saw the little girl with the baby in the perambulator and wondered if she could really have walked as fast as they had driven, but when he looked at them closely he saw that it was another little girl and another baby. Gunfire could be heard in the distance, but it did not sound really terrifying. An aeroplane came swooping down from the sky and swooped away again.

'As long as they don't bomb us,' Madame Baco said.

'They use machine-guns as well,' Madame Turbigo said.

'If only I could get back into second gear again there might be some chance of the petrol lasting out as far as Orleans,' Baco said.

'There's no two ways about it,' Latérade said. 'We'll hold them on the Loire all right.'

Bigou glanced inquiringly at Odette, but she shook a smiling head. He took her hand in his: it was wet and warm and she let him keep it there. He smiled at her again and she smiled back and happiness surged into his soul. Whatever happened Odette and he were friends forever now.

XLI

IT WAS RAINING cats and dogs when they reached Etampes early the next morning. They had almost no petrol left, but Odette's pains hadn't begun yet. The yellow tart was praying to Saint Anthony of Padua, whose feast it was next day, asking him to help them to find petrol, but Baco and Latérade were swearing. They left the car in the middle of the market-place with the women to guard it and stumbled off along the slimy soft slippy cobbles in search of hot coffee; but most of the café proprietors were already putting up their shutters, because they had been cleaned out the night before and were clearing out themselves. In one café which they found open there was no coffee, but only four bottles of beer which Baco said they might as well drink on the spot, as there was plenty of booze in the car for the others anyway. Baco also asked the boss behind the counter if he knew of anywhere in the town where he could get petrol and the boss behind the counter said that he had been a citizen of Etampes for forty years, but that he knew of nowhere in the town where Baco could get petrol because all the pumps had been emptied and padlocked up in case the Germans would get at them. Baco then said that he would give the boss behind the counter a thousand francs if he would tell him of anywhere in the town where he could get petrol, but the boss behind the counter still said that he had been a citizen of Etampes for forty years, but that he knew of nowhere in the town where Baco could get petrol because all the pumps had been emptied and padlocked up in case the Germans would get at them. At that Baco, Latérade, and Bigou stuck their mugs into their jugs and sulked, but Baco suddenly brightened and took out his bad ten-franc piece and twirled it on the counter.

'How much do I owe you for the beer, boss?' he asked.

'Twelve francs,' the boss behind the counter said.

'It's highway robbery, but bosses don't tip bosses,' he said, taking out another two francs from his pocket.

The boss behind the counter took the ten-franc piece and bounced it on the zinc. Then he tried it between his teeth.

'Even although I'm not a Parisian, you mustn't take me for a fool,' he said, as he handed the coin back to Baco.

Baco took back the bad coin and handed him another without a word. Then they all went out of the café and stood on the pavement.

'What a dirty swine that fellow in there is all the same,' he said.

Bigou looked round at the street. Householders and shop-keepers were clapping up their shutters. A swill of traffic was oozing up the causeway. Lorries, taxis, private cars, bicycles, perambulators, sludged and sloppered up the road with sticky persistence. On the railway line a high empty train rattled back to Paris and a high full one boomed out from Paris.

'People seem to be getting away still,' Latérade said.

'It's like that as far as Orleans,' a man standing beside them on the kerb said, nodding in the direction of the slowly filtering traffic.

'I'd like to see a Boche come and drop a few of his chocolates on all those civilians,' a surly soldier standing with his hands in his pockets said.

'Who the devil are you calling a civilian?' Bacqueroët said, sticking his great sore hacked face in front of the soldier. 'When I and my generation fought in a war we won it.'

'I beg your pardon, monsieur,' the soldier said. 'Believe me, I didn't see.'

'We're all soldiers, what?' Latérade said.

They stood for a few minutes longer watching the rain slumping down. Then Baco said they'd better try stopping lorries and asking them for a tow as far as Orleans, but the drivers he spoke to pretended not to hear or said their bosses had forbidden them to give tows to anybody or snarled at him and said that *il les faisait chier*. Even when he offered them a thousand francs, they still took no notice or were rude to him or drove on showing that they didn't care how much he was crushed beneath a German tank so long as they themselves weren't. Then Baco said that perhaps it would be as well if Bacqueroët were to do the asking because the lorry drivers couldn't very well refuse to give him a tow, as he was so lame and slashed about and blind, but the lorry drivers drove on just the same and told Bacqueroët that *il les faisait chier*.

They returned to the car in a despond, because Baco said that they had only enough petrol to take them another ten kilometres at most, and that perhaps the best thing for them to do would be to abandon the car and try to board a train. When they reached the car, they found Madame Turbigo waving her hands excitedly and Odette moaning and groaning because her pains had started without any warning, just

like that. Both Madame Baco and Madame Turbigo said
the only thing to do was to get Odette indoors somewhere,
but Baco said that they couldn't very well do that, as they
knew nobody in the town and most of the houses were shut
up, anyway, and were they sure that the pains were real
pains and not just imagination. Both Madame Baco and
Madame Turbigo said that they were sure that the pains
were real pains because the water had come away first. Then
Baco saw a boy walking up the pavement swinging an empty
petrol tin and said that pains or no pains he was going to
follow the boy, because he was sure he wasn't carrying an
empty petrol tin just for fun. Bigou and Latérade both got
up on the roof of the car on top of the mattress and the
luggage so as to give Odette more room to stretch out her
legs, but Madame Baco and Madame Turbigo stayed inside
to hold her hands and stroke her brow. The car lurched forward and Odette screamed and Baco swore and said that the
movement would probably make the baby come sooner and
that for all their sakes he mustn't lose sight of the boy with
the empty petrol tin.

By the time they had got going, the boy had vanished
round a bend in the road, but they overtook him again
climbing the hill. At the top of the hill they found a long
queue of cars drawn up along the grass. While Odette lay
yelling her head off, Bigou went forward to investigate and
came back to say that there was a petrol pump working, but
that it would probably take them three hours to reach it, as
there were more than forty cars in the queue and that the
petrol might give out before then, but that they would just
have to take their chance. Odette kept screaming that she
must get lying flat somehow and Madame Turbigo said the

only thing to do was to stretch her out on the grass and never mind the proprieties, but Baco said that they couldn't very well do that and that the best thing to do would be to stick her up on the roof on top of the mattress.

Bigou and Latérade got down from the roof and helped Odette out of the car and tried to heave her up, but she kept being twisted by such pains that she could not even get one foot onto the hub of the wheel, so they had to ask Baco to come and help them. While they were all three lifting her in their arms, the car in front of them in the queue shot forward ten yards and the cars behind them began to honk their horns. Bigou turned and swore at the round blob of face in the wet windscreen behind him and said that his daughter was going to have a baby and couldn't the fellow behave like a gentleman; but the man only stuck his head out into the rain and shouted that he didn't give a damn how many babies Bigou's daughter was going to have, but that she wasn't *nom de Dieu merde* going to stop him getting petrol, and that if Bigou wasn't going to move up into the gap in the queue he was going to do so. Whereupon in an endeavour to find room to incline his front wheels, he backed into the bonnet and headlamps of the car behind him. There was a crash right back along a row of six cars followed by a concatenation of '*merde*' and another brekekekexcoax-coax of klaxons and horns. Three cars from the highroad took advantage of the confusion to drive into the gap in the queue in front of Baco's car. Baco raged so much that he nearly let Odette fall, but Bigou shouted at him that they must get Odette up on the roof first and then he could go and swear at the swine afterwards.

As soon as Odette lay with her legs stretched out on the

mattress and the rain beating down on her twisted face, Bigou climbed up and knelt beside her and stroked her brow. Madame Turbigo also heaved herself up and sat at her feet and told her that she mustn't struggle against the pain, but must push with it, and that she should grip with her hands onto something behind her head. As the low rails round the luggage carrier lay far below the pile of suitcases and the mattress, Bacqueroët handed up his stick and Bigou held it between his two hands and pulled it against Odette as she wrenched and tugged at it.

Meanwhile, Baco went forward to the drivers of the three cars which had rushed the queue from the roadway and told them that they were dirty swine and that they would have to drive out again and make way for him, but they sat tightly on at their steering-wheels and called him a dirty swine back and said they would do nothing of the sort. While they were swearing and shaking their fists at one another, gunfire sounded in the distance. Baco rushed back into his seat at the steering-wheel of his own car in case the queue would move forward again and he would lose his place once more. Madame Turbigo leaned down from the roof and stuck her head in at the front window and said that they would have to get Odette down again, as she was getting soaked to the skin lying there in the rain and would catch fever and die if she were left there much longer, but Baco shouted that he wasn't going to move away from the steering-wheel again for anyone and that Odette could die a thousand times over for all that he cared, and that it was her own fault she was up there, anyway, and that the only other place she could get her legs stretched out was on the grass which was just as wet as the mattress, and what was more they would have to shift her every time the car moved forward.

Upon the roof, pulling away at Bacqueroët's stick, Bigou hated Baco when he heard him talk like this, but Odette was in such pain that she didn't seem to have heard.

'Will it be much longer now?' she asked Madame Turbigo between two bouts of pain. Madame Turbigo said that no, it wouldn't be much longer now, but when Odette was ridden with her next agony she whispered to Bigou that her deliverance was hours off yet and that the best thing Bigou could do was to go and ask the garage proprietor if he would let Odette lie up in his garage. Bigou was on the point of getting down when the queue moved forward a few metres and Baco lurched the car forward with it. Odette cried out that he mustn't leave her until he had got somebody else to come up and take his place. So when the car stopped, the yellow tart climbed up and held the stick instead of Bigou, and she said that she knew Odette must be suffering terribly because she could see there was sweat on her brow as well as raindrops, but that she would suffer less if only she would say each time the pain shook her: 'Sweet Jesus, as Thine arms were outstretched upon the cross . . .'

Bigou had to walk more than a hundred metres before he came to the petrol pump, where a man in shirtsleeves and two girls were jigging out petrol for the line of waiting cars. There were three pumps and all three were working. Although the piping from each pump was fixed to the bonnet of a car, they seemed to be pumping the petrol from one glass container into the other because as the first emptied the second filled. Bigou stood watching as he stood trying over the most suitable words in which to frame his request. The man saw him and scowled.

'You'll have to wait your turn with the others and if the petrol gives out first, it's just too bad,' he said.

'I wasn't thinking about petrol,' Bigou said. 'I was thinking about my daughter. She's in the middle of having a baby out in the rain back there.'

'That's just too bad,' the man said and went on with his pumping.

'I was wondering if you wouldn't be kind enough to let her lie in your garage for a little,' Bigou said. 'You see, the grass is wet and the mattress on top of the car is wet, and she can't stay inside the car because she can't get stretched out properly.'

'Nobody's going to have a baby in my garage because as soon as this petrol's given out I'm off myself,' the man said.

But one of the girls had a kind face and she winked at Bigou. As soon as she had finished pumping her car full, she took the money and went into the garage to put it in the till. When she came out again, she told Bigou to take her to where Odette was. When they got back to the car, Odette was still writhing away on top of the mattress and there was a group of clod-faced men watching from the grass, but they kept jumping back into their cars each time the queue moved forward. Baco said that they would have to get Odette down without his help because he had lost his place in the queue once and he wasn't going to risk losing it again. However, Bacqueroët said that he would help as much as he could, and in any case it was easier getting her down than it had been getting her up.

They carried her into the garage easily enough and laid her down in the back behind a screen of empty petrol tins. The girl with the kind face said that perhaps it would be as well if they could get a doctor, but when Bigou went back to question the drivers of the cars in the queue, they all said that they weren't doctors.

Bacqueroët and Latérade wanted to stay in the garage with Odette, but Madame Turbigo said that it wouldn't be decent if they did, so they went out again and sat with Baco in his car. Madame Turbigo then said that Bigou ought really to go outside, too, but both Madame Baco and the yellow tart agreed that as her husband couldn't be there his proper place was with Odette. So they all three sat on in the gloom round Odette as she moaned and groaned and lay still and tossed. Sometimes the guns rumbled outside and sometimes an aeroplane engine droned and always it seemed to grow darker. 'Push with the pain, don't withdraw from it,' Madame Turbigo kept saying and 'Jesus, Jesus, be to her a Jesus,' the yellow tart kept saying. There was only sweat now on Odette's brow when Bigou stroked it because the rain had long ago dried off.

Two hours later Baco came charging into the garage.

'*Bon sang*, hasn't she pupped yet?' he asked.

'Please, Auguste,' Madame Baco said.

But Baco paid no attention to his wife. He bent down over Odette and bawled in her ear:

'Push, you little bitch,' he roared. 'Push out another little Frenchman to be crushed beneath the German tanks in twenty years' time. Push, I tell you, because I've got a tankful of petrol now and if that brat isn't born in half an hour from now, I'm going to clear out and leave you to it.'

'You're quite wrong, Auguste,' Madame Baco said. 'For once in your life you're going to behave like a gentleman.'

'But the tanks,' Baco said. 'You don't seem to understand. They may overtake us any moment. We may be bombed.'

'You can do what you like, Auguste, but neither I nor Madame Turbigo is moving from here until this child has had her baby.'

'Nor I,' the yellow tart said.

Baco said no more, but went away out again. Bigou got up and followed him because he was angry with Baco for having been so unkind to Odette and wanted to tell him so, but when he stood out in the rain he was angry no longer because like Baco he was afraid.

Baco did not look round as Bigou followed him out of the garage, but went over to the car which now lay drawn up at the side of the roadway away from the queue with Bacqueroët and Latérade sitting inside. It was still raining. The queue of cars was still jerking slowly past the petrol pump and the man and the two girls were still filling them. On the highway the ooze of lorries and taxis still sucked on. Aeroplanes kept swooping through the sky, but Bigou knew they were French because they had the tricolour painted in a circle on the bottom of their wings. When he listened very hard, he could hear gunfire in the distance. Bigou ambled over to the car and stuck his head in at the window.

'It was so dark in the garage I thought it must be night,' he said.

'It soon will be at this rate,' Baco grumbled.

'Nonsense, it's only two o'clock in the afternoon,' Latérade said.

'It seems much later,' Bacqueroët said.

'The Germans have probably taken Paris by now,' Baco said.

Bigou said nothing. He knew how Baco was feeling because he was feeling the same way himself. He knew, too, that if it had been Baco's daughter who had been having a baby in the garage, he might have been just as unkind to her as Baco had been to Odette. The stream of cars slumped on and on with the same sort of faces stuck behind their windscreens. The rain made a hard sound as it fell. Nobody spoke because they were all afraid of expressing their thoughts. When they had been sitting there for a long time, Baco looked at his watch because he thought they must have been sitting there for an hour, but they had been sitting there only for twenty minutes. The rain fell on and began to make a singing noise as well as a hard noise. The proprietor of the garage filled a car and shouted to the drivers of those that were still waiting: 'That's the last of the juice,' he said and began to disconnect the piping from his pump.

The two girls pumped a little longer, but when they emptied one container the other no longer filled, so they began to disconnect their piping, too. Some of the drivers gathered round and began to protest, but they all three said that it was the last of the juice and went on disconnecting their pipes. When the proprietor of the garage had finished disconnecting his piping, he came across to Baco's car.

'Your daughter'll have to clear out of my garage now,' he said to Bigou. 'We're leaving at once.'

'But as the Germans will break open your garage anyway, surely there's no reason why you shouldn't leave it open?' Bigou said.

'I tell you I'm leaving and what's more I'm locking up my garage before I leave,' the man said.

'Monsieur is quite right,' Baco said. 'Of course he's got to lock up his garage before he leaves.'

Bigou looked at the kind-faced girl who had winked at him, but she was no longer kind-faced or winking because fear was beginning to tear through her. Even Bacqueroët looked unhappy and determined. As Baco and Latérade and he walked back to the garage with the proprietor and the two girls, Bigou wondered what he was going to do. When they entered the garage, however, Odette was no longer moaning, but was lying very still with her eyes closed. Madame Turbigo had taken off her blouse and was wrapping it round a whimpering naked red infant.

'It looks just like a monkey, doesn't it?' she said.

They all crowded round to marvel and to laugh at the child, which was a boy. They stroked the pudge of purple hands and the smear of fine silk black hair. Even Baco laughed till he showed his gold back teeth and Bigou wondered that so gentle a being as a baby could come from so rough a gesture as love. The girl with the kind face said that she must get them some warm shawls for the baby.

Because he was ashamed of himself for being so unkind to Odette while the baby was being born, Baco said that he was going back to the car to fetch some booze so that they could all drink to the new baby's health. While he was gone, the garage proprietor said that he was sorry that he had been so snifty about letting Odette have her baby in the garage, but he was sure that they quite understood that his hesitation had been due to the force of circumstances. Bigou said that of course they quite understood, and Madame Turbigo said that she had known all along that at any other time the garage proprietor would have allowed Odette to have as many babies as she wanted in his garage. Odette said nothing and lay on her back smiling with eyes as gentle as a reindeer's.

Baco came back with two bottles of champagne. He said that he hadn't been able to bring Bacqueroët with him because somebody had to stay in the car in case anyone tried to drive off in it. While he was uncorking the drink, Madame Baco and Madame Turbigo cleaned up and the girl with the kind face came down with some shawls and a blanket in which they wrapped the baby with its feet bound up tight. Then the proprietor of the garage fetched glasses and they all drank to the baby's health and laughed a great deal and said that it was funny that even in the middle of a war life had to go on as usual.

The yellow tart, however, did not laugh, and when she had finished her drink, she said that there weren't two ways about it and that they would have to baptize the baby right away, as if it were machine-gunned by a German aeroplane on the road, it would go to hell forever and ever because it had not been cleansed of the stain of original sin. The garage proprietor and Latérade grinned foolishly, and Baco said with the Germans likely to roll up at any moment they hadn't time to go careering round the countryside in search of a priest to baptize a baby; but the yellow tart said that the abbé Pécher had told her that in the hour of danger the sacrament of baptism could be validly administered by any-body, and that if Odette would tell her what name she wanted the baby called she would baptize him herself, be-cause like that she would be quite sure of fulfilling the Church's intention. Odette said that she didn't want to run the slightest risk of her baby going to hell forever and ever and that she would like her child called Jean Michel Fran-çois. The girl with the kind face went and filled a tumbler with water and the yellow tart poured it right over the baby's face, because she explained that for the sacrament to work the water must flow properly and said: 'Jean Michel François, I baptize thee in the name of the Father, and of

277 ·

the Son, and of the Holy Ghost, amen.' The babe whimp-
ered.

The garage proprietor and the two girls and Madame Turbigo and Madame Baco and Bigou all made the sign of the
cross, but Baco said that as far as he could see the baby still
looked the same as before. Whereupon the yellow tart said
that it wasn't babies' bodies that baptism changed, but their
souls. She also said that the abbé Pécher had told her that
baptism washed out not only original sin but also post-
original sin and the temporal punishment due to it, so that
if the greatest of sinners were baptized on his death-bed he
would go straight to heaven. Baco said that if that were the
case he wished his parents had omitted to have him baptized because then he could have rogered like blue stink all
his life and called in a priest when he was ninety, but
Madame Baco said that that was no way to talk and that he
ought to be ashamed of himself.

Then the guns sounded out again, louder than before, and
their terror was upon them once more. Baco said that it was
high time that they were on the move again and that if
Latérade and Bigou would ride on the roof Odette could
have the whole of the back seat to herself. The garage proprietor turned on the wireless to see if there was any news
as to where the Germans were now, but at first all that they
heard was the interval signal: *'Aux armes, aux armes, citoyens.'* Then the voice of the announcer suddenly bawled
out that the Government had cancelled its order of the previous day and that all workers in Parisian munition factories
were to return to the city at once, on foot if necessary.

'Things must be getting better, all the same,' Latérade
said.

'*Ça se peut bien,*' Baco said. 'Perhaps they've held them on the Seine, after all. Perhaps we have an army, after all, what?'

Bigou tried to smile, but his mouth was a gash because he did not want to go back to Paris and leave them all, especially Odette and her new baby. He began to shake hands immediately in case they should see how unhappy he was feeling. He shook hands with Baco and Latérade and the garage proprietor, but he kissed Madame Turbigo and Madame Baco and the yellow tart and the girl with the kind face because they had been so kind to Odette. They all said that there was nothing for him to worry about because they wouldn't be calling the munition workers back to Paris unless things were getting better and that they would all meet soon again when the Germans had been driven back. Baco said that, of course, he would have gone back to Paris with Bigou if it hadn't been for Odette and her baby, but that one couldn't afford to take risks with them, and in any case he had made an appointment with his relations in La Rochelle and couldn't very well put them off, but that Bigou could count on him to look after his daughter and his grandchild. Then Bigou kissed Odette and the baby very specially and went out of the garage. He said good-bye to Bacqueroët sitting in the car and Bacqueroët told him that if he was going back to Paris the best thing to do would be to try the station.

Bigou thanked him and moved off down the crunchy wet road. The station was not far away. When he reached it, he found the gates locked and a cram of people carrying suitcases yelling to get in. A full train came swinging down from Paris piled with windowfuls of faces and with two men sitting on the rear buffers. Then a train of trucks came chugging up filled with troops with their rifles sticking out like trees. Then the rails were empty and shining and silver again as they curved away in the rain.

'There'll be no more trains now,' a man standing beside Bigou said.

'And to think it's all the fault of the English,' another man said.

Bigou didn't wait any longer. Even if there were any trains back to Paris, he didn't want to dirty his soul scrumming with the crowd to get into the station. He turned and walked back into the town. The streets were emptier than before. The café where they had tried to get petrol was shut up and dull and dead, but there was still the same sludge of traffic stuffing through the main street. There were also heavy lorries with men and women sitting on top of machinery.

All the traffic was coming from Paris, so Bigou was alone as he trudged along in the opposite direction. It stopped raining and the sky furred and faired to blue and white. On a hill a man passed up a field making the patient holy gestures of ploughing. Then a column of painted-over Paris buses came up the road behind Bigou and he had to stand down in the ditch to let them pass. As the last bus came tumbling by, Bigou unhooked the leather strap across the doorway and jumped on the rear platform. A face on top of a scruffy uniform looked round from the back of the second-class seats.

'What the devil do you think you're doing?' the face asked.

'I'm an accountant in an armaments factory and I've been called back to Paris and I thought perhaps you'd be going that way,' Bigou said.

'If the corporal comes along, he'll throw you out,' the face said.

Bigou said nothing and the face turned into the tip of a rifle slung across a shoulder. The bus lurched on through the afternoon. On the horizon the sky became pink and green and heliotrope and then a greyish-white, like rolled down snow streaked by a broom.

XLII

THE CORPORAL didn't come along until they reached Arpajon, when it was almost dark. Instead of throwing Bigou off the bus, he suggested that he and Bigou and the face above the uniform should all go and have a quick one if they could find a café open. After rooting round all the side streets, they found one with a gloomy proprietor with a face like Bossuet sitting among his lonely bottles listening to the beginning of the news: 'Aux armes, aux armes, citoyens. The previous order of today cancelling the order of yesterday is itself cancelled. All workers in armaments factories in the Parisian district must leave the city immediately, as must also all other able-bodied men between the ages of sixteen and sixty. On the front our troops have held on to their positions in the main . . .'

When he heard this, Bigou wanted to start away back again at once, but the corporal insisted on his having a quick one first. He stayed and had four. When he took leave of the corporal and the face above the uniform, he felt that he had known them all his life and that they were the finest fellows in the world and that he would be very sorry indeed if the German tanks came along and rolled them out; but he forgot them almost as soon as the bus had borne them off into the clear sweet-smelling night. For a second or two he stood raising his cheek to the stars. Then he began to trudge away back in the direction of Etampes. The same chain of clogged traffic was chugging incessantly forward, only it was impossible to see the vehicles distinctly, because of the dark. At a distance the ribbon of their blue-shaded head-lights looked beautiful, like a garland lit in Spain to honour a saint, but close to, the lamps looked like huge eyes, leering.

As soon as he had walked out of the town, Bigou tried stopping the cars and asking for a lift. Some drivers were rude and some didn't answer and some drove on at him with harsh faces. When he tried standing in a traffic block, they were even ruder because they didn't like having to show that they didn't care how much anybody else might get shot or torn asunder so long as they themselves were safe, safe, safe. Even the drivers of the heavily laden Government factory lorries would not listen to him, saying that they were over-loaded as it was and that the Minister of the Interior had forbidden them to give a lift to anybody, even to other Gov-ernment officials. With a sore heart Bigou walked on be-neath the still sky held like a faraway lid over the world. On the footpath two invisible soldiers were talking.

'I heard from the wife last week,' one of them said. 'She says that both she and the children are well.'

Bigou took courage from the sound of the ordinary sen-tence. The German tanks couldn't be as near as all that if one French soldier could still talk to another French soldier about having heard from his wife last week. Yet a week ago

with the sun on the Champs Elysées it had seemed as though
Paris was bound to go on forever. Today the Germans were
not, and tomorrow they were, slaughtering, crushing, maim-
ing.

Searchlights suddenly sprayed all over the sky, like foun-
tains playing at a fête. Gunfire sounded with the benevolence of summer thunder. Bigou walked on quickly until he
overtook a phalanx of waiting cars in the next traffic block.
Through the window of one of them he could see the hands
of a clock and a speedometer burning a lovely lonely pale
green. The white face of a woman hung like a moon over
the speedometer. There seemed to be no other occupant of
the car, but the back was piled with luggage. Preparing to
be hated again, Bigou tapped with his finger on the glass.
To his surprise the window was pulled down and the wraith
of face floated close to his.

'Madame, I am an accountant in an armaments factory
and I must get to Saintes at once,' he began, but before he
had finished his sentence he realized that he was talking to
Mireille Arzelle. Across the darkness he could smell her
tempting rich woman's smell of fur, leather, and perfume.
'Mademoiselle, I didn't know it was you,' he said.

'Bigou!' she exclaimed. For a second she looked at him
with slumbering insolent sultry eyes and then she smiled.
'You'd better jump in,' she said. 'I expect Dupont left you
in the lurch the same way as he left me, but I'm going after
him to Saintes to make a scene. His wife won't like it, of
course, but neither will he, and that's all I care about.'

He told her his adventures and about Odette's baby, but
she did not seem interested. In the ray of light thrown by
the phosphorescent clock and speedometer she sat with
wide-apart legs.

'I expect that this will be the last time we'll ever fight a war for England,' she said at length.

'Mademoiselle, it is not for England that we are fighting; it is for France and liberty and decency,' Bigou said.

'Daladier and Reynaud seem to have taught you your lessons well,' she said. 'Listen, my friend. The real enemy of France is not Germany, but communism.'

'Monsieur Dupont seems to have been a good teacher too,' Bigou said.

'If you don't mind, we shan't talk about that,' Mireille said.

They drove on in jerks and halts. Gradually, however, the road in front of them cleared. Soon they were able to move more quickly. Mireille sat looking out over the steering-wheel. They did not speak until they reached Etampes, when Mireille declared that she was too tired to drive any farther.

'But I can drive,' Bigou said.

'I'm tired,' Mireille said. 'I must sleep between sheets.'

'But the Germans must be almost in Paris by now,' Bigou said. 'After that there probably won't be much more resistance till they reach the Loire. Those tree trunks that they're going to throw across the road won't stop tanks.'

'I tell you that I want to sleep in a bed,' Mireille said.

Bigou took the wheel from her and they trundled round and round the deserted streets looking for a hotel that was open. They found one near the station with a clump of cars drawn up outside it.

The vestibule was full of people. There was no one at the reception desk. Bigou went upstairs to look for the proprietor or a servant, but he could find nobody. When he came back Mireille was standing beside a mattress on which a

little girl of ten was sitting with a baby in her arms. Bigou
wondered if she was one of the little girls with babies whom
he had passed yesterday on the road, but when he looked
closely at her she didn't seem to have the same sort of face.

'Well?' Mireille asked.

'I can't find anyone to ask, but there doesn't seem to be
any room anyway,' Bigou said.

'The dustman's coming,' the little girl said to the baby.

Bigou smiled at the little girl and the little girl smiled
back, but Mireille did not smile at all. They went back to
the car and drove on through the brittle indigo night. After
a while Mireille made Bigou draw up at the side of the road,
saying that she thought they should both get a little sleep.
Bigou switched off the light on the dashboard and tried not
to feel excited. He liked it when Mireille made him make
love to her, but he still hated her for not having smiled at
the little girl with the baby.

XLIII

ALTHOUGH he had slept with her for four nights now, Bigou
still called Mireille 'Mademoiselle' when he said good-bye
to her on the bridge over the silver thread of river running
through Saintes. She did not look round, but raised her
gloved hand as she drove off to find Monsieur Dupont. Bigou
stood staring after the car as it jumped and bumped away
in clouds of dust. The river shone in the afternoon sun with
its surface whipped and ruffled by the wind.

Soldiers and their females were clopping to and fro on the

pavements, but they did not seem to notice the shifting beauty of the river. Bigou stopped one or two of them and asked them if they had heard of an evacuated armaments factory being located in the vicinity, but they just mooned at him out of raw faces and moved on.

There was a chemist's shop on the corner of the street, so Bigou went in there to see if he could find out where the factory was. The shop was empty except for a refugee who was buying a tube of toothpaste from a pimply-faced girl. The pimply-faced girl didn't know what the price was, so she called another pimply-faced girl out from behind a screen to tell her, and then a third pimply-faced girl appeared to take the customer's money. When the cash register had ping-ed behind the money and the door had ping-ed behind the customer, Bigou asked the three pimply-faced girls if they knew where the factory was, but they all bleared at him like cows and said that they didn't, although they had heard that important news was to be given out over the wireless at four-thirty. Bigou thanked them and left the shop.

There was a café opposite with a loud-speaker blaring away dance music. Bigou went and sat on the terrace in order to be able to listen in at four-thirty. When he ordered a half-pint of beer, he asked the waiter if he had heard of an armaments factory evacuated from Paris having rented premises in the vicinity, but the waiter said that he hadn't and that he didn't know anyone who had.

A paragraph on a beer-stained copy of *Paris-Midi* lying on the table caught Bigou's eye. It said: 'The Germans have mobile crematoria which follow up their infantry and burn the bodies of their dead, thus preventing the spread of disease. Sometimes severely wounded soldiers are burned as well.' There was also another paragraph which began: 'Frenchmen should remember that France always rises stronger from defeat. It was so after 1870; it will be so in 1940.' Bigou did not read any further because he did not want to have to think about France being defeated.

At the next table, under a hanging copy of the menu jelly-padded off in blotched purple ink, two senior officers were also ordering beer. The waiter was saying that draught beer cost two francs, but that bottled beer cost two francs-fifty. Both the officers decided that they would have bottled beer. When the waiter moved away, Bigou saw that their faces were grave and that their hands were moving excitedly. Was it possible that the great catastrophe had happened? No, it wasn't, not with the sun shining like that on the officers' pale blue képis and the girls laughing on the arms of the soldiers and the wind frilling the surface of the river. His unease returned as the dance music on the wireless trailed off into the interval signal: '*Aux armes, aux armes, citoyens.*' The signal was played over and over again and was succeeded by more dance music. The crowd which had assembled on the pavement to hear the news without having to pay for a drink shrugged their shoulders and drifted off. One of the officers next Bigou rose and walked away.

'You see, they tell us nothing,' the officer who remained said to Bigou.

'Perhaps no news is good news,' Bigou said.

'I only hope you're right,' the officer said. 'There is a cabinet meeting this afternoon at Bordeaux.' He looked away and away down into the bottom of his glass. 'And to think that they would never have got through if we had had the aeroplanes. Our seventy-fives were blowing their tanks to smithereens, but when the Germans saw that, along came their dive-bombers and there were no more seventy-fives. If we had had the fighter aeroplanes, we could have stopped that, but with "ifs" you could put Paris in a bottle. The game is up. When Spain is taken, he will take Africa. There's nothing to stop him.'

'There is England,' Bigou said.

'England will have fallen, too, in less than three months,' the officer said. 'We ought to have been on our guard ever since the last war. Things were too good to be true. So perhaps our grandchildren will say that it wasn't only because of the lack of seventy-fives and aeroplanes that France fell in 1940, but also because Frenchmen didn't listen to the still, small voice in time of peace.'

Bigou watched him walk away up the street in his faded tunic, a lonely man who loved France. Perhaps the other soldiers in the street were also lonely men who loved France, but they didn't look it as they strutted with their girls. Then he caught sight of Monsieur Terrasse behind a fat colonel and his wife and ran out onto the pavement to greet him.

'Where on earth have you been all this time?' Monsieur Terrasse grumbled. 'I've been looking for you everywhere.'

'I arrived here only this afternoon,' Bigou said. 'I've been trying to find the factory, but nobody seemed to know where it was. I left Paris in a car with friends the moment I heard the order and then I started back on foot again the moment I heard the next order and then . . . ' He stopped as he realized that Monsieur Terrasse wasn't interested and that he had better say nothing about having met Mireille. 'And you must have had quite a few adventures too, monsieur?'

'The main thing is that I've found a site for a factory,'

Monsieur Terrasse said. 'Naturally there's no machinery. That's why I want you to go to La Rochelle first thing to-morrow morning and see if you can arrange about getting a permit to purchase sterling. It seems that some of the Treasury officials have been evacuated there. You must find them and explain to them that it is important that you get a permit to purchase sterling with as little delay as possible. Tell them that we've been evacuated, that we can't make munitions without English machine tools, and that we can't purchase English machine tools without English money. If you explain matters to them clearly, I am sure that they will understand.'

They were crossing the bridge as Monsieur Terrasse spoke. Below them the silver river ran on beneath the silver sky. The officer was wrong, Bigou thought; France was great and could never die.

XLIV

NEXT MORNING Bigou managed to get a lift in an army lorry as far as Châtelaillon, where to his joy he found Baco, Madame Baco, Bacqueroët, Latérade, Madame Turbigo, the yellow tart, and Odette stretched along the terrace of a café sticking their mugs into steaming cups of coffee. The baby was there, too, sucking away blandly at Odette's bare breast. They all waved frantically at Bigou as they saw him, but Odette waved more frantically than anybody else.

'Fancy meeting you,' Baco said. 'We were afraid that the Boches might have pinched you in Paris.'

'I got the next announcement in time,' Bigou said. 'I was lucky enough to get a lift to Saintes in a private car.' He felt a blush on his cheek as he said this and hurried on: 'And now I'm on my way to La Rochelle to get a permit to purchase sterling for our new factory. The war goes on.'

'Of course the war goes on,' Baco said, and handed Bigou a newspaper.

The newspaper said in great headlines that Marshal Pétain was now Prime Minister, and gave the names of the other members of his cabinet. It said that the Marshal had been entrusted by Monsieur Albert Lebrun with the task of defending the fatherland. It said also that the Germans had mobile crematoria which followed their infantry and burned the bodies of their dead and sometimes of their severely wounded as well. It said also that Frenchmen should remember that France always rose stronger from defeat. Bigou handed the paper back to Baco.

'And it's not only Pétain,' Baco said. 'Just look at all the other generals and admirals in the cabinet: Weygand and Huntziger and Darlan. You'll see, things'll go like smoke now, because after all it's generals and admirals and not politicians that win wars. And then yesterday I walked in dog's mess with my left foot. That's always lucky. The only thing that worries me is that I haven't been able to get rid of that bad ten-franc piece yet, eh, mother?' He beamed at his wife.

'The Germans are, all the same, at Dreux and Dijon,' Latérade said. 'It looks as though they were going to turn the Maginot Line.'

'Pétain, conqueror of Verdun,' Bacqueroët said. 'It's a great name certainly, but it comes a little late in the day.'

'What do you think, Madame Baco?' Latérade asked.

'You ought to know by this time, monsieur, that I never discuss politics,' Madame Baco said.

This made Baco laugh so loudly that he insisted on standing drinks all round and didn't even try to work off his bad ten-franc piece on the waitress when he paid for them. Bigou stood the next round and Bacqueroët the next round and Latérade the round after that because he suddenly remembered that everybody knew that he was in receipt of two Government pensions and had a commercial job in Paris into the bargain. When Baco started to stand his second round, they were all so cheerful that even Bacqueroët began to admit that with a fellow like Pétain at the head of affairs there was still a hope of conquering Germany and keeping her down and out world without end amen as they sang in church.

'And on the day of victory how we'll all dance in the street,' Madame Turbigo said.

'All the same with Pétain,' Latérade said.

'All the same with Pétain,' Bigou said.

'Monsieur the Marshal Pétain looks the dead spit of monsieur, my late husband's, late uncle,' Madame Turbigo said.

'With the left foot, I tell you,' Baco said. 'That's always lucky.'

'I must be getting into La Rochelle all the same,' Bigou said. 'I must be seeing about purchasing that sterling.'

'We'll drive you there,' Baco said. 'And we'll have a whale of a good lunch at the station restaurant and we'll all get as drunk as Poles. It's not every day of the week that they elect a field-marshal Prime Minister of France, what?'

The proprietor was standing on the pavement talking to a customer as they went out. 'And to think that we'll have to come to terms with swine like these,' he was saying. Baco wanted to slosh the proprietor one on the jaw, but Bacqueroët stopped him. Bacqueroët liked the proprietor because he had allowed him to use the ladies' sit-down lavatory on the ground floor instead of the men's stand-up lavatory in the basement as it was easier for him.

Odette had to be helped into the car because she was still rather weak on her legs. Latérade climbed up on the roof to give her more room. Bigou sat with Baco and Bacqueroët in front. As they drove along, Baco explained that they had had to sleep out on the road in Châtelaillon because his relations in La Rochelle had turned out to be swine in their souls and wouldn't take them in because they had let out their spare rooms to other refugees at high prices.

There were cars with mattresses and luggage on top of them parked all round the square when they reached La Rochelle, but Baco managed to squeeze in by denting somebody else's mudguard. They left Odette and her baby in the car. Baco said that he would have her lunch sent out to her, but Odette said that she wasn't really hungry and would prefer to sit in peace and look at her baby. The rest all trooped into the restaurant, but it was so crowded that they had to stand about looking for a table. When at length they dived at one that had just been vacated, the rubber tip on the end of Bacqueroët's stick slid on a splash of soup, but the yellow tart managed to steady him in time. The waitress came and asked them what they wanted to eat, but she didn't seem to pay much attention to what they said, and walked away without brushing the previous customers' breadcrumbs from the tablecloth. Baco began to drink the dregs of wine left in the dirty glasses. A whistle sounded long and piercingly in the station. Then the manager came in and said that they must all clear out at once, as a Red Cross train had just come in and the medical authorities wanted to use the restaurant as a clearing centre.

Most of the customers went readily enough with cowed resigned looks on their faces, but Baco swore at the top of his voice until his wife called him to order. The yellow tart walked out of the restaurant with her face raised and her lips moving like a nun's. Baco started to swear again as soon as they got out on the pavement, but Madame Turbigo called him to order this time, pointing out that it was much sorer to be wounded than to go without one's lunch. Baco said that he knew that as well as she did, but that as far as he knew nobody had to go without his lunch when he had been wounded in the last war.

When Odette heard that there were wounded arriving at the station, she asked Bigou to go and see if François was among them. She said that she knew it was silly of her to think that he might be there, but, after all, the world was a small place and she hadn't heard from him for more than a month now, and she would never forgive herself afterwards if she learnt that he had been there all along and she so near and not comforting him. Bigou said that of course he would go and see if François were there and the yellow tart said that she would come with him.

It was such a long time since Bigou had been alone with the yellow tart that he didn't know quite what to talk to her about. He wanted to ask her if she had really found peace in God and if she never wanted to be a tart again; but he knew that he couldn't, because it would be asking a question that really mattered, and questions that really mattered never got answered even if they got asked.

Inside the station the wounded were laid out in a line of stretchers along the platform where the train had drawn in. At first the officials didn't want to let Bigou and the yellow tart in, but when Bigou said that he was looking for his son-in-law they let him pass. Grey faces, grey faces, they all looked alike to Bigou, but none of them was the grey face of François. As they passed down the line again, one of the grey faces smiled at the yellow tart and the yellow tart smiled back ever so beautifully.

'Have you been very bady wounded, monsieur?' she asked.

'They say it's in the base of the spine,' the young boy on the stretcher said. 'The general sent us a message in hospital afterwards. He said: "The glorious spirit of your sacrifice will live forever in the golden scrolls of history." But will it? Won't there ever be stock exchanges and unemployment and unkindness again?'

The yellow tart knelt down beside the boy and stroked his head with long cool fingers. She nodded to Bigou to leave her. Bigou walked out of the station with tears in his eyes. What could one do for the afflicted but feel for them? And there were so many people to feel for in France. And could one feel *for* without feeling *with* them? He walked out into the sun wishing that he could feel nails sticking into his belly, but he felt no nails sticking into his belly. He found Baco, Madame Baco, Bacqueroët, Latérade, and Madame Turbigo still cluttered round the car, with Odette sitting in the back holding her infant in sweet sacrament to her breast. He shook his head dolefully at Odette as he came and then he saw that she and they and all the people in the square were all crying their eyes out.

'It's just come over the wireless that Pétain has asked the Germans for an armistice,' Latérade explained.

Bigou said nothing. He made the sign of the cross. There seemed to be nothing else to do. Then he, too, started to cry. All around him people were crying. Poured down within themselves, clapped down, trapped down, each alone with God forever, Baco, Madame Baco, Madame Turbigo, Latérade, Bacqueroët, Odette, and Bigou sat and cried.

'And to think that I stepped in dog's mess this morning,' Baco said. 'And with my left foot too.'

'The English betrayed us,' Latérade said.

'We betrayed ourselves,' Bacqueroët said.

'And, after all, what could a people of forty millions do against a people of eighty millions?' Baco said.

'And we mustn't forget that France always rises stronger from defeat,' Madame Turbigo said. 'It says so in the papers.'

'Perhaps Hitler won't be so hard on us as we imagine,' Baco said. 'After all, the Germans are human beings like ourselves.'

Bacqueroët's tears were the last to dry. He did not bother to wipe them away, but sat with them making the wounded skin on his face look more stretched than ever.

'This is the day of our greatest shame,' he said.

Bigou said nothing. Both Bacqueroët and the abbé Pécher were right, he thought: the greatness of a nation was the sum total of the invisible goodness of its inhabitants. He wanted to tell them all that, but he didn't, in case they should think him a prig. Instead he thought of Paris, which was now a city of roofs, and her sweet evening streets. At his mother's breast the babe, inheritor of Jeanne d'Arc, Napoleon and Foch, sucked on with a vast blue eye.

THE END